Recipe for
a Happy Life

Also by Brenda Janowitz

Jack with a Twist

Scot on the Rocks

This is a work of fiction. All of the characters, organizations, and events portrayed in this novel are either products of the author's imagination or are used fictitiously.

Design by Omar Chapa

www.stmartins.com

Library of Congress Cataloging-in-Publication Data

Janowitz, Brenda.
    Recipe for a happy life : a novel / Brenda Janowitz.—1st ed.
        p. cm.
    ISBN 978-1-250-00786-5 (trade pbk.)
    ISBN 978-1-4668-4022-5 (e-book)
    I. Title.
    PS3610.A584R43 2013
    813'.6—dc23

                                                                2013009321

St. Martin's Griffin books may be purchased for educational, business, or promotional use. For information on bulk purchases, please contact Macmillan Corporate and Premium Sales Department at 1-800-221-7945 extension 5442 or write specialmarkets@macmillan.com.

First Edition: July 2013

10 9 8 7 6 5 4 3 2 1

Recipe for a Happy Life

Brenda Janowitz

ST. MARTIN'S GRIFFIN ♔ NEW YORK

To my mother: You are the mom Hannah always longed for.
I am so lucky that you are mine.

In memory of my grandmothers, Dorothy Waldman and
Florence Janowitz. Two of the most glamorous ladies
I've ever known.

One

My grandmother's seventh husband, the one with the title, is the one she remembers most fondly. We call him "the one with the title" because he was the Mattress King of Canarsie. But even a self-appointed title, my grandmother always says, is a title nonetheless.

He's the one who left her the estate out in the Hamptons—the one where we're staying this summer—but that's not why she remembers him as her favorite. It's because, she says, he was a true gentleman, not a cad the way most men are nowadays, and he knew how to treat a lady like a lady. He would open doors and tell you how beautiful you looked. He would stand up when a woman entered a room or left a table. He would never let a woman pay. Never let a woman leave a party without seeing her home. Things that delighted my grandmother to no end, and about which I'm still forming an opinion.

The doctors told us that the Mattress King simply died of old age. There was nothing we could have done, they said. Nothing we could have prevented. They were trying to comfort us. Then the youngest doctor of the bunch, probably still a resident, discreetly pulled me aside to warn me that oftentimes, when an older person dies, his or her "mate" follows soon after, having succumbed to grief. So, clutching my hand, he told me that I should mentally prepare myself for what may come. I laughed out loud. Clearly, these doctors had never met my grandmother.

Her sixth husband was a former teen idol. I'm not going to say who he was, but you know him. Your mother knows him, too. He died three weeks after getting a diagnosis of mouth cancer. A lifelong cigar smoker, he puffed away right until his very last day. My grandmother always said that he died in the best possible way, if there is a "best possible way." You find out you're dying, say good-bye to all your loved ones, get your affairs in order, and then you're out. Quick and easy. No long suffering. No sudden shock.

If anyone is an expert on the best way to die, it's my grandmother. She's buried six husbands already and she's only seventy-six. There's still plenty of time for her to find someone else, marry him, and have him die on her watch. Not exactly a ringing endorsement for dating my grandmother, but she's always got men lining up, so I guess it hasn't exactly cramped her style.

My grandmother's fifth husband—the prince from a tiny French municipality just west of Monaco—died in a freak hang gliding accident while they were on vacation in Majorca. We called him "the one with the title" until the Mattress King came along. Now we just call him the Prince, or "the man formerly known as my husband," in my grandmother's case. She didn't really love him. Not much, anyway. To hear her tell it, she was simply caught up in the moment. I should mention here that this was in the sixties and that it was a Grace Kelly moment she was caught up in.

My grandmother was off shopping for pearls when the news broke. The French newspapers went absolutely crazy over the fact that, upon hearing the news of her husband's demise, she completed her purchase of the sixteen-inch double-strand she'd been trying on. ("He was dead," she later said of the controversy. "It wasn't like he was going anywhere.") To this day, she is still persona non grata in certain parts of the South of France.

Some people say that it was my grandmother who killed her fourth husband, the Senator, but that was never proven. Even though he died in a room full of four hundred Republican contributors, there was not one witness to support the allegation. But my grandmother knew what happened that night. And she told me.

It was just a few well-chosen words that brought down the Senator, and with him a legacy of three generations—his father, his father's father, and him. All United States senators by the time they'd reached forty. All staunch Republicans. Quite a feat for a woman who hardly ever voted.

The Senator himself had a kid at Yale, just biding his time until he could claim his birthright, his seat in the United States Senate. Junior the Third had considered everything in setting himself up for his rightful place in the family dynasty. He'd befriended all the right people, dated the right women, and volunteered for all the right candidates during high school and college. Of course, he also got a coveted spot in the Order of Skull and Bones, Yale's secret society, which has produced at least ten U.S. senators and three presidents. Even if two of them were George Bush Senior and Junior, it's still impressive.

But for all of his planning, even Junior the Third couldn't have seen my grandmother coming. It's her eyes, I think. They lull people into a false sense of security. A faint blue that looks violet in certain light, they make my grandmother look sweet. Angelic, almost. And she's anything but. They should have seen her coming that night—her eyes lined in black liquid liner, lashes glistening with two coats of mascara. But they didn't. The Senator

smiled broadly as my grandmother walked over to him. Five minutes later he was dead.

Seems old grandma threatened to expose the fact that the
Senator, for all of his preaching on family values and America's
moral compass, was gay. Upon hearing her threat, the Senator
grabbed his chest and promptly fell to the ground, never to get
back up again. Now, you must understand, my grandmother was
not actually upset about the fact that the Senator had married
her under false pretenses. "You can't expect your husband to tell
you the truth about *everything*," she would say. But she was rather
peeved when she found out that she wasn't drawing the same
weekly salary her predecessor got for her years of service. My
grandmother is nothing if not business savvy.

Her third husband, the Italian race car driver, was the one
with the most passion. Everything about their relationship was an
extreme: their fights were the harshest, their makeups the most
delicious. He was the one who taught her to follow her heart. And
he was the one who died the quickest into their marriage—just
four months to the day. Ironically, he died in a simple household
accident when he slipped on a bar of soap in the shower and hit
his head on the faucet. They do say that the majority of accidents
happen in the home.

My grandmother's second husband was my grandfather, my
mother's father. He was a trusts and estates lawyer from a good
family. A solid man. A good provider. The type of man *I* should
be looking for, she'd say.

My grandfather died in a car accident at the hands of a drunk
driver when my mother was twelve years old. That was when, my
grandmother believes, her run of bad luck started. You see, she's
always blamed herself for what happened to him that night:

It was well past 10:00 p.m. when my grandmother got a craving for an Ebinger's black-and-white cake. They were already in for the night, already had my mother tucked into her bed and asleep. There was no reason for my grandfather to have been on the road that late. No reason for him to be on the corner of Front Street and Broadway, car idling at a red light like a big bull's-eye. But it was a romantic gesture for him to indulge my grandmother in this way—she often said that she knew they were perfect for each other the moment they shared their first Ebinger's. When he only wanted to eat the vanilla half and she would only eat the chocolate, she just knew. A match made in heaven. My grandmother still can't look at cake without getting all misty.

In the end, she outlived them all. Just about every husband. The only one who did not widow her was her first. The one who looked like Rhett Butler. They ran away and got married when she was just sixteen. The details have always been fuzzy, but I do know that he was the only one who broke her heart.

Some people would call a woman like her unlucky. Others might call her cursed. But to me, she's just Grandma.

My grandmother's been there for me through everything. She stood proudly as I was sworn in at the New York State Bar; she lent me her shoulder as she nursed me through my first broken heart. She helped me pick out my clothes for my first day of school.

My mother, on the other hand, couldn't be bothered with such parochial things. She's a world-class photojournalist, so her life consists of constant movement. It's served her well—she has the Pulitzer to prove it—but I think she sometimes uses work as an excuse. A way to get out of commitments she has changed her mind about.

I know this because I do it, too. Sometime into my first year of law school, when I had so much work that I couldn't keep a set plan to save my life, I realized that no one ever balked when I broke plans because I had to study. They knew the drill, they knew how punishing the hours could be in law school. So they'd always let it slide.

I began taking advantage. Too tired to go out? Plead moot court. Want to skip that movie with a college friend you wish you hadn't kept in touch with? Cry about how many pages you have to read before criminal law class at 8:00 a.m.

Looking back on my childhood, I wonder how much my mother used this little trick of mine. There was the skipped third-grade play when I was cast as the second lead. My grandmother sat beaming from the front row, but my mother was "stuck on assignment" in the Soviet Union. Or my high school graduation, when my mother was "stuck in an editing bay" for a Ronald Reagan retrospective. ABC News was using over twenty images that she'd shot during the Iran-Contra affair, and her contract stipulated final creative control. Her images couldn't be trusted in just anyone's hands, she would later tell me, as I took off my cap and gown and folded them quietly in my lap.

In my heart of hearts, I know she did it all the time, used work as an excuse. A way to avoid reality. I know it because we're so much the same. I wish we weren't, but we are.

My grandmother and I are not the same, not by a long shot, and maybe that's the reason we're so close. My grandmother has an entirely different set of values, a different set of skills, and I like to think that we learn a lot from each other. She finds it charming the way I take my work seriously and always strive to be the best. She just doesn't think it's particularly important. My work, that is. She's the kind of woman who thinks that letter writing is an important art. The type who still thinks that penmanship is a very valuable skill for a woman to have. (Hers, of course, is impeccable.) But more important, and more to the point, she is a woman who has never in her life held down a real job.

My grandmother attributes much to her feminine wiles. She thinks I need to work on mine.

Two

The moment I step off the Hampton Jitney, I have the sense that it was a mistake to come out here. The big beautiful trees and all around hopeful attitude of Southampton are getting to me already. The last time I was out here, I was one of those happy smiling people you see walking down Main Street, enjoying the day without a care in the world. But that was years ago, and for the past few summers I haven't been able to drag myself back. Instead, my grandmother and I meet up anywhere but here. She'll stay at the Pierre during the week so we can have quiet dinners together, go to the theater. We'll take two-week trips to Paris, long weekends at Canyon Ranch, or a lazy cruise through the Mediterranean.

I wasn't sure I'd ever come back. But right now, I have nowhere else to go. The police are swarming my Manhattan apartment, so if I want to get away from all of that (and still stay in New York State, as instructed by Detective Moretti), then this is my only option.

I notice that my grandmother is all gussied up for the occasion, as if I am disembarking from the *Queen Mary* and not the Hampton Jitney, a cross between an oversized minivan and a bus. She's a vision—as always—in her white capri pants (starched to perfection) and teal tunic top. She's got on a huge chunky necklace with some sort of large white stones, arranged in a way that's supposed to look haphazard but is clearly purposeful in the way it highlights her long graceful neck.

She raises her arm and moves her hand slightly. Dozens of tiny bangle bracelets chime in the breeze. It's not a wave, exactly; it's more like an acknowledgment. *I'm right here*, it says. *You come to me*, it says, *I don't come to you.*

I give my grandmother a big hug. She hugs me back, tightly, and my eyes tear up. She tries to release me from the hug, but I won't let go. I don't want her to see that I'm crying, even though she's been the one to dry my tears for as long as I can remember. But I also just don't want to let go. Not yet.

Finally, she pats me on the back; that's my cue to gather my bags. After all, her driver, Raoul, is patiently waiting for us. When you are a widow six times over, you tend to accumulate things over time. Raoul is one such thing.

As is the navy blue Maybach Raoul is driving today. Just one of the fleet that my grandmother keeps back at the house. I don't remember the last time I saw her actually drive one of her cars herself.

We drive through town toward the Mattress King's estate and I can't help but think about the first time I was out here to visit. But the memories of that are far too painful, so I push them away, like I always do.

Main Street is bustling, as it usually is on a summer Saturday afternoon. The throngs of people walking around just make me want to get into bed, dive under the covers, and hide. But as we move south of the highway, past Agawam Park, through the tree-lined streets of the estate section of Southampton, everything changes. All you see is green—enormous trees, perfectly trimmed hedges, and freshly cut grass abound. The only people here are the parents and children riding their bikes along the street, and it gets calmer with each street closer to the beach. I notice the fresh, cool air and feel the breeze coming off the ocean.

Once we turn onto my grandmother's block, it's completely quiet. You can hear the birds chirping, the ocean waves breaking. This is why I came out here, I think. This is what I needed.

My heart seizes just the tiniest bit as we pull through the gates—I'm forced to remember the last time I was out here, with him. I can feel a panic attack coming on, just thinking about all that I've lost, so I take a deep breath, close my eyes, and concentrate on being present. The smell of the beach, the gentle hum of the car's engine, the crushing of the gravel as we pull onto the driveway. I open my eyes and look around in wonder. The front lawn is even more like an arboretum than I remember. And my grandmother has acquired some rosebushes and an enormous weeping willow that I'll later learn is over a hundred years old. But my favorites are the trees filled with hydrangeas.

Of course, no one really cares about the front of the house in Southampton. Out here, the real excitement is around the back. The Mattress King's estate is beachfront property, the best you can get anywhere in the Hamptons, not just Southampton.

My grandmother describes the place as a "beach cottage," but it's anything but. Sure, it evokes a cottage feel with its charming details, like beadboard cabinets in the kitchen, whitewashed wood as far as the eye can see, and copious amounts of wicker furniture. But most cottages don't have an elevator. Or seven bathrooms for that matter. Or a guest house with another three bedrooms and four bathrooms. Or another cottage over the garage to house the staff. Beach cottages are not over six thousand square feet.

But the thing I've come to learn about the Hamptons is that there's an entirely different set of rules out here.

"It's so wonderful to have you back. We're going to have a marvelous summer together. I have you set up in the room next to mine," my grandmother says as Raoul helps us upstairs with my bags. Well, bag I should say. I only packed one.

"Great," I say, and then to Raoul, "Thanks." He smiles back at me, nodding as if to say, "You're welcome," and I remember something my grandmother used to tell me when I was growing up: you should always speak to everyone in the same way. From the man who shines your shoes to the president of the United States, you should give each one the same amount of kindness and respect.

"Is this okay up here?" my grandmother asks. "I didn't think you'd want to be in the guest house all by yourself."

"This is perfect," I say. "I'm right next door to you. I'm like your lady-in-waiting." My grandmother gives my outfit the once over.

"Would you like to change for lunch, darling?" She smiles at me innocently, but I know that what she is really saying is: *You need to change for lunch.*

To be clear, my outfit isn't all that offensive—I'm wearing a pair of dark-colored jeans and a pocket tee. Not the height of fashion, I know, but hardly a distasteful ensemble. More to the point, of course, is the fact that we are having lunch here, at the house. Just the two of us. No one to impress. But my grandmother feels that you should always be dressed to the nines, even if you're all alone. After all, you should dress for yourself. To please yourself.

I could, right now, make a crack about how you can take the girl out of France, but you can't take France out of the girl, but my grandmother wouldn't appreciate that. She feels that I spend far too much time coming up with what she refers to as my "clever little quips."

"Of course I was going to change," I say, and then take a mental inventory of what I've brought. I packed in such a hurry this morning that I'm not even sure if I brought a sundress or white jeans or anything that my grandmother would deem even slightly appropriate.

"I can see by your face that we must immediately go shopping," she says. "Immediately! I'll call Raoul." And with that, she spins on her heel and leaves the room.

I suppose that lunch is off for the time being.

Working as a lawyer in Manhattan doesn't allot you the time you need to amass the sort of wardrobe my grandmother would deem necessary for a summer in the Hamptons. So I don't really mind that she's dragging me to Georges Mandel after tempting me with the idea of lunch, even though I was on that Jitney for over three hours and can't remember the last time I ate.

Since my mother would never let my grandmother set up a trust fund for me, or give me money without reason ("If you don't work for something, you won't appreciate it," my mother always argued), shopping and showering me with presents is one of the ways my grandmother can unload some of that pesky cash she has too much of. I don't love shopping, but I do love bathing in the glow of my grandmother's attention, so going shopping together is generally a win-win proposition for us.

Raoul drops us off right in front of Mandel's, and I open the door for my grandmother. Salespeople from every department practically fall over themselves as they see my grandmother walk into the store. It's a virtual chorus of "Oh, Mrs. Morganfelder! So lovely to see you!" and "Mrs. Morganfelder! What can I help you with today?" and even one "Mrs. Morganfelder, is this that fabulous granddaughter you've told us so much about?" No one dares call her by her first name, Vivienne.

We start in the makeup department, where one kind soul is nice enough to offer us a cup of tea and some cookies. My grandmother takes the tea, passes on the cookies. I do not pass on the cookies.

In twenty minutes flat, I've got a new beauty regimen that will take me twenty-five minutes to complete each night. It involves a face cream that costs more than most people make in a week, an eye cream that's made with caviar (I didn't catch why this would be desirable), and copious amounts of makeup remover. Apparently the key is to fully remove all of your makeup before bedtime. Wearing makeup while you sleep is strictly verboten.

I also get a new makeup "look," which I'm sure I will never be able to replicate once I'm home. It involves a product called a "corrector," which I find funny. The salesperson does not seem to find this quite as funny as I do—she takes the banishing of undereye circles very seriously. She does not realize that I need a corrector for my life, not just my face.

The corrector goes on first, followed by a cream concealer, and then you finish with a powder. I want to tell my grandmother that I have neither the time nor inclination to indulge in such a detailed morning ritual, but then I see her beaming at me, so happy to see me looking undereye-circle-free, and I just don't have the heart. Once my complexion is evened out, and only then, do we move on to the actual makeup part of my new look. There are powders and liners and a whole lot of mascara that go into making me look "natural," and the salesperson writes it all down for me since it is such an extensive set of instructions. I know that I will lose this sheet of paper the second I get back to the house, but I take it anyway.

Next, we move on to clothes. It's a blinding assortment. For starters, all of the pants are white. Nary a blue, black, or gray to be found. Jeans, capris, Bermuda shorts, trousers—all of them white. There is seemingly no black clothing of any kind in the Hamptons. Instead, there is an array of cheery pinks, bright greens, and lively yellows. I grab a subdued lavender top to contrast with what the salesperson has already picked out for me, under my grandmother's gentle guidance. I look at a bright orange shift dress and my grandmother gently shakes her head no.

From there, it's just a short hop over to swimwear, and in no time, I've got four new "appropriate" bathing suits, along with coordinating cover-ups. My grandmother makes a comment about us coming back for more, and I can't help but giggle at the fact that four bathing suits is not enough in the Hamptons. It doesn't seem like too much of anything is enough out here.

Then it's on to footwear. As a woman living in New York City, I've got quite a shoe collection, but most of it is work-appropriate, and my grandmother shuns all of the sensible shoes that I've already got. (Which is funny, in that my grandmother helped me pick out most of those, too.) Apparently, a woman simply cannot survive in Southampton unless she has the perfect strappy three-inch sandal, a sexy high-heeled wedge, and a pretty flat. I did not know that.

I am Audrey Hepburn to my grandmother's Professor Higgins, only my grandmother is the one with the gamine looks and hypnotizing eyes.

After we hit accessories and I have more necklaces, scarves, and handbags than I know what to do with, and only after that, do we head home to—finally!—eat lunch. But it's a light lunch today, since, as my grandmother casually informs me, we have a double date this very evening.

Three

Here's what I know about husband number one. They met as children in Vichy, France, the town where my grandmother was born. They both had very rich fathers (hers, a jeweler; his, a lawyer) who disapproved of their career aspirations (hers, to be a playwright; his, to be an artist). Sometime before her sixteenth birthday, they hatched a plan to get married and run away to Paris to live among the artists in Montmartre.

Which is exactly what they did.

It didn't last long, though. The day Germany invaded Poland, my great-grandfather had my great-grandmother take all of the gems and jewelry from the house safe, and stuff it into her bra and corset. It was a scary time and no one knew what would happen. They only knew that jewelry was a currency that would always hold value, always help you out of a sticky situation.

The diamonds were the easiest to hide. The hardest stone, they are nearly impossible to damage. My great-grandmother stuffed dozens of tiny little bags filled with loose diamonds anywhere they would fit. Her bra held most of them. Many of the rubies were already set into jewelry, so those were packed in larger bags and tucked into her girdle. Emeralds aren't supposed to be exposed to moisture, so they were hidden in a secret compartment in my great-grandfather's hat, far away from the heat of his head. The pearls were another story entirely. Delicate. Prone to damage. Those went into secret inside pockets sewn into my great-grandfather's jacket.

Then, just as if it were an ordinary day, they drove to Paris where they carried my grandmother, kicking and screaming, into the car. Since her husband wasn't Jewish, he wasn't in any danger, so there was no real reason for him to come with them. My grandmother still remembers telling her parents that they were overreacting, that Jews would always be safe in France. But her parents ignored her protests. And my grandmother never saw her first husband again.

Four

I suppose I brought this upon myself. If I hadn't fled my life in the city I wouldn't be out here in the Hamptons with my grandmother. It would follow, then, that I wouldn't be at this dinner, and I'd really rather not be at this dinner.

"So, a lawyer?" he says. "That must be interesting." There's a tiny speck of salad dressing on his lip, and I can't take my eyes off it.

We're at the Palm in East Hampton. I happen to love the Palm—it's one of my favorite restaurants—but the company tonight is taking away from my enjoyment of my Gigi salad. I notice how different the décor in this Palm is from the one in midtown Manhattan, much airier and beachier with the ceiling fans and open glass doors, but that doesn't detract from the fact that my date is a boor. He barely looked at me when we were introduced, and has been gawking at other women since we sat down at the table. My grandmother's date, on the other hand, is quite charming. He looked me in the eye as we were introduced, complimented my outfit, and took my wrap so that it could be checked. I wish some of that had rubbed off on my partner for the evening. Still, my grandmother always taught me to be polite, so I answer the question.

"It can be," I start to reply, but before the words are completely out of my mouth, he is already talking about his job in finance (and he's one of those people who pronounces it finnance as opposed to figh-nance, which I detest). Seems the Boor is well bred enough to know he is supposed to ask me what I do for a living, but simply doesn't care enough to listen to my answer.

My eyes float around to the rest of the dining room. It's a sea of dull men, all of whom look like carbon copies of the Boor. Most of them are wearing pastel-colored chinos. Their companions are a more varied bunch, with one thing in common: they seem to have more interest in their cell phones than they do in their dates. Not that I could blame them. If I didn't think my grandmother would pull me away from our table by my ear, I'd be playing on my cell phone, too. For a moment I wonder what someone looking at my table would think of me, but then I realize that an onlooker glancing at my table wouldn't look at me at all.

They'd be looking at my grandmother.

Some people would be intimidated by having a showstopper of a grandmother like I do. They certainly wouldn't agree to double date with her. (Although "strong-armed" is more like it.) But I love basking in my grandmother's glow. I don't care that I'm a plain Jane compared to her glamour-puss. I am, and always have been, happy to be in her presence.

I would just rather not be on a double date with her. But it's not because she got the better date than me. It's because I'd rather have her all to myself.

The secret truth, the thing that I don't want anyone to know, not even my grandmother herself, is that I really like when she plays dress up with me. As much as I argue with her about going shopping together, I enjoy it when she tries to make me over in her image. Which is precisely what she did before we went out on this date. Everything that I am wearing tonight, from the borrowed gold hoop earrings down to the brand-new platform cork wedges, has been carefully vetted by my grandmother. She told me that I looked drop-dead gorgeous in the outfit she selected for me—a coral-colored tunic and white jeans. The perfect Southampton chic, she called it.

And still, everyone at the table—at the restaurant really—is fawning over her. It's not just her humongous diamond stud earrings that get her the attention. (Four carats in each ear, given to her by her sixth husband, Dallas Jones. I know I said I didn't want to mention his name, but something about the town of Southampton just makes you want to name-drop.) Nor is it her gigantic ruby cocktail ring, given to her by the Mattress King himself.

No, it's something in the way she looks at you. It's something about the way she always has a sly little smile playing on her lips, as if she's privy to something that no one else is, but if you get into her good graces, she just might tell you.

It's her aura.

"And what do you think, Anna?" my grandmother's date asks me. My first thought is: *I have no idea what they were all talking about just now.* My second is: *Should I correct him and tell him that my name is actually Hannah?*

"Hannah, dear," my grandmother corrects, her hand patting his gently.

"Oh, Hannah," he says, unembarrassed. "An even *more* beautiful name." I can see that my grandmother's date has taken this embarrassing social situation and turned it into a way to compliment my grandmother. He leans into her when he tells her how beautiful my name is, as if to say: "You are so lovely that you managed to have a daughter who gave her *own* daughter a beautiful name." But my grandmother isn't looking at him. She's looking at me.

I run a hand through my hair and then remember that my grandmother told me not to do that. Touching your hair at the table is rude, she said at lunch today. Personal grooming should be taken care of in the restroom, lest a stray hair end up where food is served. She furrows her brow and I can see in her eyes that she's just realized that I haven't been listening to the last five minutes of conversation. I just know that she's about to save me from this awkwardness. In fact, now that the main course has been served, surely she'll excuse us from this dinner and we can leave before dessert.

"I have an idea," my grandmother says. I smile in anticipation. I blot the sides of my mouth with my napkin and place it on the table. Just as I'm about to thank my (humorless) date for dinner, my grandmother announces: "Why don't you fellows come back to the house for a nightcap?"

Five

"Is the State of New York allowing you to be this far from the house?" my grandmother asks in her slight French accent, smiling, arranging herself on a chaise longue next to mine. Today she's wearing a bright blue mailot. Her whole life, she's managed to keep herself remarkably thin (probably owing to her lifelong ban on baked goods, enacted after the death of my grandfather). As usual, she looks fantastic. The blue brings out the color of her eyes and the cut of her swimsuit flatters her every angle.

"I'm not under house arrest," I remind her for the umpteenth time. It comes out sounding angrier than I had intended. I never get angry with my grandmother, but she knows how upset I am about what happened in Manhattan, and I don't think I'm quite ready to be so blithe about it. I feel her eyes on me, and I drape my right hand self-consciously over my tummy. "I spoke to Jaime yesterday and he's not pressing charges. The officers told me not to leave the state while the investigation is pending, and we're still in New York State."

"Well, good," my grandmother says, "because I don't want any men in blue showing up at our party."

My grandmother is always in the midst of planning a party.

And this week is no exception. To celebrate my arrival at the Mattress King's estate, my grandmother has planned a

Gatsby-esque extravaganza to which she's invited two hundred of her closest friends. Which is to say, each and every family who lives South of the Highway got an engraved invitation.

My grandmother is a very friendly gal.

"Oh, darn," I say, "then in that case, I'll have to fire those strippers I hired for you. They were going to pretend they were cops before taking it all off. In a classy way, of course."

My grandmother turns her head and regards me skeptically. She doesn't have to tell me what she's thinking. I know what she's thinking. All my life, she's been telling me: "Men don't like funny."

I'm often told that I'm funny.

But, I've never really had a problem attracting men, funny or not. Keeping them around is generally the rub.

I turn from my grandmother's glare and stare out to the pool. It's glorious. My grandmother explains to me that it is a "negative edge" pool, meaning that it gives the appearance of disappearing into the horizon. From our vantage point, it looks like it bleeds right into the ocean.

Also glorious is Sonny, the pool boy. He's twenty-two if he's a day, but what he lacks in age he makes up for in muscle tone. He is a perfect physical specimen, a striking contrast to the entitled rich kids you see running around the town of Southampton with their foreign cars and soft guts. Sonny looks up and catches me staring at him just a bit too intently, and I quickly look down and examine my nails. My grandmother insisted that I accompany her on her weekly trip to the nail salon this morning, so today my nails are light pink.

I am oogling the pool boy, I think, staring at my perfectly manicured cuticles. How did I end up as such a cliché? I'm not even forty yet. Yet.

I sink into my chaise longue and can't help but melt into the luxurious cushions, which are covered with thick Egyptian cotton towels, monogrammed with the Mattress King's initials. The Mattress King's estate in the Hamptons is nothing if not cozy. I slept like a baby last night on a king-sized bed with six-hundred thread count sheets. Of course the mattresses are comfy. But it's not just the beds. *Everything* about the Mattress King's estate is exceedingly comfortable. Even the carpeted runners going up the staircases are plush and tickle your feet.

The estate—five acres of pure unbridled beauty—was a wedding gift to my grandmother who had once casually mentioned that she liked the beach. The Mattress King spent an entire year building the main house, guest house, and a pool, each created with an eye toward making its inhabitants totally, completely, and blissfully relaxed.

It even has a golf cart to take you from one end of the property to the other. There are no tired feet at the Mattress King's estate.

I've spent my life in equal parts between beautiful surroundings like this and more unsavory ones. You see, I grew up in hotels. Just like Eloise, only the hotels my mother and I stayed in were never quite as posh as the Plaza—our home base was a suite at the Hotel Chelsea, and when we traveled, the accommodations went downhill from there. Because my mother was a photojournalist, my childhood was a blur of jetting off to the latest news story. We were never in one place for very long.

The only time my mother left me behind was when she photographed a story in Nicaragua, which she felt was too dangerous for me to tag along. In November of that year, the Iran-Contra affair became public and my mother won a Pulitzer for her work.

It was the best summer of my life, a summer of firsts for

me—my first kiss, my first period, my first real home. My grand-mother and I lived in a house in the Caymans that was left to her by the Italian race car driver, and it was the first time I ever had a bedroom to call my own. My own room. My own bathroom. My own space.

I learned so much from my grandmother that summer. She would never tell me I was wrong or right. She would never say I told you so; she would never judge. If she disagreed with some-thing you said or something you did, she would simply turn to you and say, "Well, darling, that's not the recipe for a happy life."

"Southampton doesn't have strippers," my grandmother fi-nally says.

"Every town has strippers," I say, making a mental note to find a strip club to lure my grandmother to. This will be a first in the life of Vivienne Brushard Goodman Finelli Worthington Rudolph Jones Morganfelder.

A night of debauchery. Actually, she's probably had plenty of those. I should say: a night of debauchery that doesn't end in marriage.

"What are you planning to wear to the party?" my grand-mother says, turning onto her side and putting her head in her hand.

"I brought a sundress with me, so maybe that," I say. "What are you wearing?"

"I'm not worried about what I'm wearing," she says. "I'm wor-ried about what *you're* wearing. I don't think there's anything in that sack you brought that would be suitable for a garden party."

First of all, I did not pack my things in a sack. True, I fled the city with record speed, but I tossed a few things into a very re-spectable tote bag, not a potato sack, as my grandmother seems to think. When she picked me up at the jitney stop, she asked the jitney driver to help me with my valise, and then, upon discovering that I had brought a tote bag and not a suitcase, tut-tutted about "you young people" all the way back to the house. I wasn't sure which she was more annoyed about: that I was able to pack for an entire summer in one tiny little tote bag, or that the jitney driver had no idea what a valise was.

Second of all, she's not throwing a simple little garden party. She makes it sound like she's having an impromptu backyard barbecue with a few neighbors, when in fact, she's throwing a huge extravaganza that required the acquisition of party and noise permits from the Village of Southampton. (Yes, in the Village of Southampton, you not only need a permit to party, but you also need one to be loud.) Not to mention the massive white tent that's being set up to house twenty tables, three fully stocked bars, an ornate white wood dance floor, and the best twelve-piece orchestra on Long Island. And don't even get me started on the flowers.

There will be a fifty-minute-long cocktail hour ("one hour is just a touch too long, darling") on the front lawn during which seventeen different types of hors d'oeuvres will be served, followed by a five-course tasting menu under the tents. The valet parking station will be manned by a five-person team. But I guess, to a certain type of person, that's just a garden party.

"I'll wear the white dress we got at Georges Mandel," I assure her. "I promise that I won't embarrass you."

"The only person who can embarrass you, dear, is you," my grandmother says. "What I meant was . . . I just thought there might be some nice gentlemen at this party and so you should look your best."

"Grandma, this time off isn't about meeting someone," I say.

"Then what is it about?" she asks. "It seems to me that the

reason you came out here is because you are thirty-four years old; you no longer have a job and you no longer have a man in your life. In my experience, you need to have at least one of those. I can help you with the meeting-a-man part. Meeting men is a thing at which I excel."

"Yes, I'm aware," I say. "But I think that this summer's really more about figuring out my life and what to do about a job."

"So, no men?" she asks. She asks it like she doesn't really understand how that can be the answer. As if she were Sir Paul McCartney and I've just announced that I have no interest in rock 'n' roll.

"Right," I say, clarifying the point. "No men."

"Yes," she says, "of course. I went through exactly the same thing when I was your age."

I'm about to say something that I've been wanting to say for quite a while, something that I've never quite had the heart to say to her, when she beats me to it.

"I don't know why you like to play this little game where you pretend we're so different," she says, adjusting her hat so that her face is out of the sun. "You and I are turning out to be very much alike."

Six

"So, are we shopping for husband number eight?"

My grandmother and I are at a restaurant called Roman's, where the diet Cokes cost twelve dollars.

"I don't shop for husbands," my grandmother replies, not missing a beat. I can tell that she is not annoyed by my snarky comment. Rather, she is about to turn it into a teachable moment. "I shop for diamonds, pearls. I don't shop for husbands. That would be tacky."

My grandmother takes a slow sip of her water, eyes on me the whole time.

"Is that what *you* are doing this evening?" my grandmother asks, eyes narrowing. "Shopping for your next husband?"

"No," I reply, "it is not."

The waitress comes to our table and we place our orders— for me, chicken parmesan, for my grandmother, a mixed green salad topped with goat cheese and pecans.

"People don't really *eat* here," she explains once the waitress is out of earshot. "You don't come to Roman's for the food, you come for the view."

I look out to see just what view my grandmother is refer- ring to, but all that I see is a parking lot filled with a lot of very expensive cars. Surely a woman who uses four different eye creams has no interest in cars. I turn back to face my grandmother.

She laughs at me and says: "No darling, I mean *the view*," and throws her arm out to show me the bar area. It is crawling with twenty- and thirty-something singles. A view indeed: rich boys, trustafarians living off daddy's dime; girls looking to marry rich, desperate wannabes, aching to fit in with all the money; a few lonely looking divorcées.

"That one's cute," my grandmother says, pointing at a nondescript guy my age. He's wearing seersucker pants.

"He's not really my type," I say, and take a sip of my diet Coke.

"And what exactly is your type?" my grandmother asks, lips pointing upward into a sly smirk.

"Well, I don't really like the same type as you."

"And what type is that?"

"Rich," I say. "Well off. You know, established."

"That's just a lot of different ways to say that I'm a gold digger."

"No," I say, my eyes widening to prove my innocence. "I don't mean that at all. I don't think that. I just mean that my type wouldn't be out here in the Hamptons."

"If I recall correctly," my grandmother says, "your type used to be someone who really went for things in life and got them. A big-time lawyer who wanted to change the world. The type of man who most certainly would be in the Hamptons."

"I don't want to talk about that."

"I only bring it up to point out the fact that your type now seems to be 'loser.' But it didn't used to be."

I feel myself losing my temper, something I almost never do

in front of my grandmother, and I take a sip of my ice water and grind down the ice cube with my teeth.

As if on cue, the waitress brings our main courses. *I'm complaining about the spoiled brat man-children out here, but I just ordered a forty-two-dollar chicken parmesan.*

My grandmother takes tiny bites of her salad, and as I watch her eat her salad gracefully, I'm reminded of her European heritage. As for me, there is just no graceful way to eat a huge slab of chicken parmesan. So I just dig in, letting the cheese drip everywhere, scooping up sauce with every bite.

"You're not going to get anywhere with your attitude. You can't look down your nose at everyone you meet. Men need to feel important, like they are successful."

"Not every man you married actually was successful," I say.

"Yes," my grandmother concedes, "that's right. But they all *thought* they were. Even the Prince truly believed that the people loved him for him, and not because of his father's crown."

My grandmother looks over my shoulder, to catch what my eye has just seen.

"Are you still scared of those kids?"

"What kids?" I ask, and whip my eyes back to my chicken parm.

"Those young men over there," my grandmother says with a slight tilt of her head. "They look like the sort of people you went to school with."

"I'm not scared of them."

"Well, that's good," she says.

"I was never scared of them," I tell my grandmother. She looks back at me and smiles, but it's a smile that says she feels sorry for me, that she knows I'm lying to myself and to her, and that she doesn't care. She understands.

I was very different from all of the other kids who attended Pearce, the private school on the Upper East Side where I was a student from kindergarten through the twelfth grade. My attendance was spotty, for one thing, but the trustees loved that my mother was this award-winning photojournalist, so the school always let it slide.

The differences weren't something you could see. I always had the right clothing, the right haircuts to fit in—my grandmother saw to that. But it was the subtle things that made me stand out. Being the only one in class without a father to speak at Career Day. Having my grandmother be the one to serve as "class mom."

I'd be at the dinner table with a classmate in her family's Upper East Side brownstone and her mother would innocently ask, "So, where do you live, dear?" My one word answer always shut them up: downtown.

Downtown New York City is a very cool place to live now, probably more desirable than the Upper East Side even, but when I grew up, with the people I grew up with, no one dared live below Fifty-Seventh Street. In fact, most people wouldn't even travel below Fifty-Seventh Street, what with the gang violence, porn theaters, and crack epidemic raging in the eighties. The New York City I grew up in was pre-Disney Times Square, before people really lived all over the city, before every neighborhood in town was completely gentrified.

So telling someone that I was from downtown usually put a stop to the conversation. And my playdates.

But it wasn't that I was scared of those kids. In fact, some of them I liked quite a lot.

Every Christmas break, my grandmother would take me away to somewhere warm. Sometimes it would be the vacation home of one of her husbands, sometimes she'd be between husbands and would cherry-pick a fabulous resort with beach access and lots of families vacationing so that I'd have other kids to hang out with.

When I was in ninth grade, we went to the Four Seasons on the Big Island of Hawaii. I loved going to Hawaii, where I usually met kids from California, rather than New York, as most New Yorkers opted for the three-hour plane ride to the Caribbean as opposed to the eleven-hour trek to Hawaii. I found that in these two weeks of vacation, I could reinvent myself to be whoever I wanted to be. Also, it was my second year in a row on the Big Island, so I knew a bunch of the kids from the year before. We hadn't kept in touch at all—in a pre–email/Facebook/Internet world, the only mode of communication was letter writing—but when we saw one another again down at the lagoon, it was as if no time had passed.

The second night of vacation, we all gathered in the lobby after dinner, which was our custom, and began talking about what sort of mischief we could create that night. The boy from Texas said that the valet would give him his parents' rental car so we could drive into town and try to get into a bar. Just as a quorum was being reached, a new kid joined our group. Mitzy from New Jersey immediately began chatting him up and discovered he was from New York City.

"Hannah's from the City," she announced loudly, and then presented him to me, as if I were in charge.

"I go to Dalton," he said, name-dropping his top-tier school. This was a game I could play.

"I go to Pearce," I said back. He smiled and told the group that I was a "real smart cookie." Everyone laughed at this since, of course, they already knew that.

From that moment, Logan and I became inseparable. The rest of the kids doted on us as if we were their king and queen, which I suppose we were. But we only had eyes for each other. Every day, we met for breakfast before heading out to the lagoon. We'd sit side by side in lounge chairs all morning, then break at twelve-thirty for lunch, which we'd eat with the whole group. Then we'd disappear for a bit, exploring the grounds of the resort together. Late afternoons were spent wrapped up together in a hammock, gazing up at the perfect Hawaiian sky and, of course, kissing. I couldn't kiss him enough and the feeling seemed to be mutual.

Luckily for me, my grandmother was busy with husband number six, the former teen idol, so she allowed me to eat dinners with the group almost every night.

By the time Christmas Eve rolled around, Logan asked me to spend it with his family. They even invited my grandmother and her husband to come along, too.

Christmas Eve was magical. Which is saying a lot, coming from a Jewish girl. My grandmother later told me that I was beaming the whole night. Positively beaming. Everything just seemed so perfect. Logan's parents were kind to me. They didn't ask where in the city I lived, just went on and on to my grandmother about how smart I must be to attend Pearce. My grandmother never once mentioned that I only got in because of my mother. She simply smiled to accept the compliment.

There were even presents—a photo album from the gift shop from Logan's parents and a delicate necklace with a pink shell dangling in the center from Logan. As he put the necklace around my neck, I remember thinking, *I will never take this necklace off. Ever.*

That night we had sex under the banana tree by the lagoon.

Me, for the first time ever. Him, for the third. I was utterly, completely in love.

I'd be lying if I said that a tiny little part of me wasn't also thrilled at the prospect of going back to school with a real-life, bona fide boyfriend. Better still, a Dalton boy. One who went to the right school, wore the right clothes, lived in the right part of town. Maybe having Logan would make me feel less like a social pariah.

And I knew just when I'd show him off. Melissa Rowan, the richest girl at school, was having a New Year's Eve party. She hadn't really invited me, per se, but she was throwing flyers around the hallways before break, so how strict could the guest list be? News of the party had reached Dalton, and Logan and his friends were planning to attend. On the last night of vacation, we said our tearful good-byes and told each other that we'd meet at the party.

I literally had to bribe my best friend Libby to come with me. I had to agree to do her geometry homework for an entire month just to get her to walk in the front door.

It was a simple bargain: I knew I couldn't go to the party by myself, and she knew that the second I met up with Logan, I'd be off making out with him for the rest of the night, leaving her completely alone at a party she didn't want to attend in the first place.

We walked in and I tried to keep my head high, tried to act like the leader of the pack I was when I was in Hawaii. But the moment I walked into Melissa's brownstone, I was transformed back into Hannah Goodman, class outcast. No one turned around when I entered the room like they'd done in Hawaii. No one even noticed at all. The huge smile I wore was greeted with blank stares. My tanned skin, which I thought made me glow, was becoming warm and itchy. I quickly downed a beer to get a bit of a buzz—I figured that if I felt giddy enough, I could fake my confidence.

By the time Logan and his friends walked in, Libby and I were firmly ensconced in a corner. I turned to see him—you could feel his presence as he walked into the room—and he looked even more handsome than he had in Hawaii. I fingered my shell necklace and walked over to him, but it was already too late. It was obvious. I may have been the coolest girl in Hawaii, but back here in Manhattan, I was a nobody. And no one in the New York City prep school scene wants to be with a nobody.

He walked by me and pretended he had no idea who I was. I would like to say that I was crushed, that my heart was broken, but the truth is, I had a feeling that this would happen all along.

Seven

It's raining. I figure that my grandmother will take this as an op-portunity to have her event planner come by and work on my welcome-to-the-Hamptons garden party, but she has something else in mind.

My grandmother wants to organize her photo collection. I didn't even know she had a photo collection, but it seems she does. And a quite extensive one, at that.

In her bedroom there is an enormous trunk, the kind that people used for trips on cruise liners across the Atlantic. A trav-eling chest. The sort of thing that isn't used anymore because it's too large and bulky to travel with. When I saw it in her bedroom on my first day here, I'd assumed that it was part of the décor—it's a Louis Vuitton with faded leather, beech-wood slats, and a "V" hand painted on the top. Then there are the labels: Greece, Cannes, Spain, the Bahamas. They read like a diary from her life.

"What is this?" I ask, running my fingers over the customs stickers.

"My photographs," my grandmother answers, and inserts a key. The trunk squeaks open, and as I peer in, I can see that it's filled with old photographs and albums.

"I never knew you had this," I say, and my grandmother gives me a sly smile. She is very much an open book, so I'm surprised to have discovered something about her that I didn't know before. Why would she store all of these old photographs in a trunk? Why is she traveling with them?

"Makes me look like an old lady," my grandmother says, almost under her breath.

"No," I say, "it doesn't. You know, people who've lost their homes in fires say that the thing they most wish they'd run back for is their photos. Photographs are important."

We sit down on her bedroom floor, next to the trunk, thousands of pictures splayed at our feet.

It is like a map of my grandmother's life. And my life, too. My grandmother is seated over by the black-and-white photos, but I'm surrounded by swaths of color. I see a few of her past husbands—the Mattress King with a glass of sangria in one hand and my grandmother in the other; the pop star, performing at the Carlyle in New York City; and even one of the Senator, when they were at an NRA fund-raiser in upstate New York. My grandmother stops and stares at one photo in particular, so I lean over and snatch it from her hands. It's a picture of her with her first husband.

"Rhett Butler," I say.

"Oh, him," she says. "I was just looking at that photo to remind myself of how young I once was." And then, before I can formulate my next thought: "Look at this photo."

I scoot over.

"It's all of you, isn't it?" I ask.

"Yes," she says. "That's me, that's your grandfather, and that's your mother."

"Wow," I say. They all look so happy. I'm not accustomed to seeing my mother look happy.

"I think you look like your mother here," my grandmother says.

"I think I look like you."

She pulls me to her for a hug.

"If that's what you think," she whispers into my ear, "then you do."

I do not look like my grandmother. I'm nowhere near as pretty. I look just like my mother. Unfortunately, she's the one person in the world who I don't want to look like. Don't want to be like. Growing up, I used to wish that my grandmother was my real mother. I can't say that much has changed. My grandmother wishes that I could be closer to my mom, not resent her quite as much as I do, but I know that she secretly cherishes our close relationship. I'm not sure we'd have that if my mother was fully in the picture.

It's hard to look in the mirror and see my mother staring back at me. I see the parts of her I wish I hadn't inherited—her inability to stay in one place for too long, her instinct to run at the first sign of a problem. She was always running. And sometimes I feel like I always want to run, too. After all, isn't that how I got out here this summer? My life in the city got a bit too complicated, so I ran to the one safe place I could go, the one place I knew I would be secure.

I'd much rather resemble my grandmother. She never judges my life choices. She always lets me be. With my mother, it was always as if I couldn't live up to some ideal that she had made up in her mind for me. Nothing was ever cool enough or hip enough for her. What I always longed for throughout my entire childhood was to be normal. To be like all the other kids who populated my school. But she lived outside of normal.

It was a cruel joke, really, to put me in an Upper East Side prep school and then expect me to stand out. To not follow the crowd. I ended up an outcast who was desperate to fit in, and I'm not sure I've ever entirely escaped that feeling.

My grandmother, on the other hand, saw the importance of living a "normal" life. She understood why a little girl needed the jeans everyone else was wearing, or why it was important to be invited to the sleepover party that everyone else was attending. She didn't see living a normal life as a sin. She thought you could live a normal life and make it extraordinary for yourself. Which I suppose is what she does. She makes a casual lunch at home, just the two of us, into something exciting. Into an event. "Life gives you enough to cry about," she always tells me, "so you have to celebrate the times when you can be happy."

It's what I would like to do for myself. But I don't really know how.

Eight

I never knew my father. Never even met him.

As my mother explained to me—years before it was actually appropriate to have done so—my father was a man who didn't want to be a father. He was a friend to my mother, and when she decided that she wanted to have a baby, he agreed to help her under the condition that he would not have a role in my life, that he wouldn't have to actually *be* my father.

The best way to characterize their relationship would be to say they were work colleagues. He was a reporter for the *Washington Post*, and they often found themselves on assignment together. Through the years, I'd ask my mother to tell me the story of how they met. I was desperate to romanticize it, make it something more than it was, but my mother never let me. "He was a friend, nothing more," she would say, even though she could tell how badly I wanted to turn it into a fairy tale, to make it something grand.

I'm not angry about it anymore. At least not like I used to be. As a child, I'd sneak off to the New York Public Library and comb through old issues of the *Washington Post* on microfiche, looking for my father's bylines. I'd sit in the stacks and make up elaborate stories about how my father, when I was born, realized that he really did want to be a dad, and had only stayed away for so long because of his important work. I wouldn't hold it against him when he finally came back for me, I vowed, I would just run to him and hug him and tell him that everything was okay, since we were a real family now.

These fantasies kept me going for much of my young life. They kept me warm at night, helped me fall asleep. I'd be on a school trip to the Bronx Zoo and I could practically see my father coming toward me from Tiger Mountain, ready to be my dad. Or I'd be with a friend at the Aquarium in Brooklyn, and I'd imagine my father surprising us and then taking us to the Coney Island boardwalk for a hot dog and a ride on the Cyclone.

I don't have fantasies like that anymore. Now that I'm an adult, I understand that we all make decisions in life. Some are good, some are bad, but we make the decisions. And my father made his.

Still, I like to believe that my father feels that not knowing me was one of the bad ones.

Nine

Raoul is taking us wine tasting today, although my grandmother would probably disagree with that statement. It's not so much that he's taking us, which my grandmother would take to mean that he's invited us, it's that he's driving so we can drink whatever we like. If you ask me, that's even better.

"Notes of berry and wood," my grandmother says, swishing a glass of pinot noir around her mouth.

My grandmother knows how to taste wine properly. You take a sip, swirl it around your mouth, then open your mouth slightly and breathe in some air, so that you can then taste the wine once it's been aerated. Then, for your grand finale, you are to spit the contents of your mouth out into a bucket, aptly named the "spit bucket." Since I have decided that getting drunk is the whole point of wine tasting, I refuse to spit. My grandmother, also, refuses to spit, but for altogether different reasons. She thinks it's unladylike.

"Berry and wood," the sommelier says. "That's very good."

The sommelier has taken a liking to my grandmother. When we first walked in, he said that he couldn't place her trace accent. She explained that she was born in France, and he was immediately enchanted. Apparently, he studied wine in France for four years. Ever since he said that, my grandmother has been playing up her French accent. "Feminine wiles," she will later tell me.

"This wine is very good," my grandmother says. "Don't you think, Hannah?"

"It's very good," I say. For a minute I consider whether I'm slurring my words, but then decide that I am not. I take another bite of aged brie on a hearty seven-grain cracker, just for good measure—and to make sure I don't embarrass my family by falling over drunk at the Southampton Vineyard.

I do not taste berry and wood. I just taste wine.

"We'll take a case of this, too, dear," my grandmother says, and the sommelier smiles. There's a sparkle in his eye and I'm not sure if it's because my grandmother is flirting with him, or because he just sold another case of wine. We already have three cases in the car.

The sommelier uncorks another bottle.

"Dessert wine?" he asks, even though it's not really a question. He's just about done uncorking the wine, so even if we didn't really want it, it seems that dessert wine is in our future.

"I love sweet wine," my grandmother says. "I grew up on Rieslings from Alsace."

"Ah"— the sommelier nods— "the Alsacian Riesling. Perfection." And then to me: "Your grandmother has a very fine palate."

"Yes," I say, downing the rest of my pinot noir. "That's one of my favorite things about her."

The sommelier furrows his brow and my grandmother regards me skeptically. I wonder what she will be more annoyed about later: that I made one of my "clever quips," or that I wasn't flirting with the sommelier, whose age is somewhere between my grandmother's and mine.

"Shall I pour?" the sommelier asks.

"Yes, please," my grandmother says with a smile. She's very good at brushing things off. I wish I could be like that. If something annoys me, I'm likely to sulk about it for days.

The sommelier motions to the back, and the chef brings out dates stuffed with goat cheese and almonds. I take one and let it melt in my mouth.

"Great pairing with this wine, isn't it?" the sommelier asks.

"Great," I say, even though I haven't yet touched my glass.

We sip wine and eat our dates (my grandmother, one; me, four), and talk about how wonderful the pairing is. Once the dates are gone, I move back to the baked brie and seven-grain crackers. I keep my eyes down, lest anyone see me pairing a Muscat with the wrong cheese.

"That's very good, Hannah," the sommelier says. "I think brie is a wonderful complement to this wine."

My grandmother beams. *See, I knew we could teach my class-less granddaughter something if we stuffed her full of enough wine!*

"Yes," I say, and nod soberly. "Very good complement."

"You know," the sommelier says, "when I was in culinary school, I used to think my beverage classes were a real joke. I used to get drunk in wine class and not even pay attention!"

He looks at me. Clearly, that was the punch line.

"That's so funny," I say, without actually laughing. My grandmother smiles broadly. She will later remind me of the importance of laughing at a man's jokes, even if they aren't funny.

"But then I went to France to study pastry and I just fell in love with wine. I'm not sure when it happened exactly, but it changed my whole life's course."

"Hannah knows a little something about that," my grandmother chimes in.

"Oh?" he asks. "Did something change your life's course recently?"

"Hannah got arrested," my grandmother says.

I feel my face getting very red. I'm not sure if it's the wine or my grandmother's declaration, but I take a sip of water, just to be safe.

The sommelier is riveted. He's practically sitting at the edge of his chair. I would have thought that someone who works with fine wines, who has dedicated his life to the finer things in life, would find this story somewhat distasteful, but my grandmother has piqued his interest.

"She's wanted by the State of New York for attempted murder," my grandmother says.

"No, I'm not," I say, but the sommelier still has his mouth on the ground. He's practically panting. He's like one of those dogs you see in a cartoon whose mouth drops to the ground and tongue unrolls while his eyes pop out of his head. "I was *questioned* by the New York City police. I was not arrested."

"For attempted murder," my grandmother says.

"For attempted murder?" the sommelier asks.

"For attempted murder," I say.

"Who did you try to kill?" he asks.

"I didn't try to *kill* anyone," I explain. "It was an accident and his mother completely overreacted and tried to press charges."

"Whose mother?" he asks.

"Her ex-boyfriend," my grandmother says, in a hushed tone. "So, you'd better watch your step. Don't get too close to this one."

I'm about to explain that this all wasn't really such a big deal—my ex is completely fine, and I only came out here to try to get a little rest and relaxation before rebooting my life in the city—

but we're interrupted by the winemaker who has a case of wine on each shoulder.

"I've got a case of the pinot noir, good choice," he says. "And I also brought out the Muscat, just in case you wanted that, too."

"Sure," my grandmother says, "why not?"

The winemaker retreats to the car.

"We should be going," my grandmother says. "It was so nice to meet you."

"It was my pleasure," the sommelier says, taking her hand and kissing it.

"Thank you for everything," I say. I think about trying to explain, telling him that I'm not an attempted murderess, but then decide otherwise. After all, it's not like I'm going to be seeing him again. I walk toward the door.

"I'd love to see you again," the sommelier says, taking my hand.

"Oh, sure," I say. "This was fun. Maybe we'll come back again."

"I mean just you and me," he says. "May I have your telephone number?"

"Who me?" I say. "Don't you mean my grandmother?"

"Why would I mean your grandmother?" he asks, laughing.

"Oh, right," I say. We just stand there for a minute, staring at each other. I don't particularly want to give him my number—the truth is that before my grandmother started in with all of the joking around about my legal situation, I was not having a good time with this man. I found him a bit pedantic. He does have nice hair, especially for his age, whatever that might be. It's full and wavy with a sprinkling of gray. He's got wrinkles next to his eyes, but for some reason, on men, that's always so sexy. But when he told me that my beloved Santa Margherta pinot grigio was overproduced and awful, I wanted to punch him.

It's as if we are both waiting for the other one to speak. Technically, since I was the one to speak last, the onus of conversation should be on him. But he stands there, just staring at me with a stupid grin, presumably waiting for me to hand over my phone number.

Since I don't know what else to do, I give it to him.

Ten

My last relationship ended badly.

When I woke up that morning, I had no idea that by the end of the day my relationship would be over. If I'd known that the ending was so near, I might have made sure that the last kiss we'd shared was more special, or that my hair was more perfect as he watched me leaving his apartment. Instead, I'd overslept and left the apartment in a hurry with my unwashed hair and unmade-up face. I still can't remember whether or not I even kissed Jaime good-bye.

It was a few minutes after ten when I got to my office. A few minutes after that when the administrative partner of my firm appeared in my door.

"Hey, Tim."

"Hannah." He stood, leaning on the frame, his arms and legs crossed neatly over his body. It's never a good thing when the administrative partner of a law firm comes to see you. It either means that someone has criticized your work or, worse, wants to give you more work.

"What's up, Tim?" I asked as nonchalantly as I could muster. I made it a habit never to make small talk with him. When he appeared in my doorway, I generally just wanted him to say what he was going to say and then go.

"The New York State Attorney General's Office has an opening," he said, and looked down at his shoes for an instant.

When you're a ninth-year associate at a large Manhattan law firm, that's not the administrative partner being nice and showing concern over your career—that's the firm's gentle way of telling you that you're not making partner. That you no longer have a career.

"I'd be happy to make some introductions," he continued, "and set up some meetings over there for you."

All the while he was telling me this, I couldn't help thinking about what he would be like in bed. In fact, whenever I meet a man, all I can think about at first is whether or not he'd be good in bed. I look at his lips, the way he holds himself, the way he looks when he thinks I'm not looking at him. And I always look at his hands. Not because most women my age look at a man's hands to see if he's married or not, but because my mother always told me when I was young to look at a man's hands so that you can see how hard he has had to work in his life. She was always telling me things like that that were inappropriate for my age.

I look at a man's hands and think about what they would feel like on my skin. Tim's hands were soft and gentle and didn't have a scratch on them. They had that prep-school-haven't-worked-a-day-in-his-life feel to them that I abhorred. I think that a man's hands should feel like a man's hands. Big, strong, masculine. Jaime's hands were rough and calloused, more a product of playing the bass guitar than actual real-life hard work, but sexy nonetheless.

"I think this could be a really great fit," he said. "Hannah?"

"I haven't taken any of my vacation time in the last two years," I said.

"So, should I make a few calls?" he asked, trying to get me back on track.

"That's twelve weeks altogether."

"Yes," Tim said. "But the Attorney General's Office?"

"What?" I asked.

"I'll give you some time to think about it," he said before leaving. It took me the rest of the morning and most of the early afternoon to digest what Tim had said to me—the gravity of it. I was not making partner at this law firm. I'd given up the last nine years of my life to this place and now it was all over with nothing to show for it. Just like that. I couldn't stay at the firm if I wasn't making partner and no other firm would want me, since they would know that any ninth-year associate who is looking for a new job is only looking because she didn't make partner at her own firm.

By 3:30 p.m., I'd called Jaime to tell him the whole story in gory detail. I knew he'd be around—he was always around—just like any starving artist in New York would be.

"Could you swing by my office?" I asked. "I need to talk."

"Those bastards," he said. "How dare they?"

At 4:00 p.m., I stood on the corner of Fifty-Third and Fifth with my unwashed hair waiting for my boyfriend, ready for the sympathy to pour over me as I told him again about how horrible my day was. As I stood waiting, I realized that with the drama of the day, I'd entirely forgotten to eat lunch.

Four-fifteen and still no sign of Jaime. I figured it should only take him about thirty minutes to get from downtown to midtown, but I couldn't wait. I was beginning to see spots before my eyes. I looked around for the closest candy store, certain that a large frozen yogurt with chocolate sprinkles would get my blood sugar under control.

I walked down Fifth Avenue in search of a candy store, my head throbbing from hunger, but it being midtown Manhattan, I found a street vendor selling nuts first. I bought a bag of salted cashews and a bottle of water from the vendor. I practically swallowed them whole, chugging the water down with the nuts as they were still in my mouth. As the water went down my throat, I could feel my body thanking me. The spots went away and I felt stronger. I took a deep breath and looked up. Jaime was coming my way. The sight of him, of his broad shoulders, long hair, and rough hands, always put a smile on my face.

"Hey, baby," I said, and put my arms around him for a kiss. Not one of those "hello" peck-on-the-lips kisses, but a real kiss. A thank-God-you're-here kiss. He gave me a heavenly kiss back and I could feel my day getting better. I pulled away and smiled at him.

His eyes rolled back into his head and he passed out. I tried to hold on to him so he wouldn't hit the pavement, but my five-foot-four frame was no match for all six-one of him.

I didn't realize he'd take the news that badly.

I fell to my knees and put my hand to his face. He was out cold, but sweating profusely. Trying my best to remember my health class lessons from junior high school, I began to perform CPR. A crowd gathered around us and I heard people on their cell phones, calling 911. Suggestions came flying from the crowd. Give him food! Give him water! I took the water bottle I'd been drinking from and tried to pour some into his mouth, which did nothing but get his face wet.

Just as I felt panic sinking in, I heard an ambulance come roaring down Fifth Avenue. It stopped right in front of us, blocking an entire lane of traffic. Two EMTs jumped out and carefully loaded Jaime, still unconscious, into the ambulance, with me following. Inside, the EMTs began drilling me with questions about Jaime.

"Age?" they asked.

"Twenty-seven," I replied, grabbing his hand. It was hot and sticky to my touch.

"Does he have any medical conditions?"

"No," I said, stroking his hand, "Oh, wait, yes. He has a weak left shoulder." The EMTs looked at me. The older one furrowed his brow.

"Any allergies?" the older EMT asked, and I felt my stomach fall through my body, straight to the ground. The world had temporarily stopped, yet I could feel the room inside the tiny ambulance spin. When it stopped spinning, I had two very concerned EMTs still staring at me. "Any allergies?" the older one asked again.

"Yes," I said. "Nuts."

The EMTs didn't say a word, rather looked at my face and then looked down at my left hand, still clutching the bag of cashews and bottle of water.

"I didn't give him any nuts," I said, feeling my face heat up. The younger EMT reached back into the supply drawer and took out a needle. "But I did kiss him. He couldn't possibly have had an allergic reaction from my eating nuts and then kissing him." The older EMT rolled up Jaime's sleeve while the younger one flicked the needle twice. "Could he?" He drew down the needle— hard—and Jaime woke up with a start. His body lurched forward as the older EMT helped him sit up and then lay back down.

"Where am I?" he asked.

"You're going to be all right, honey," I said.

"You lost consciousness," the older EMT told him. "We're just going to take you to the hospital for observation."

Moments later the EMTs were lowering Jaime's gurney onto

the ground and into the emergency room doors. I ran alongside them, holding Jaime's hand as we entered the hospital.

"What relationship are you to the patient?" a hospital employee asked me, furiously scribbling on his clipboard as we wheeled Jaime toward an empty bed in the emergency room.

"I'm his fiancée," I lied. I was afraid that only family was allowed to be in the emergency room with patients, and I didn't want to leave Jaime alone. Jaime pretended not to hear, the way any single man in his late twenties pretends not to hear when his girlfriend mentions marriage and/or engagement. The attending physician came in to examine Jaime and a nurse showed me to an area where I could sit down. A sign above me indicated that cell phone use was not allowed in the hospital and I reached into my bag to turn mine off.

"Excuse me, miss, do you know a Priya St. John?" a different nurse asked me. I ran out to the reception area and threw my arms around my friend Priya.

"What the hell are you doing here?" she asked me. "Donnie in the mail room saw the whole thing and now the entire firm is talking about it."

"You know how Jaime's allergic to nuts?" I said, and Priya nodded her head. Anyone who had ever been out to dinner with Jaime and me knew that he was allergic to nuts. Anyone who had ever sat at a table next to Jaime and me at dinner knew that he was allergic to nuts. I showed her the bag of nuts, still curled up in my hand.

"You are not having a very good day," she said, grabbing them and throwing them in the nearest garbage. *She's a good lawyer*, I thought. *Getting rid of the evidence.*

As I shook my head, looking for further sympathy from

Priya, I felt a presence behind me, a set of angry eyes on my back. I turned around to find Jaime's mother, Celia, staring me down.

"Wot deed you do to my son?" she asked me in her thick Cuban accent, still shooting a deadly stare my way. She always looked at me with hatred, as if I had been personally responsible for the Bay of Pigs invasion.

"Jaime's back here," I said, bringing her back to Jaime's bed. Priya wisely stayed behind. Most of my friends were mortally afraid of Celia. The smart ones, anyway.

"Ay, dios mio!" she called out when she saw Jaime lying helplessly on the bed. She began praying very quickly in Spanish.

Our ER doctor, a woman who looked a little too young to actually be a doctor, came over to tell me that Jaime had stabilized and that he would be all right. Celia practically pushed me aside and announced that she "was ze boy's mother" and that the doctor should be speaking to her, and not to someone who wasn't family.

"With all due respect, Mrs. Castillo, I think that Jaime's fiancée should be here for this," the doctor said, giving an encouraging smile in my direction. Maybe she, too, has to deal with a woman like Celia. Celia grabbed my ringless hand and thrust it into the doctor's face.

"Dey are *not* engaged," she said. The ER doctor looked at me as if I'd just informed her that I would not be donating my kidney to my twin sister. "And he was about to break up with her anyway."

As if the humiliation of being broken up with by your boyfriend's mother isn't enough, I was asked to leave the Emergency Room. But apparently, that wasn't enough, either, because Mrs. Castillo then demanded that I be removed from the hospital. As I was being escorted down the hallway by a very burly candy striper, Celia called out to me: "How come every time my son ees with you he either ends up een the hospital or jail?"

That whole jail thing wasn't really my fault, either.

I got back to my apartment at a little bit past six o'clock and threw my bags down next to the door. I stood, frozen in the entrance-way, feeling an overwhelming sense of déjà vu. I tried to take a deep breath, but I couldn't escape the sensation of the walls clos-ing in around me. The feeling was back. I had to get out.

As I walked into my bedroom to change out of my work clothes, it dawned on me that I could leave. I could pack a bag and leave New York. Tonight. My job was gone. My boyfriend was gone, and I didn't have much else besides a Redweld folder filled with take-out menus.

I'd done it before.

The summer after my first year of law school, I packed up and went to live in the South of France for three months on a whim. Before that, I'd moved to Prague for a year during college, waiting until I'd found myself a place to stay before even letting anyone know I was gone. I'd even run off for two weeks in high school, leaving my mother in Brazil while I flew off to Greece to spend time with my grandmother.

The wanderlust was hitting me again.

The last time I felt like this was seven years ago, after *him*. The love of my life. The one I couldn't live without. The one I thought I'd grow old with. Once he was gone, it felt like my in-sides had been ripped out and I couldn't bear to sit still, not even for a minute.

I never say his name anymore. Never even hear it. Everyone around me is careful never to mention it. They call Adam "him" in hushed tones. Steer me away from buying books with characters named Adam. Anything not to upset me.

Turning over my options in my mind—Should I stay? Should I go? Where would I go if I left? What would I do if I stayed?—I poured myself a glass of wine and walked out to my balcony. Sitting outside, watching the world go by, I told myself that I did not want to be my mother. Never putting down roots, never staying too long. Running. Always running. *That* was not the recipe for a happy life.

The doorbell rang and I popped up from my seat, hoping that it would be Jaime. For a moment, I was afraid that it might be Celia, but I put that thought aside and rushed to the door. Standing there was a New York City detective.

"May I help you?" I asked, wondering why my doorman hadn't called ahead to announce him and why I hadn't answered the door through the chain instead of swinging the door wide open as I had.

"Detective Moretti, Eighteenth Precinct. May I come in?" he asked. He showed me his badge and didn't even try to enter my apartment until he'd been granted permission. I called the police and checked out his badge number as he stood patiently at my door. As I waited for the dispatcher to make sure that Detective Moretti was who he said he was, my eyes fell down to his hands. They were rough and leathery.

"What can I help you with, Detective?" I asked as I showed him to a chair in my kitchen.

"Where were you at four-thirty p.m. today?" he asked, taking out a pad and a pen.

"What?" I said. I was struck by how *Law and Order* it all was. Detective Moretti looked up and waited for my answer, pen poised at his pad. "Taking my boyfriend to the hospital for an allergic reaction to nuts," I said. "I was in an ambulance. Why?"

"You're being investigated for the attempted murder of Jaime Castillo," he said, looking up at me again. I assumed he was gauging my reaction to this news.

"What?" I said, thanking the gods above that Detective Moretti said "attempted murder" and not "murder." "That's ridiculous!"

"With all due respect, Ms. Goodman, you had a motive," the detective said. "He was going to break up with you." I never understood the expression "with all due respect." Clearly he did not respect me—he was accusing me of assaulting a man with my deadly lips.

"You can call me Hannah. And who told you that he was going to break up with me?" I asked.

"Jaime's mother," he said, and I resisted the urge to roll my eyes.

"Well, that is a total surprise to me," I said, speaking very quickly. "I had *no idea* that we were breaking up." I tried to remember something valuable from criminal law class. "And even if I *did* know, trying to kill him would not exactly be the best way to get Jaime to stay together with me, now would it?"

I spoke very quickly, saying anything that came to my head while I tried to remember my first year of law school. I got an A in criminal law; surely something should have stuck. Finally, I remembered something valuable: always lawyer up.

"I think I'd like to see my lawyer," I said, and Detective Moretti stopped scribbling and put down his pen.

"This is only questioning, Ms. Goodman. Do you really think you need a lawyer?"

"I'm sorry, Detective Moretti," I said, "I really think that I do."

The next morning, I went downtown with Priya, who was acting as my attorney even though she actually practiced tax law. As we got closer to the Eighteenth Precinct, I was beginning to doubt my very juvenile plan to get out of this mess. I was counting on the fact that Detective Moretti would be awestruck by Priya's beauty and let me out of the whole thing. Because if anyone could get you out of a mess just by being herself, it would be Priya.

Three years of law school and the best strategy I could come up with was to throw the detective off guard with a gorgeous tax attorney? No wonder my firm didn't want to make me partner.

Priya pulled her tiny Mini Cooper up to the precinct and parked it right in front. Her father is a diplomat, which means that she can park anywhere she wants in the city, a fact she takes full advantage of. Priya touched up her pout—a quintessential part of our defense strategy—and we were off to face the detective.

We waited for about fifteen minutes in what I could only guess was an interrogation room from its similarity to one I had seen on an episode of *CSI:NY*. Two cups of decaf later, the detective strolled in. Try as he did to focus on the investigation, he couldn't take his eyes off Priya. My plan was working perfectly. He and Priya made flirty chitchat as she crossed and uncrossed her legs in a very PG-13 *Basic Instinct* fashion. The swoosh of her nylons seemed to have the intended effect: Detective Moretti was awestruck.

"Sorry I'm late," the assistant DA said as he flew into the room. "Hi, I'm Nate—"

"Sugarman," I finished.

"Hannah," he said, with a look on his face that I couldn't quite decipher.

"You two know each other?" the detective asked.

"Yeah," Nate said, smoothing back his hair and setting his

briefcase on the table, "we went to law school together. I never thought we'd be adversaries in court, though. I didn't even know that you did criminal law."

"I don't," I said. "I'm the defendant." Nate shot a perplexed look in the detective's direction.

"You haven't been charged with anything," Priya piped in. "You're just in for questioning on these totally baseless and defamatory allegations." I was too shocked to see Nate to actually register that Priya was being a very good lawyer for someone who didn't even litigate for a living.

"I think there may be some kind of conflict of interest here," Nate said, motioning for the detective to leave the room with him.

"If he's an ex-boyfriend," Priya said as soon as the door slammed shut, "I'm recusing myself."

"You can't recuse yourself," I said through gritted teeth. "You're not really my lawyer, you're my friend."

"You're not paying me for this?"

"Anyway, he's not an ex-boyfriend, I never would have dated him. We hated each other in law school," I said, putting my head in my hands.

"Why?" she asked. "He's cute."

"He's not cute," I said back through gritted teeth. "He's the epitome of everything I hate about the kids I grew up with in the city. Rich, entitled brats. The types who think they hit a home run when they were born on third base."

"Is that what you think of *me*?" she asked.

"No," I said, as I caught a glimpse of her diamond pendant, a sixteenth-birthday gift from her father. "We work hard. We don't rely on trust funds."

"He works for a living," she said. "He's the DA assigned to your case."

"That's not the point," I said.

"Isn't that exactly the point?" she asked.

"I can't believe I'm about to get arrested."

"I know," Priya said. "This is going to be really embarrassing."

I picked my head up to shoot her a dirty look just as Nate walked back into the room with Detective Moretti. I folded my hands primly and tried not to look like an attempted murderess.

"I think there has been a huge misunderstanding here," Nate said. "You're free to go, Hannah." Priya and I sat still for a minute, unsure of what to say or do.

"Of course there has been," Priya said as she stood up and adjusted her suit. She grabbed me by the arm and led me out of the interrogation room. "Bye, Detective," she added with a flirty smile.

As we walked to Priya's car, she said, "So, I guess he didn't hate you all that much."

Eleven

"It's all about figuring out what someone wants and giving it to them," my grandmother says.

"You sound like a con man," I say.

"I sound like a good conversationalist."

"I'm still detecting notes of con man."

"When you meet these men today, focus on the one who is most enchanted by you. A relationship works best when the man wants the woman more than she wants the man."

"What if they all want me desperately?" I ask.

"Then you date all of them," my grandmother says, matter-of-factly. She's completely missed my joke. Or maybe she's just pretending she didn't hear it. "It's important to have lots of men hanging around. That way, you can never get too caught up in any one of them."

I see her point. When you just have one romantic prospect, you tend to put everything into that one. Maybe if you have three or four going at the same time, you take a good hard look at each of them.

What I normally do is put all of my eggs into one basket, become obsessed with that basket, and then wonder why I end up brokenhearted and alone. Never a contingency plan, never a thought as to what I'll do if things don't work out. The last time things didn't work out, with *him*, I never fully recovered.

Maybe my grandmother is on to something. She has a different date for each day of the week and she's happy. She's having fun and not getting hurt. Eventually, I suppose, one will step up to the plate and she'll marry him, but until then, she can just enjoy her summer. Maybe I should be more like my grandmother.

"Should I be playing the bad-girl angle?" I ask. We are on a one-hundred-fifty-foot yacht in Sag Harbor with another one of my grandmother's gentleman callers. This one has—count 'em!— three grandsons, so I want to figure out the game plan before I get caught off balance again.

"You should—" she begins, but gets cut off.

"So that's where you've been hiding," our host says as he joins us. Here, on the top level of the yacht, there is a hot tub that seats eight with bench seating around the perimeter.

"We're not hiding," my grandmother responds with her eyes sparkling. Even through sunglasses, her eyes sparkle. "We're just having some girl time."

"Well, maybe it's time for some coed time," he says with a big puppy-dog grin. "We missed you two."

Harold is really quite nice. He's wearing a hat with the name of his boat on it, *Zelda May*, along with a polo shirt with the same insignia. I've noticed the towels are embossed with the boat's name, as well, so I've made it my goal today to see how many things are monogrammed with this namesake. His yacht is named for his wife, dead four years now, and he refuses to change it. Refuses to apologize for it. I like Harold. So does my grandmother.

"We've missed you, too, darling," my grandmother says as

we make our way down to the main level. From the top level, where we were, down to the second floor, you need to walk down a tiny spiral staircase. All I could think as I walked up was: I hope no one is staring up my cover-up. It would not be a flattering view. And now, I see that, indeed, I have an audience on my way down: all three of Harold's grandsons are waiting for us just under the staircase.

I try to emulate the way my grandmother walks down the stairs—with her legs completely closed, sliding against each other as she takes each step. I'm reminded of her teaching me to sit like a lady, over tea at the Plaza Hotel when I was six years old. Knees together, ankles crossed, letting your legs fall lazily to one side.

It's an enormous living room space. It doesn't look like a boat at all. It's nicer than most people's homes. Beautiful mahogany cabinetry; soft, supple carpet; elegant custom-made couches arranged in a comfortable design that really encourages conversation; and a playful card table with mismatched antique chairs. And, of course, a sixty-inch flat-screen television that looks like a mirror, but reveals itself at the simple touch of a button.

I wonder for a moment how all of these heavy materials can float. Harold makes the introductions and his eldest grandson offers to show me around the yacht.

"Let's go to the bow first," he says, and opens the cabin door for me with the push of a button. All of the doors are automatic sliding doors due to the high winds out on the water. I walk out to the side of the boat but then realize I don't know where the bow is.

"You lead the way," I say.

"The bow is the front," he says, smiling. "I see we have a boating virgin here."

I have no response to that. But that's okay, since Trey continues: "Starboard is the right side, the left side is called port."

"Wouldn't it just be easier to say right and left?"

He laughs. "Yes, I suppose it would.

"The stern is the back of the boat," he says. "So, let's go to the bow. These close quarters are starting to get to me. Let's get away from everyone for a second."

When my grandmother and I first boarded the yacht, before the grandsons were back from town, Harold showed us around the lower part of the boat, where all the bedrooms are. This boat has four bedrooms, each equipped with its own en suite bathroom. And that's not including the servant's quarters, which are under the hull (not a part of the tour) and house a staff of eight.

Close quarters? The bedrooms on this yacht are bigger than the bedroom in my Manhattan apartment. Still, I humor him, since that's what I imagine my grandmother would do in this situation.

"Have you been out here all summer?" I ask as we approach the bow. We're pulling out of the harbor, so it's fun to be at the front of the boat. It's set up with two lounge chairs (outfitted with towels monogrammed with *Zelda May* and neck rolls that simply have a Z), so we each lie down on a chair.

"We started the summer in Cape Cod," he says. "And then we docked in Nantucket for a bit before coming down here. In a week or so, we're going to double back to hit the Vineyard and then Newport. We like to be in Newport at the end of the summer to hit the boating show."

I'm dying to know if these guys work—I assume Harold is retired—but I can't seem to formulate a way to ask that doesn't sound judgmental. Probably because I want to know so that I can judge them.

"That's amazing, you and your brothers can get so much time off," I say.

"Yeah," he says, "when you work for yourself, you can set your own schedule. You must know what I mean, right?"

Of course he assumes that I know what he means. We're out on a yacht on a Wednesday. And now we are out on the open sea, without a care in the world.

"Actually, I'm a lawyer. I don't work for myself. I work for a firm in Manhattan."

I'm not sure why I'm so intent on explaining that I work for a living, emphasizing why we are different.

After all, I do work as a lawyer, but I have the luxury of living debt-free due to my grandmother's largesse: she paid for all of my schooling from Pearce straight through to law school. Technically, I'm not a trust-fund baby since my mother refused to ever let my grandmother set up a trust fund for me, but what's the difference? She's paid vast sums of money over the years to make sure I could live debt-free. She even made the down payment on my apartment.

But still, it feels different.

"My grandfather said you were staying out here all summer," he asks, clearly confused.

"I am."

"So you're not working right now," he says.

"It's complicated."

"My life is *complicated,* too," he says, giving me a wink. "My brothers and I don't actually work for ourselves, per se. We live off our trust funds."

I furrow my brow. Clearly, he thinks that I'm a trust-fund baby, too.

"Oh, no, it's not like that," he says, allaying my fears. I breathe out a sigh of relief. "We're not blowing through them like some of the morons you see out here. No, we just live off the dividends."

Dividends? His trust fund is so large that he doesn't even need to dip into it. He can live large off the mere dividends. I can barely process this information.

"Is that what you do?" he asks me.

I say yes just to end the conversation. Trey points out parts of Connecticut we can see from the boat and I start wondering exactly how long this day cruise is going to last. Maybe I should have pled seasickness to keep us docked in their slip? I hear footsteps coming from the starboard side of the boat.

"Excuse me, please," one of the staff members says. She's wearing the yacht's uniform: khaki short shorts along with a polo monogrammed with *Zelda May* with her name embroidered under it: Inga. Her long blond hair is braided into two pigtails. "It's time for lunch, if that's okay with you."

"Fine," Trey says. "Grab me a Sam Adams Summer Ale and meet me at the table with it."

"Of course, Mr. Pennington," she says.

"Do you want anything?" he asks me.

"Oh, okay," I say. "May I please have a glass of white wine?"

"Certainly."

"I like a girl who drinks during the day," Trey says, smiling as he helps me up from my chaise longue.

I think but don't say, *I'll need to drink if I'm going to get through the rest of this trip.* And then I do.

Twelve

Mornings in the Hamptons are different from mornings in New York City. In the city, it's a hurried affair—a quick shower, throw on clothes that aren't too wrinkled, grab a bite to eat as you run out the door.

But here, morning is a ritual. We wake, and slowly get out of bed. I wear actual pajamas that have coordinating robes, so I can be covered up for breakfast. I have slippers. I put them on and then pad into the bathroom. I freshen up, then put on my robe and make my way to the breakfast table.

Breakfast is always a buffet with two or three choices of hot meals (today: pancakes and scrambled eggs) and a few choices of cold (granola and blueberry muffins). My grandmother's chef makes coffee to order, even though my grandmother and I drink the same thing every day (she, espresso; me, black coffee). We have three different newspapers to read (the *New York Times*, the *New York Post*, and the *Washington Post*).

The staff does not eat with us.

My grandmother has maintained a large staff for as long as I can remember. There's Raoul, her driver, and his wife, Martine, who works as housekeeper. In the summers, they live on the top floor of the garage in a small two-bedroom apartment. In the winters, they live in their own house in Queens.

She had two chefs, both formally trained in the classic French technique, although they could both do any type of food you might like. Alec, the older of the two, had been working for my grandmother since she was married to the Italian race car driver. On their honeymoon, he told my grandmother that he really appreciated home-cooked meals, which my grandmother took to mean that she should hire a chef. Jean-Marie, the younger of the two chefs, came aboard when my grandmother married the Mattress King. He really loved French food—the Mattress King never met a heavy sauce he didn't like—so Jean-Marie was hired to infuse healthy alternatives into his diet. Alec strenuously objected to a hollandaise with low-fat cream, so he gave my grand-mother an ultimatum: it was either Jean-Marie or him. Alec had been with her for years, but my grandmother had fallen in love with Jean-Marie's avocado salad, so Jean-Marie got to stay on, and Alec left. Also, my grandmother doesn't take kindly to threats.

There is one person whose job it is to "run the house." What that means exactly, I'm not quite sure, but I think Eleanor's for-mal title is social secretary (think 1940s screwball comedy star-ring Cary Grant and Katharine Hepburn). I think part of her job responsibilities include paying bills and maintaining certain ac-counts, like the phone and cable, but I could never be sure about that, since my grandmother doesn't like to talk about money. She's very good at acquiring it, but doesn't think it's seemly to talk about it.

Eleanor is in charge of the rest of the staff and she loves be-ing in charge. I see her walk around the house, looking down her nose at everything, making sure that each task is done with an eye toward perfection. She often travels with my grandmother, since one of her main responsibilities is to maintain my grand-mother's social calendar.

There are also two other housekeepers who come in two days a week to keep things clean. My grandmother likes a clean house. When she was married to my grandfather she took her role of suburban housewife very seriously, and takes tremendous pride in her home (or homes, I should say). Even though she no longer does the cleaning herself, she sees no reason why her homes shouldn't be immaculate.

Finally, there is a groundskeeper, who lives out at the estate year-round. During the colder months, when my grandmother isn't here, it's his job to maintain the grounds and the houses—to make sure that no pipes freeze, that no animals take up residence in any of the buildings, that the toilets get flushed once a week. For the months when my grandmother is out here full time, he concentrates on the landscaping and does small repairs on an as-needed basis.

Each staff member has been around for years, but I can't say that I know any one of them all that well. They do a very good job at remaining invisible—doing large amounts of their work when my grandmother and I are out shopping or strolling on the beach, remaining mostly in the kitchen when we are around.

My grandmother has decided to cook tonight. Which means that we have the kitchen to ourselves today. In fact, we have the whole house to ourselves, because she's given the staff the day off. Raoul and Martine are spending the morning relaxing in their apartment, but mostly everyone else has gone to the beach.

We don't spend a lot of time in the kitchen, my grandmother and I. Generally, breakfast is set out on the enormous butcher block that serves as the centerpiece to the kitchen, and my grandmother and I eat our breakfast in the adjoining sunroom. But today, after breakfast, we get ready quickly, and meet back at the butcher block to discuss our plan for dinner.

She's making coq au vin. I've been informed that it takes the entire day to cook, so I'm prepared. We sit on stools at the butcher block, and make a list of the ingredients we will need. I check the pantry as my grandmother calls out various ingredients that we may already have in the house, as she compiles a list of the things we will need to pick up in town.

I see a newspaper clipping taped to the back of the pantry door. It's old, the edges are so yellow that I'm almost afraid to touch it. The clipping reads:

RECIPE FOR A HAPPY LIFE

INGREDIENTS:
One cup of love
Two cups of friends and family
One tablespoon of understanding
Two tablespoons of compassion
Three teaspoons of generosity

Mix together and serve with a dash of humility. The recipe won't work out the same each time, but the important part is that you try your best and enjoy yourself.

"What is this?" I ask.

"Oh, that silly thing?" she says. "I'd almost forgotten all about it. My mother clipped it out of a newspaper when we first got to America."

"But you saved it," I say. "It must have been important."

"It reminds me of my mother," she says. "She wanted so badly to be American. For all of us to be American. So she would clip things like this out of the paper all the time."

"You say it to me," I say.

"What's that?"

"You say, 'That's not the recipe for a happy life.'"

"My mother used to say that to me when I was a girl," she says with a smile on her lips.

"Your mother said it to you and now you say it to me," I say.

"I used to say it to your mother, too, you know," she says.

"So, then, what *is* the recipe for a happy life?"

"I don't know," she says. "Maybe you and I will discover it this summer."

It's a beautiful day. I'm surprised she doesn't want to spend it out-doors as she normally does, but I'm thrilled that she's teaching me to cook. I really don't know my way around a kitchen, but even though my grandmother seldom prepares her own meals anymore, she's still an amazing chef. It's one of the things my mother recalls most fondly from her childhood, and I do, too. In between all of the jet-setting, my grandmother and I had lots of days like this, when we would stay in and she would cook for me. She used to make a truly amazing cheese sauce that I loved when I was younger. She'd pour it over pasta, cauliflower, really anything she had in the house. A nice contrast to the room service meals I was accustomed to.

We get to the market and stroll the aisles. I'm glad that she insisted we dress to go to the market—it seems everyone here is dressed to impress. I know my grandmother would have been disappointed if I'd come in what I normally wear to the super-market in the city, sweatpants and a T-shirt.

"Is this something your mother used to make for you?" I ask, excited about the thought of a shared history with my grand-mother. Her mother made it for her, now she's making it for me.

"No," my grandmother says simply. "We were rich. My mother never would have made this. Coq au vin is something I made for my first husband, the one who looked like Rhett Butler, after we ran off and were living in Montmartre with no money."

"Oh," I say, and put my head down into the produce.

"Coq au vin and beef bourguignon were two staples back then," my grandmother explains. "But they were considered peasant food, so my mother would never have made them. They're only now coming into vogue. Back then, we ate it because it was cheap; you could use inexpensive cuts of meat since the braising made them soft."

I want to ask her why, then, we are making it now, but I don't. I assume she has her reasons. I wonder how closely linked they might be to looking at the old photographs of her first husband.

My grandmother picks up a few sprigs of thyme and smells them.

"Fresh," she says, and holds them out for me to smell. I take a whiff, but I can't tell whether they smell fresh or not, so I simply smile and nod my head.

In the car ride home, I learn that her secret ingredient, the thing that makes her coq au vin special, is using riesling in place of red wine.

Once we get back to the house and unload the groceries, we take a break for lunch. I never saw either of my grandmother's chefs taking a break for lunch, but she assures me that the dish should be served hot, so we have a bit of time before we begin cooking.

We bring our chicken, pepper, and avocado wrap sandwiches (prepared by Jean-Marie before she left for the day) outside and eat by the pool. We don't talk much, which is a big change from the usual. I try to just smile and eat my sandwich and pretend that everything is normal, but my grandmother is somewhere else today.

After lunch, we come back to the kitchen and begin our prep work. As I stand at the butcher block chopping carrots and cremini mushrooms, my grandmother prepares the chicken. I want to say something to her, but I get caught up in the chopping. As I chop, my mind wanders and I begin to feel calm. Calmer than I've felt in a while. Maybe this is why people love cooking. I've heard people say that cooking relaxes them, but I always found that it wasn't worth the effort to cook for hours on end, only to eat the product of your hard work in under half an hour.

My grandmother, of course, doesn't eat like that. She makes every meal last a long time. Savors every bite. She takes long sips of her wine and enjoys the meal. Before coming out here, I ate most of my meals standing up or on the go. My grandmother thinks that eating a meal without sitting down at a table is barbaric.

With all of our prep work done, it's finally time to start cooking. My grandmother guides me through how to brown my pancetta perfectly, and I feel such a sense of accomplishment at doing a task well. That's another thing I'm learning about cooking: I love completing tasks, checking things off a list. It makes me feel good to have browned my pancetta perfectly, that my grandmother now trusts me with browning an entire chicken.

Next, we add the carrots, onions, garlic, salt, and pepper to the pan and cook the mixture until the onions are lightly browned. We add the cognac and put the pancetta and chicken back into the pot. Then, my grandmother takes over for the next part, while I watch. She adds the wine, chicken stock, and fresh thyme, bringing the whole thing to a simmer, carefully adjusting the heat on the burner to get just the right amount of fire. Once she's happy with the simmer, we cover the pot and put it into the oven. It needs about forty minutes in the oven, so my grandmother suggests a quick swim while we wait.

She takes her time in the pool to relax and stretch her legs out. I, on the other hand, am checking my watch like a maniac.

"What will happen if it overcooks?" I ask my grandmother. I'm trying for a leisurely tone, but it comes out anything but.

"It won't overcook," my grandmother says.

"But we're in the pool," I say, feeling my pulse racing. "How will we know?"

"If it overcooks, we can always make it again," my grandmother says, waving her arms out in the water. She looks like a beautiful mermaid.

"But when you cooked it for Rhett, you couldn't afford to buy the ingredients again," I say. "What would you do if you overcooked it?"

"I didn't have a pool to relax in while it cooked," she says, smiling. "Back then I used to sit in the kitchen and wait."

"So, should we be waiting?"

"No," she says. "We should be relaxing. We worked hard to cook a beautiful meal, and in forty minutes, we'll take it out of the oven and finish it off. There's nothing to worry about. It will be delicious. Or it won't be. But anyway, it's just dinner. It's not the end of the world."

"What would you do with Rhett if you overcooked the dinner?"

"We would throw it away and spend the night making love."

I look away and then float off to the edge of the pool. Suddenly, I am no longer interested in the time.

The chicken does not overcook. It comes out of the oven perfectly done. And it turns out that we have more than enough
time to take a leisurely swim, and then take quick showers to get
ready for dinner. I set the table outside while my grandmother
finishes off the coq au vin. She apparently didn't think I was
ready to master the rest of the recipe after my near-breakdown in
the pool.

The table looks beautiful—my grandmother's china is the
perfect complement to the outdoor setting. A white bone china
with delicate yellow flowers, it's a nice contrast to the lush green-
ery outside. I set the glasses and silverware down on the table, but
still, it looks like something is missing. I decide we need a centerpiece. I've never once before in my life looked at a set table and
decided that it needed more, needed a centerpiece, but something inside of me is telling me that we simply cannot eat dinner
without some flowers adorning the table.

I walk around the house toward the front lawn, telling myself that I'm just looking for some pretty flowers to pick. But I'm
walking toward those hydrangea bushes as if I'm on autopilot. It's
not a conscious decision. One minute I'm thinking about a floral
centerpiece, the next moment, I'm there. I've completely disre-
garded the rosebushes and sunflowers. It's like I didn't even see
them there.

I stand before the hydrangea shrubs, mesmerized. All I
can think about is the last time I stood in front of these bushes,
the last time I was out here at the Mattress King's estate. But life
doesn't ever work out quite the way you plan it, and back then I
didn't know how precious happiness was. How happiness shouldn't
just be assumed—you may have it, only to lose it in an instant.

In my head, I'm telling myself to cut a few branches of flowers for the centerpiece, just enough to put into that bright yellow

Tiffany vase my grandmother has in the sunroom, but it's as if I can't move. All I can think about is him. How he knew I loved hydrangea, so he dragged that hammock, heavy brass stand and all, over to these bushes so we could lay here in the afternoons and stare at the flowers. How many afternoons did we spend in that hammock? I should remember that. But at the time, I took it for granted. I thought we could always come back here, always gaze out at the flowers, always spend a lazy afternoon together.

I don't know how long I'm out in the front of the house. I've completely forgotten about my grandmother, and the coq au vin, and our plan to have a lovely quiet dinner together. When my grandmother comes to find me, I've completely lost track of the time.

"Are you ready to eat?" she says. Her voice startles me, and it takes me a minute to remember where I am, what I'm supposed to be doing.

"Yes," I say. "Sure."

"I brought you a glass of wine," she says. It's a glass of sparkling rosé. Sparkling rosé, my grandmother told me on my first night out here, is what everyone drinks in the Hamptons. I've developed quite a taste for it in the past week. I take the glass from her and take a sip.

We walk together to the backyard in silence. Now we're both somewhere else, I suppose. My grandmother's brought out the huge pot with the coq au vin. She removes the lid with a flourish and we enjoy the fruits of our labors.

Thirteen

"The key to a happy marriage is for the man to be more in love with the woman than she is with the man," my grandmother tells me as we walk along the beach.

"Shouldn't the man and woman be equally in love?" I ask.

My grandmother looks down her nose at me. She removes her sunglasses, and slowly says: "Not if the woman wants her marriage to last."

I'm not sure what to make of this bit of advice.

I feel her eyes burning into me, so I turn to her. "You didn't love any of your husbands?" I ask. "Not even my grandfather?"

"Don't misunderstand me," she says. "I loved all of them. I loved each and every one of my husbands with all my heart. That's not what I'm saying at all."

"Then what are you saying?" I ask, but I'm not sure I really want to know.

"I loved them, but the truth is each one of them loved me more. Marriage can't be successful if the man doesn't love the woman more. The woman is the one who holds a marriage together, who works at it day after day, but she can't do it if the man is not fully, completely committed. You can't keep a man if he's only lukewarm about you. Eventually the marriage will collapse. Eventually, he will leave."

"And how would you know that?"

"I think I've been married enough times to know," she says.

"Someone who's been married seven times either knows quite a lot about marriage, or very, very little," I say back, almost under my breath. Even as the words trip out of my mouth, I'm still not sure if I want my grandmother to hear them.

We're walking along the beach in these enormous floppy hats ("A woman should never let her face get any sun after thirty," she told me earlier), so it's easy to let my hat fall and just block my face from my grandmother's view. With the combination of the hat and the wind blowing, I don't even think my grandmother can hear what I'm saying.

Except she does. "I've never been divorced, let me remind you," she says. She tilts the side of my hat so that she can speak directly into my ear.

"Your first husband," I say, turning to face her.

"That was annulled," she explains. "Every other husband widowed me. As I said my vows each time, I truly believed that that was the man I was meant to grow old with."

"Well, then, I guess you know quite a lot."

"I know enough," she says. "I think that you should just look for someone who is head over heels for you and give him a shot."

"And Jaime wasn't?" I say.

"He didn't love you enough," she says.

"And how, exactly, would you know that?"

"He didn't delight in everything you said. His eyes didn't follow you when you left a room. He didn't particularly care if you stayed or went."

"That's because we had a normal, healthy relationship," I say. "He wasn't jealous. He knew if I said I was going home, I was actually going home. We didn't have to be attached at the hip to show that we cared for each other."

"A man should miss you when you're gone," my grandmother says. "He hasn't even called you once since you've been out here."

"I don't want to play this game anymore," I say.

"It's not a game," she says.

"We're here," I say, as we approach another beachside estate.

"Why don't we keep walking?" my grandmother suggests. "I don't think we're done with this conversation."

"We're done," I say, and walk onto the bridge that connects the beach to the house. A sign alerts us that the estate is called Easy Money. So tacky, but having class isn't necessarily a prerequisite to owning beachfront property in the Hamptons.

My grandmother is friendly with the father of the owner of the house. She met Walter at a charity golf event right before I came out here. She wasn't there for the golf, just the black-tie party that went on afterward.

And now there's a party going on today.

As we walk along the bridge over the dunes, I can already hear the party. There's apparently a DJ and he's playing a remix of Justin Timberlake's "I'm Bringing Sexy Back." I look at my grandmother and she's doing a little dance-walk with a broad smile playing on her lips. It appears that she is, indeed, trying to bring sexy back this very minute. And me, I'm just walking, as if I were a little kid going to take a test.

But this party is a test, isn't it? Everything I do with my grandmother in the Hamptons is a test, it seems to me: how I dress, how I speak, how I act. It's all a test to figure out where I am in my life. What's going on with me. What I want. But I inevitably fail each one. How can you prepare for a test when you don't know what the proper answers are?

My grandmother, still dance-walking, grabs my hand and leads me straight into the heart of the party. It's like a scene out of a movie: there must be over a hundred people hanging out on the backyard deck. People are all over, dancing, holding frosty cocktails everywhere I look. The pool is filled with floating candles and the adjoining hot tub is filled with happy party guests. Waitresses flit about, carrying trays filled with tiny delicacies: mini hot dogs, mini hamburgers, mini bags of French fries. It's as if we are at a party for a small child, only the birthday boy is actually a forty-three-year-old man. And it's not his birthday.

Enormous lamps around the perimeter of the deck release a fine mist. It's a hot day and I suppose the party would be a huge failure if any of the guests were to overheat. My grandmother has to bob and weave ever so slightly, so as to avoid the misters, lest they disturb her hairdresser's handiwork, and since Jacques came to the house this morning in anticipation of this party, that would be a sin.

I have never been to a party like this. But clearly my grandmother has. She flashes a smile at the first man she sees and asks him where the bar is. I take a slightly different approach and avoid eye contact with virtually every party guest I encounter. Out of the corner of my eye, I see the man point to the bar and my grandmother takes my hand and drags me toward it.

I want to kill my grandmother for forcing me to wear this tiny baby blue bikini with white lace trim. I feel ridiculous. For starters, the salesperson told me that I shouldn't really get this suit wet, in light of the lace. But more to the point, there is no possible way that I can suck in my tummy for the entire party. I edge the matching sarong up my hips and closer to my belly, but my grandmother catches me and readjusts my outfit. I wish I were wearing her little ensemble instead: a navy one-piece with detailing around the neck. Hers has a matching sarong, too, but it goes down to her ankles, as opposed to mine, which hits mid thigh. If I drop something, I will not be able to pick it up.

She can't swim today, either, only it's not because of her suit. It's because she's chosen to come to this party in full jewelry. She's wearing emerald studs, not the most practical decision for a poolside party, and a chunky gold cuff bracelet.

She hands me a glass of white wine and we clink glasses. I consider asking her why we haven't ordered frosty beverages—there's an assortment of seven different coolers carrying every color of the rainbow—but I know what her answer will be. "Too many calories." She also thinks that drinks like piña coladas and daiquiris are too down-market.

"Vivienne!" I hear a voice call out. We both spin around at the same time and see Walter waving at us from across the pool. He exudes Hamptons cool with his kelly green Bermuda shorts and white button-down shirt with the sleeves rolled up. He could have walked right out of a Ralph Lauren catalog. He runs a hand through his mess of gray hair and smiles at us. He's got a mouth full of capped teeth, but on him, it doesn't look ridiculous. It just looks handsome, like he's a movie star. Walter also has a really deep tan, probably owing to his regular tee time at Southampton Golf Club, but his skin doesn't look leathery. Everything about him says refinement.

He takes my grandmother's hand and kisses her on both cheeks. I know that he is doing this because he is charmed by the fact that she is French, but since he, himself, is not, I consider this to be affected. My grandmother does the introductions and then Walter insists I meet his son, the owner of this house. I smell another fix-up.

Walter's son approaches and I can barely catch my breath. Only it's not that I'm swooning—it's the Cuban cigar he's smoking. It envelops us in a cloud of smoke, and I feel my eyes water. I look to my grandmother, but she doesn't seem to notice. The smoke has no effect on her; she stands there composed and acts riveted by everything that Joseph says to us. I, on the other hand, can feel the eyeliner and sunscreen dripping down my face.

Joseph ("Don't call me Joey") is short and unattractive and doesn't look like he belongs here at all. His skin is so pale he looks translucent. He speaks much louder than everyone else around us. His eyes stay planted on my chest, even as he speaks to his father and my grandmother. He has no hair on his chest or arms, but he has very bushy eyebrows. And that damned cigar.

"My sixth husband was a cigar smoker," my grandmother says. My grandmother is never at a loss for conversation. "He puffed away until his dying day."

She omits the part about the cigars being the thing that killed him. My grandmother will later tell me that it is in bad taste to say something like that in polite company.

Joseph explains to me that he owns tanning salons all across the Jersey area. I can tell by the way he describes his business that he looks down on his clientele, that he finds them to be classless and tasteless, and I hear my grandmother's voice echo in my mind when I think to myself: *It only lowers you to speak unkindly of others, especially those who provide your lifestyle.*

I smile and pretend to be engaged in the conversation, but my eyes dart nervously around the party. Perhaps if I find someone I know, I can excuse myself from this conversation and get out of this doomed fix-up.

But I'm really just fooling myself. I don't have a ton of friends in the city, especially the types of friends who might come out to the Hamptons, so instead I end up looking like one of those rude people who talks to you while trying to find someone more important to talk to. But Joseph doesn't seem to notice, since his eyes are still focused on my breasts.

"Hannah?"

I turn to see who has just called my name and through the throngs of people, I can't really see his face.

He weaves his way through the crowd, and I'm instantly deflated. I was hoping that it would be someone I could ditch Joseph for, but it's Nate Sugarman.

I hate Nate Sugarman. I loathe Nate Sugarman. I despise Nate Sugarman, and people like him. The men who act like boys by still wearing baseball caps and ironic T-shirts long after they've graduated college. The types of guys who still call one another by childish nicknames like Broseph or Animal or the more to the point, Beaver. The sorts of men who have so much family money they never really had to worry about making a living, so they rely on daddy's dime and connections to carry them through life.

Nate and I met at a mixer on the first day of law school. His reputation had proceeded him. The girls all whispered about his looks and his family money, the guys all talked about his father, the chairman of his family's multimillion-dollar corporation, whose name was often bandied about when discussing possible candidates for New York City mayor.

"Law is just a first step for me," he told me the first time we met. "After practicing for a few years, I'd like to make a bid for a judgeship at some point or a move into politics."

"That's great," I said. But I didn't think it was great. It just reinforced what I already hated about him: of course he can try for a judgeship or a move into politics. For others, that would be a pipe dream. But when you have the Upper West Side Sugarmans backing you, anything is possible.

Our second year of law school, we were matched up against each other in the Moot Court Competition. It was a semester-long competition that entailed massive amounts of research, the drafting of a twenty-page brief, and culminated in an hour-long oral argument against your adversary.

What I recall most about it was how Nate and his friends didn't take it at all seriously—they didn't take most of law school seriously either, but this was the one thing I felt was important. It was a chance to actually test out our lawyering skills in a mock setting, before we had a real client and stood before an impatient judge. But Nate and his minions did subpar research, and adjusted the margins on their briefs so they could write less but make it appear as if they'd completed the assignment properly. All throughout prep, I told myself that it was great that Nate didn't take this exercise seriously. I could beat him with my eyes closed.

But then, the day of our argument, he threw me for a loop. We arrived at oral argument, both of us in our navy blue lawyer suits, ready to go. His hair was slicked back, and I had mine in a bun. We looked just like real lawyers.

"Best of luck, Goodman," he said to me, hand outstretched to shake as we made our way toward the bench.

"Best of luck to you, too," I said, confident that I was going to win.

And then I saw them. Beneath that tailored blue suit was something that just didn't belong.

Sneakers. Nate Sugarman was wearing sneakers.

I just couldn't get over his footwear and I told him so. I told him that Moot Court was to be taken seriously. He laughed and told me that no one could see his feet as he stood behind the bar, but that wasn't the point. I could see them. Our classmates could see them. It was as if the rules didn't apply to Nate Sugarman. We all had to dress up in our uncomfortable lawyer shoes, but not Nate. Nate could just glide by in life in a pair of tennis shoes.

In hindsight, I tell myself that the shoes are what annoy me most about that day. Not the fact that Nate won our oral argument.

And then, of course, there's the fact that Nate Sugarman is the one member of my graduating class who knows I was recently accused of murder. Ahem, attempted murder. Not exactly fodder for pleasant cocktail hour conversation.

"Oh, hi," I say, remembering that the host of the party, Joseph, is standing next to me. "This is Joey."

Now I'm stuck. I don't want to be with Joseph, or his cigar, but I certainly don't want to ditch him and get stuck with Nate Sugarman. My only true play here is to pretend I'm on a date with Joseph. He may be slightly slimy, but he is the party's host, and Nate's at this party, so who is he to judge?

"Do you want a cigar?" Joseph asks Nate.

"Oh, thanks, man," Nate says. "But I don't smoke."

Joseph nods his head and resumes staring at my chest. A woman with much larger breasts walks by, and Joseph excuses himself.

"Well, I'll just let the two of you reconnect," Joseph says, and makes a hasty exit.

"Do you need a drink?" Nate asks me. I hold up my glass to show him that I don't.

"So, are you still with your firm?" Nate asks. I know he's just trying to make small talk, but this seemingly innocuous question is the crux of what's wrong with my life; the reason why I'm out here in the first place.

"Yes," I fib. It's not really a lie. It's more of a half-truth. "Are you still with the DA?"

"Yup," he says. "I love it."

"Great," I say, feeling a surge of anger as I realize that Nate's life plan, as laid out for me on our first day of law school, is going off without a hitch. Today, the DA's office. Tomorrow, a bid for a judgeship or a move into politics. The Oval Office awaits. Why does his life get to move along perfectly as mine continues to fall apart? My eyes dart around for an exit strategy. "Would you please excuse me?"

I turn on my heel and make a beeline for the house. I tell my grandmother that I'm going to the bathroom and breeze by her before she has a chance to say a word.

There's a long line for the guest bathroom. But waiting on a long line is much better than the alternative—mingling at the party—so I lean against the wall and wait my turn.

Twenty-five minutes later, I walk out of the bathroom, ready to face the party.

"What are you doing?" my grandmother asks. I'm not even five feet from the bathroom when she accosts me.

"Using the ladies room," I say. We walk together down the hallway. I try to adopt the dance-walk move I saw my grandmother doing earlier, but on me, it just looks silly.

"You were talking to two different young men," she says, "and you rejected both of them within ten minutes."

"Oh," I said. "I already know the tall one from law school. And I hate him."

"Well, he doesn't seem to hate you," she says. "Not at all. Why didn't you dance with him?"

"Because I don't want to dance," I say.

"You don't want to dance. You don't want to make new friends. What, exactly, do you want to do?"

"Have a frosty beverage," I say as I sail out of the house and toward the bar.

I make my way through the crowd on the deck, determined not to look back to see what my grandmother is doing. My plan is this: I will order and then down one of those delicious-looking high-calorie cocktails, then I will tell my grandmother I have a headache, and make my way home. I look down to check the time (*You should never leave a party in less than ninety minutes—it's simply rude to the host,* my grandmother would say), but then remember that my grandmother wouldn't let me wear my watch. *Why do you need to constantly check your watch if you're out having fun?* And, owing to the tiny size of my sarong, there was nowhere to put a cell phone.

As I sip my strawberry daiquiri, I do a mental calculation: it must have taken about half an hour to walk into the party, meet the host and his father, and then bump into Nate. Then, I was on the bathroom line for another half hour, so if I drink this daiquiri slowly, I can leave this party when I'm done without provoking the ire of my grandmother.

Thinking about all of this, I can't help but laugh to myself. Some people have grandmothers who stay at home and bake all day. I have a grandmother who goes out all day to party, and gets angry if I don't do the same. Double if I don't flirt with every eligible man I see.

"What's so funny?" Nate Sugarman again.

"Oh, nothing," I say. "I was just thinking about something my grandmother said."

"What?"

"Nothing."

"Oh," he says. And then, to the bartender: "I'll have what she's having."

I can tell by the look on his face as he waits for his drink that Nate Sugarman is not used to awkward silences. I bet he's also not used to girls who aren't charmed by him either. But I specialize in awkward silences, awkward silences actually make me feel comfortable, and I am not charmed by Nate Sugarman.

"Sweet," he says. I turn to face him and I can see his mouth trying to fight off a wince. He's talking about the strawberry daiquiri. So maybe he's a little charming.

I suppose he's attractive in a certain way. Today he's wearing a pink polo shirt and matching patchwork shorts, and it shows off how tall and lean he is. I say lean, because lean is different from skinny. Lean is something you become by having a standing tennis date or a set tee time. Skinny is something you become by being a starving musician living on the Lower East Side, unsure if you'll have enough money to buy yourself dinner that night. My ex, the musician, was skinny.

As I stand next to him at the bar, I notice that Nate Sugarman has a lot of freckles. And I mean a lot. They dot his nose and part of his cheeks and cover his arms. He is fair, but you can tell his skin would still tan easily, and he has very, very dark brown hair. Almost black. And it's straight, not like my unruly mane.

"Do you want to dance?" he says.

"Oh, no thank you," I say, because that's what I always say when someone asks me to dance.

"C'mon," he says, grabbing my arm. "It will be fun."

I generally don't hang out with men who ask me to dance, or would grab my arm to get me to dance. Or have fun of any variety, really. It wouldn't seem cool. But Nate, as it turns out, is hard to say no to.

So we dance. And it's not half bad. I can't remember the last time I surrendered to a moment like this. Danced, smiled. Enjoyed myself without thinking about it.

Everyone on the deck is bouncing around unself-consciously, and people are genuinely having a great time. Nate and I are still holding our big frosty glasses and the iced glass feels good in my hand. Nate takes his and puts it to the back of his neck, then waves his hand in front of his face to denote: it's hot out here. It makes me laugh.

The song changes over to another pop song, one of those songs the radio stations play on overdrive during the summer. Nate points to the speakers, as if to acknowledge that this is *that* song. He's probably the type who has a favorite summer song each summer.

I feel a presence beside me, and I look to my right. It's my grandmother cutting a rug with Walter. And they seem to be having a great time. I smile and turn to face them. My grandmother grabs my glass and I think she's about to put it down on a nearby table. Instead, she takes a sip of my strawberry daiquiri.

"Too sweet," she yells, over the blaring music, and makes a mild grimace.

"I agree," Nate says, also yelling. He puts his drink down on the table next to where my grandmother has deposited mine.

"This is Nate," I say. And then, to Nate: "This is my grandmother and her friend Walter."

"Good to see you again, Mrs. Morganfelder," Nate says. "Hi, Walter."

I'm impressed. I thought my grandmother knew every single man out here who was over sixty, but it appears that she has not discriminated. She knows every single man out here, period. It is only later that I'll realize that I mentioned Nate by name when I told her the story about being questioned by the DA and then wonder why she didn't mention to me at the time that she knew him.

The song changes again, but this one has a Latin beat to it, and somehow, all of the party guests take this as their cue to grab their partners for the merengue.

My grandmother and Walter are dancing, twirling, and then Nate grabs my hand. He puts his other hand around my waist, and then, just like that, we, too, are doing the merengue. At least I learned something from my Cuban ex, even if our relationship did end in attempted homicide. I think about asking Nate how he knows how to do this dance, but then I do something else. Something I never do.

I let Nate lead. He pulls me close and I can smell the sunscreen on his skin. He puts his cheek to mine and it feels rough, like he didn't shave this morning. When he twirls me just so, I enjoy the view out to the beach. I look over and smile when I see my grandmother enjoying herself. And then, as much as I hate to admit, I begin enjoying myself, too.

Fourteen

My grandmother's party is days away. I know this because Eleanor is running around the house like a chicken without its head. Even though my grandmother has hired a party planner—the best on the East End, of course—Eleanor's job is to oversee her work. Eleanor takes her job very seriously. Especially when it comes to bossing other people around.

"She wants to use paper napkins for the cocktail hour," Eleanor tells us, as my grandmother and I sit by the pool. "Paper!"

"What's wrong with paper?" I ask.

Eleanor looks at me with horror. The party planner walks over to my grandmother's chaise longue.

"I just thought it would be fun to create a monogram and then use that throughout the party. Like a theme. A signature. It would appear on the paper napkins for the cocktail hour and the paper guest towels in the bathroom."

"You want to use paper in the bathrooms as well?" Eleanor asks.

I can't help but suppress a giggle. I have a vision of Eleanor stripping the bathrooms of toilet paper and having everyone use linen to wipe their behinds.

"This is not funny," Eleanor says. "The party is in a few days."

"I think what Eleanor is trying to say," my grandmother explains, "is that we prefer to use linen napkins for the cocktail hour, as well as linen guest towels in the bathrooms. We had discussed a rental. Can we still make that happen?"

"Of course," the party planner says. "I have a hold for linens, let me just call to let them know it's a go." She gets on her cell phone.

"Does anyone ever say no to you?" I ask my grandmother.

"There have been one or two along the way who have been immune to my charms," she says with a smile.

The loud beeping of a truck backing up tells us the tent rental is here. Eleanor rushes off—thrilled to have another group of people to boss around—and my grandmother and I sit back in our lounge chairs and look out toward the ocean.

"Are you excited for the party?" my grandmother asks me.

"I guess so." I'm not sure what she's fishing for, so I figure that noncommittal is my best bet.

"Well, I couldn't let an occasion like you coming to visit me for the entire summer pass me by."

"Heaven forbid," I say. I take a sip of my iced tea and my grandmother does the same.

"It's beautiful out here, isn't it?" she asks.

"It's perfect," I say. Because it is. "The umbrellas give just the right amount of shade and the breeze coming off the ocean is amazing."

"Your mother likes it out here, too," my grandmother says.

I keep my gaze toward the ocean. I don't know how to respond. I simply sit there, perfectly still, like a gazelle caught in the gaze of a lion. Maybe if I sit still enough, the comment will just pass me by and leave me unscathed.

My grandmother knows this little trick of mine. She doesn't fill the void of conversation, just lets it lie. So I do the same. And then we sit like that for a while, staring out at the ocean, sipping our iced teas and waiting for the other to speak first.

Our silence is interrupted when the tents come into the backyard. A huge team of men invades our space.

"Why don't we move the two of you inside?" Eleanor asks, one eye on the men working in the backyard.

"Oh, I think we're fine out here," my grandmother says.

All at once, a dozen different industrial-sized power tools go on and the tents begin to take form. Another team brings in the wood that will eventually make up the dance floor.

"Did you invite her?" I ask. "Is that what you're trying to tell me?"

"No," my grandmother says. "If I'd invited her, I wouldn't *try* to tell you, I'd just say it outright. This is my party and I can invite whomever I want."

"A party that you're throwing for me."

"Don't be ungrateful," she says, turning to me. "It's not attractive."

I laugh. "So, this party is really for you."

"It's my party and you are the guest of honor."

"Oh, I see."

"Would it be so bad if I'd invited your mother?" she asks.

What I want to say is: yes, it would. I haven't spoken to her for months, and now is certainly not the time to start. I don't want to hear what she thinks of my taking the summer off to lounge around the pool in the Hamptons. But instead I say: "No, not at all."

"Well, I'm glad to hear that," my grandmother says.

Another group of men begin wheeling in tables and chairs, and the combination of steel being erected, wood being hammered into the floor, and Eleanor's screechy voice as she tries to coordinate all of this gets to be too much for us.

"Walk on the beach?" my grandmother asks.

"Great idea."

The beaches in the Hamptons tend to get a bit quiet during the week, especially by the private estates. My grandmother technically does not own the land from the bluff to the water—neither do any of her neighbors—but still, people tend not to congregate near the beachfront homes.

If we walk to the left, we'll be walking along more beach-front property. I've walked that stretch before and it's beautiful, just beautiful. It's so much fun to see the various estates. I like to walk by and imagine which one I'd buy for myself if I had tens of millions just sitting around burning a hole in my pocket. Some are way too modern for my tastes, with pointy lines and copious amounts of chrome. I prefer the more traditional Hamptons homes, with the wood siding and clean overall look. Some are way too exposed, with floor-to-ceiling windows everywhere you look, designed, no doubt, to take in the view. Others take advantage of the view with an "upside-down traditional" layout, which means that the bedrooms are downstairs, with the shared spaces— living room, dining room, kitchen—upstairs. My favorite house that I've seen so far is the one just to the left of us. It's a yellow farmhouse with charming little details, like a wraparound porch and widow's walk. I wish I could see the interior. I'd love to know what it looks like, see every little detail. Is it modern inside, or did they stay true to the architectural details they have on the outside?

Today, instead, we walk right. If you keep going in that direction, eventually you'll hit the public beaches, which is where all the action is. Don't let the term "public" fool you, though. Not just anyone can come to the public beaches in the Hamptons. In order to park in the lots here, you need to have a special sticker that indicates you own a home in Southampton. Without the sticker, you'll pay forty dollars a day. For your forty bucks, you get access to the beach and also the little snack bar that serves breakfast and lunch. For another forty, you can also rent beach chairs and umbrellas if you haven't brought your own. The kids in the share houses usually take a taxi to and from the beach—it's cheaper than parking for the day. And anyway, if you show up after 11:00 a.m., good luck getting a spot.

It's a half mile to Coopers Beach (my grandmother once had Raoul track it for her), so my grandmother likes taking the walk this way. I prefer walking along the quieter route, but I can see why she likes the action. In just half an hour, you can go from the calm of our backyard, crashing waves as your only sound track, to the insanity of hundreds of people setting up camp on a stretch of five hundred feet. It's crowded. It's alive. It's a total scene. No wonder my grandmother loves it there.

We walk along the white sand and the scenery changes in an instant. As we approach Coopers, there are children running wild in the waves, a few boogie boarders, and girls in bikinis. Not as crowded as the weekend, but a very decent showing for a weekday.

"Want to get some ice cream?" my grandmother asks me.

"Yes," I say. We walk up to the snack bar. There's a huge line at the ice cream window, so we get on line. My grandmother adjusts her floppy hat and I do the same. I'm secretly happy that she insisted on the hats: where we're standing there's no shade, and if you just stand directly in the sun like this, it can get hot. I'm glad to have the tiny bit of respite.

"Vivienne? Is that you?"

My grandmother and I turn around.

"Oh, Charlie," my grandmother says. She allows him to kiss her on both cheeks and then makes the introductions.

"I've been sent to get ice cream for my little one," he says. He pats his pockets. "If I wasn't wearing this swimsuit, I'd whip out a picture to show you," he says, smiling. "Do you have children?"

It takes me a moment to realize that this question is directed toward me. He's speaking about his grandchild and he wants to know if my grandmother has a grandchild, too. Little does he know, her grandchild is me. She really does look great for her age. Or maybe he just doesn't think that it's appropriate for two grown women to be standing at the ice-cream window at a snack bar.

"No," I say. "I don't have kids."

"You never know," my grandmother says to me. "Maybe soon."

"Are you and your husband trying?" Charlie says to me, smiling a conspiratorial smile.

"I'm not married," I say.

"Oh," he says, "I'm sorry. I thought you were. I thought I was at your wedding a few years back, but I must have been mistaken. Your grandmother throws so many parties, it's easy to get confused."

"You never know when your life can change," my grandmother says. "One day you wake up and it's a regular day. But that could be the day everything changes for you. That's what's so wonderful about life, don't you think?"

Charlie looks a bit dazed from this whole exchange. He smiles and says: "I can't wait for your party this weekend."

"Neither can we," my grandmother says, not missing a beat.

"Your grandmother throws the best parties," Charlie says to me.

"I know," I say. Because it's true.

Fifteen

"I'd like her to wear white," my grandmother tells the salesperson. We are at a tiny boutique in town where there's hardly any clothing on display. Even though it's a beautiful day outside, my grandmother wants to go shopping. She has decided that nothing in my closet is party appropriate.

"Were you thinking a dress or pants?" the salesperson asks my grandmother. I look around at the racks. There are only four of them. It's like a carefully curated art exhibit.

"Dress," my grandmother says.

"Long or short?"

"Let's look at both," my grandmother replies.

It's like I don't even have to be here.

"This suit is really nice," I say, pulling a white linen suit off the rack. My grandmother has already declared that white is the color I'll be wearing that night, so I don't dare go too far off program.

"That's lovely," my grandmother says. "It's just not right for this party. If you want to try it on, maybe you could wear it to a Sunday brunch or to the polo matches later this summer."

The salesperson rounds the corner with an armful of dresses: white eyelet, starched white cotton, off-white silk, and white rayon.

The starched white cotton is first. I put it on and take a look at my reflection. The white makes my skin glow, but the dress is too tight. It has no give to it.

I walk out to the three-way mirror, but I don't need to look. My grandmother tells me everything I need to know.

"Do you like it?" she asks me.

"I can't lift my arms," I say, and make a big show of trying, and failing.

"Why would you need to lift your arms?" she asks, and motions for me to put the next dress on.

I put the silk dress on, and immediately feel self-conscious. First, it hugs my every curve, but I'm not sure if it's in a way that is desirable. Second, I fear that if someone touches me, the entire thing will unravel. I slowly walk out of the dressing room, careful not to let the fabric snag on anything.

"Why don't you put on the next one?" my grandmother says.

"Oh, okay," I say, and make a hasty retreat.

"Did you like that one?" she asks, but I'm already slipping on the white rayon.

It has a plunging neckline and a swingy skirt. The fabric is soft and falls nicely on my frame. I feel a little like Marilyn Monroe in it.

"Happy birthday, Mr. President," I say as I walk out for judgment.

"Do you like it?" my grandmother asks. I'm not sure if she doesn't get the reference, or just doesn't appreciate it.

"I guess so," I say, and swivel my hips so that the skirt swings around.

"Don't do that," my grandmother says. "It looks nice. Try on the next one."

The second I put on the eyelet dress, I know it's the one. It's sweet, it fits me perfectly, and I think it's the way my grand-mother sees me. Youthful, cute, nice.

"I like that," she says. "Do you like it?"

"It's very comfortable," I say. "And I like that it has sleeves."

"Comfortable is not what one should look for in a party dress," my grandmother says.

"What should I be looking for?" I ask. "I like to be able to raise my arms."

My grandmother purses her lips. She motions for me to go back to the fitting room to get dressed.

"Which one do you want?" she asks as I walk out of the dressing room.

"I really have no idea," I say, and I don't.

"Let's go with this one, then," she says, holding it up for me to see.

I'm surprised that the rayon Marilyn Monroe number is my grandmother's choice—it's a bit on the sexy side. I would've bet that she would have chosen the white eyelet with the bell sleeves.

"Silver or gold?" the salesperson asks me as I walk out of the fitting room.

"Silver or gold what?" I ask.

She laughs, turning to my grandmother to say: "Mrs. Mor-ganfelder, your granddaughter is such a breath of fresh air." And then to me: "Shoes, silly. Do you want to wear silver or gold shoes?"

"I already have shoes," I say.

"She's already got silver," my grandmother pipes in. "Let's do gold."

"Gold, it is!" the salesperson says, feigning excitement.

We walk toward a wall of shoes at the back of the store. I go into sensory overload and can barely look at it. I feel a headache coming on. Now I remember why I hate shopping so much.

"She'll take these," my grandmother says, pointing at a pair of gold strappy heels.

I wish I could be like that: look at an entire wall of choices, hone in on one thing, and know it's the right one. Me, I'd spend an hour just staring at the wall, overwhelmed by it. Then, when forced to make a decision, I'd randomly choose ten different pairs, try on each one, and still have no idea which one would suit me best. Eventually, I'd choose a pair, only to find out a few days later that they don't fit me properly.

But the shoes my grandmother has selected fit me perfectly and I can see how they would look great with the dress. And a few other things I have hanging in my closet.

I let my grandmother choose where we go for lunch.

Sixteen

"What are you doing here?" I say as I open the front door. I'm not accustomed to having visitors here in the Hamptons. Let alone gentleman callers. Let alone Nate.

"Nice to see you, too." He seems to find my churlish attitude cute. "May I come in?"

I don't know what to say. I don't really want Nate Sugarman to come into the house. Sure, we had a nice time dancing at the party the other night, but that doesn't really change the fact that I find him arrogant and entitled.

"Nate, darling," my grandmother says, walking over to greet him. "Come in!"

"You look nice today," he says to me. And then to my grandmother: "Mrs. Morganfelder, you look fetching as always."

"Oh, Nate," my grandmother says. She is completely taken by his boyish charms. "We were just about to eat. You simply must stay for lunch."

"Grandma, I'm sure he has a lot of things to do," I say. "Don't you, Nate?"

"No, not really," he says.

"A golf tee time? A tennis date? Don't you play tennis? You look like you play tennis."

"We can play tennis later if you want," he says. "We have a court at my place."

"I don't play tennis." I say.

Nate furrows his brow, but quickly regains his composure. "I stopped by to see if you needed anything for the big party."

"You're coming?" I say.

"You say that like it's a bad thing." He leans in to me as he says this.

"Why don't you meet us outside and I'll help my grandmother get us set up for lunch."

My grandmother is about to say something about the chef bringing lunch out to us, but I am able to maneuver her into the kitchen before the thought is fully out of her mouth.

"You invited Nate Sugarman?" I ask her. "I told you that I hate Nate Sugarman."

"When you were dancing at Walter's son's party, it didn't seem to me like you hated him so much," she says.

"But you knew he was the DA from the story I told you?"

"I might have figured that out."

"Yet you still invited him to the party?"

My grandmother laughs and brushes past me. Jean-Marie has already set out iced tea and lemonade on the table, and I see Nate take my grandmother's glass and then pour her some iced tea.

"The tents look amazing," I hear Nate say as I walk outside.

"They've been working on them for days," my grandmother says.

"Well, actually one day," I say, sitting down at the table next to my grandmother. "Didn't they finish in one day?"

"Yes," my grandmother says. "I suppose they did." She regards me.

"Well, they look great," Nate says. "I love how they're open on the sides, so we can take advantage of the breeze coming off the water."

"Yes, I thought that would be nice," my grandmother says.

"It was really the party planner's idea," I interrupt.

"Yes," my grandmother adds. "We've worked together on all of my parties out here and it seems that the tent with the open sides works best for this venue."

And then, there it is: complete and utter silence. A very uncomfortable silence as we all end up averting our eyes, careful not to stare at one another, sipping our drinks because there really isn't anything else to do. Or say.

It's moments like these I savor. I guess it's because I feel uncomfortable all the time, so when I can sit in a group where we all feel uncomfortable, I feel a little less lonely.

Nate excuses himself to use the restroom and I feel my grandmother's eyes bore into me.

"What exactly are you doing?" she says.

"I have no idea what you mean."

"Why are you acting like this?"

"Like what?" I ask.

"Like a petulant teenager," she says, regarding me. "You're embarrassing yourself."

"I thought that the only person who can embarrass you is you," I say, recalling one of my grandmother's many life lessons.

"Yes, that's right," she says. "And *you* are embarrassing *yourself*."

It's only then that I understand what she's saying—that I'm not embarrassing her, but I'm embarrassing myself. Why did I misunderstand what she was saying to me? Is it because I was trying to embarrass her? And if so, why? Why am I acting this way?

Nate walks back out of the house with Jean-Marie. I can see in my grandmother's face that she is charmed by the fact that Nate helps bring the food out to the table, even though he doesn't have to do so. She'll later tell me that he's a good man—the type of man you want to marry.

"For lunch today, we have tuna tartar on these tiny little crispy things," Nate says, playing the role of chef.

"I've prepared them on wonton chips, but I also have lettuce wraps, if you'd prefer," Jean-Marie says. "And then I have this Asian summer salad, which I've prepared in a peanut-soy dressing, which has glass noodles, peppers, red onions, and peanuts."

"You're not allergic to peanuts, are you?" my grandmother asks Nate. I narrow my eyes at her, but she simply laughs. Nate misses the joke completely.

"No," he says. "It looks great!"

"Yes, it does," I say, and serve the salad.

Nate nods his head in agreement as he stuffs a wonton filled with tuna into his mouth. I watch him as he eats his food and I'm struck by how manly he is about it. To look at him, all gangly arms and legs, freckles all over, you wouldn't think he was an eater, but he really devours his food. Almost like an animal, but an animal with extremely good table manners. His napkin is in his lap. His hands are manicured, neat, but there's a roughness to them. Like if he touched you, it might hurt. When he tears a piece of bread and bites into it—he has a tiny chip on one of his front teeth—I have a fleeting thought about what it would be like to have those hands on my body. I feel my face flush and take a long swallow of my lemonade.

"I think you're getting red out here," Nate says as he looks at me.

My hands fly instinctively to my face.

"Are you wearing sunscreen?" my grandmother asks.

"Yes," I quickly reply.

"Your face is turning bright red," she says. "Maybe you need to get out of the sun."

"You have to be really careful in the sun out here," he says.

"I'd better go get more sunscreen," I say, and make a hasty exit into the house.

"You should come over some time," Nate says after lunch, after I walk him to the door to leave the house. "Maybe I could teach you to play tennis."

"I don't really have the time," I say, almost on autopilot. It's true, I did have fun at lunch with Nate, but what's the point in starting something I know won't last? Nothing ever does.

But I can see in his eyes that Nate might be harder to get rid of than your average suitor. I try to channel my grandmother as I come up with my next comment. "How about this? I'll call you the next time I'm in your neck of the woods." I figure this gives me an out if I want one, and an opening should I change my mind about the whole thing.

"Are you calling me right now, then?" he says.

"What?" For some reason, a girlish giggle escapes my mouth.

"I live next door," Nate says, laughing. "Your grandmother didn't tell you?"

"No," I say, slowly. "She did not."

"Well, I do," he says. "I live in the yellow house next door."

"The yellow farmhouse with the widow's walk?" I ask.

"The very one."

"Maybe I will come over sometime."

Seventeen

The day of the party. T minus eight hours until the big event. In my old life, if I had a party invitation for seven o'clock, I would hop in the shower at six, run my fingers through my hair, throw on some clothes, and arrive at the party by seven-thirty.

But in my new incarnation as a lady of leisure, that routine simply won't cut it. For starters, since we are the hostesses, we need to be downstairs, ready to greet guests, at six-forty-five. Not a minute later, my grandmother insists. That would be rude.

The day starts and we are immediately on the clock. We rise sometime around nine, as we usually do, and have our breakfast. After we are done with our coffees, my grandmother informs me that I ought to bathe quickly, since our appointments begin at eleven. Specifically, our nail appointments are at eleven and noon, Jacques will be coming to do our hair at one and two. After our hair is perfectly coiffed, we will take a short break for a light lunch. Nothing too heavy, since we don't want to be tired or bloated for the party. Then, our makeup artist will arrive for appointments at four and five, giving us enough time to go upstairs and dress once the beautification process is complete.

All of the last-minute details of the day will be handled by Eleanor, which explains why she is already running around like a complete and utter lunatic.

I decide to take a bath. My grandmother has graciously offered to take the first appointments of the day so that I can leisurely bathe and come down to get started at noon, instead of eleven. Since coming out here, I have learned to enjoy baths. In the city, I never took a bath because my tub wasn't big enough to sprawl out in, but here, all of the baths are oversized soaking tubs, designed for you to stretch out and stay awhile. They all have hundreds of tiny jets, which make perfect little bubbles. My grandmother takes a bath every day and has done so since she was married to her third husband, the race car driver. He was the one, she says, who taught her how indulgent a bath could be—your one respite in a busy, crazy day. She says that just hearing the faucet pour water into the tub and watching the bubbles take form is enough to relax her, prepare her for the day. She also says that bathing with salts will make the fine lines around your eyes disappear. (I hadn't realized I had any of those.)

I ease myself into the tub and immediately feel calm. This is what my grandmother was talking about—the warm water and lavender-scented bubbles have a way of making you feel like you can handle anything that comes your way. Even fine lines around your eyes. I use the remote control to open the cellular shades and look out the window at the perfect blue Hamptons sky. Even the clouds are perfectly shaped out here. It's as if the residents of Southampton wouldn't stand for any misshapen clouds.

As I look out the window, I try to catch a glimpse of Nate's house—that beautiful yellow farmhouse that I always think about, always wondering about the people who live inside. Then I think about Nate's hands—how big they are, how they tore apart that bread. And his mouth. How he devoured his food. What those hands and that mouth would do to me.

All at once, I'm uneasy, like someone's watching me. I jump out of the tub and wrap myself in an oversized towel.

When I come downstairs, my grandmother's manicurist is hard at work on her feet. My grandmother is regaling her with a story about her last fête when I sit down next to her.

"So, are you excited for the big event?" the manicurist asks.

I'm not excited. Not excited about it by a long shot. But my grandmother is looking at me, waiting for my answer, and I just don't want to disappoint her.

"Yes," I say with a smile.

My grandmother can see right through me. Right to my core. She always does.

"Why do you hate parties so much?" she asks. "I would think you'd do well in a social situation like that."

"I don't hate parties," I say, and my grandmother rolls her eyes. She never rolls her eyes.

"I just never know what to do, what to say," I say.

"Well, I can help you with that," my grandmother says. "Give me an example of a situation you were in the last time you were at an affair."

I don't go to a lot of parties. Certainly never a bash like the one my grandmother is throwing. The last time I was at a get-together was on a rooftop of a building in Williamsburg. There were kegs of beer and copious amounts of pot.

"I always get stuck talking to the biggest bore in the room," I say, thinking about the last time my law firm threw a reception. "I can never extricate myself. Usually, I end up telling him I have somewhere to go and then I just leave to get away from him. But I can't very well do that here. Can I?"

"That's an easy one," my grandmother says as her manicurist starts in on a foot massage. I look down and see that she is listening, too, waiting, just as I am, for my grandmother's good advice. "I learned this from the Senator. You just put your hand on the person's arm and then look him or her right in the eye as you say: 'Well, I don't want to monopolize you all night. It was lovely talking to you.' The sincere look in the eye is important. It doesn't work without the look in the eye."

"I don't know if I can do that."

"Try it right now," she says. "Try it on me."

"It was very nice talking to you," I say to my grandmother, my hand firmly planted on her forearm, "but I don't want to monopolize you all night."

"You're not monopolizing me," my grandmother says back to me, smiling.

"Oh," I say. "Well, then, I guess—"

"Do you see where you went wrong there?" my grandmother asks.

I shake my head no. Her manicurist does the same.

"You lead with the 'monopolizing' line. Not the 'nice to meet you' line. The 'pleasure talking to you' should come last, so the person understands that the conversation is over. Try it again."

"I don't want to monopolize you all night," I say. "It was a pleasure speaking to you."

"And you as well," my grandmother responds. "That one was better. But you need to work on your sincerity. They really have to buy the fact that you liked talking to them. I can see that this will be the challenge for you."

"I like talking to people," I say, and my grandmother laughs a big throaty laugh.

"During cocktail hour don't sit down," my grandmother says. "It's easier to extricate yourself if you're standing up. And by all means, mingle! Talk to as many party guests as you can."

"I hate mingling. I'm not a good mingler. I never know what to talk about," I protest.

"Another easy one," my grandmother says. "Stick to light topics. The weather, the food, the wines that are being served. We just went wine tasting, so that would be a fun thing to talk about."

"I can talk about that yacht we went on," I say, catching on.

"Well, you don't want to gossip," my grandmother says. "And since you thought those young men were spoiled and awful, that probably wouldn't be a good thing to talk about."

"But the yacht was pretty fabulous," I say. "If only those boys weren't on it . . ."

"You've just proven my point," she says. "Stick to topics where you won't be tempted to judge others. Talk about the view of the ocean, what a beautiful night it is. Try it."

"The view of the ocean is so pretty," I say. "I love living beachside."

"Now *you* sound like the spoiled brat," she says. "Keep it light, act like your conversation is going to be broadcast on the evening news. Never say anything you wouldn't want your grandmother to hear." Her eyes light up at that last part.

"But I don't mind if you hear anything I say."

"Never say anything you wouldn't want printed on the front page of the newspaper, then."

I look down and see that my grandmother's manicurist has stopped working on her toes. She's just looking up at my grandmother, soaking in every word.

"The breeze off the ocean is just beautiful, isn't it?" I say. "We really are having a delightful summer."

"Yes, we are," my grandmother says.

"And the food!" I say. "Have you tried the lobster rolls? Truly delicious. They would pair perfectly with the cabernet they are serving. Very strong notes of nutmeg and vanilla. Did you have a chance to taste it?"

"Well done," my grandmother says smiling. "Although I think a lobster roll would pair better with a white wine."

"Noted," I say.

"I think you're ready for the party," she says.

I suppress a giggle, since in fact, I won't be ready for the party until my nails are buffed, my hair is teased, and face is made up, but I decide that now is not the time for one of my "clever little quips." So, instead I say, "Yes, I think I am."

Eighteen

It's a myth that black widows eat the male after mating—that only happens a very small percentage of the time. Often times, the female spider will leave the male alive and he can go on to mate with other females. Still, black widows have a large red hourglass on their bodies, a sign to predators that they are poisonous.

This is just a small sampling of the information I've learned so far by talking with Hunter J. Kensington IV, for all of ten minutes. Since Priya hasn't yet arrived, I've been trying to be inconspicuous, hanging out in the kitchen with the caterers. Apparently, this is also a trick used by fourteen-year-old boys who walk into a party, only to discover that they've been lured to a gathering for adults. ("I had no idea Hunter would be so young! His father is so old," my grandmother would tell me later.)

Hunter's been rambling off factoid after factoid about black widows gleaned from his eighth-grade science class (their webs lack shape and form, their venom is more dangerous than that of a rattlesnake), under the guise of making conversation with me. I'm not sure whether it's that he's too young to realize that a conversation entails a bit of give and take—that you should expect the other person to speak occasionally—or if it's that when you are a Kensington, you're simply not accustomed to caring what other people have to say.

I give Hunter the benefit of the doubt and he moves in for the kill.

"So, that's why people say," Hunter explains, "that Mr. Morganfelder named this place Viuda Negra. It means Black Widow. Because Mrs. Morganfelder killed all of her other husbands."

"Who?" I say, momentarily distracted by the mention of the Mattress King's actual name. I often forget that the Mattress King has a name. That they all had names.

"Your grandfather?" Hunter says, making it sound like a question, even though I know he's actually telling me.

"He wasn't my grandfather," I say. "He was my grandmother's seventh husband."

"That's what I said," he says.

"No," I say. "You said he was my grandfather. He was my grandmother's husband. There's a difference."

Hunter shrugs.

"Do you want to get something to drink?" Hunter asks, and I say yes.

We walk toward the tent where tonight's party is being held and I'm struck by the sheer excess of it all. The tent alone took an entire day to construct. Imported caviar, lobster served two different ways, three different types of vodka, hundred-dollar bottles of champagne—it's all too much. As are the men in their white dinner jackets and the women in their designer cocktail dresses. I look at the party guests and immediately see that I don't fit in. I am the Sabrina to their Larrabee.

I stand on the grass, just outside of the tents. Looking into the tent is surreal—it doesn't look like real life at all. And it certainly doesn't look like a party that I'm about to walk in to. What it looks like is a movie set. I hear the orchestra in echoes, and the tent casts a faint glow on all of the partygoers.

There are three large chandeliers hung inside the tent, and lights set up strategically to give the inside of the tent a pinkish glow. Each table is outfitted with a gigantic floral arrangement—roses, peonies, and hydrangeas float atop tall glass vessels, filled with rose-colored water. The columns that hold up the tent are draped in white fabric; in fact, there's white fabric everywhere you look. On the bars, on the stage where the band is set up and already playing, on the tables and chairs.

"It's beautiful, isn't it?" Hunter asks with a smile as he guides me toward the first of the three bars set up outside. Hunter orders two glasses of champagne and the bartender pours them for him without a second thought. Having been in Southampton for a couple of weeks now, I feel like nothing can surprise me. Certainly not serving alcohol to minors.

"Hannah?" I spin around and see Nate Sugarman.

"Nate," Hunter says, putting his body between Nate and me. "How are you? I see you've met my date."

"Your date?" Nate asks Hunter, trying to conceal a little giggle. "Well, good for you."

"Thank you," Hunter says to Nate, then looks up at me with a crooked smile. "Hannah, let me get you another drink. Nate, would you like something?" Nate shakes his head no, and Hunter is off at the bar. I hadn't realized that I needed another drink, but when I look down at my champagne flute it turns out Hunter was right—I need another.

"Hunter lost his mother this winter," Nate whispers in my ear. "So be nice to him."

"I'd be nice to him anyway," I say, and look over at Hunter. He's just a few feet away, talking to an adult, but he keeps looking over his shoulder to make sure I'm still there. I smile back at him and he blushes.

"It's just, he probably thinks you're a mother figure or something," Nate says.

"I'm not old enough to be his mother," I say, and feel my face flush.

As Nate warbles his way through an apology ("No, of course you're not . . . And even if you were, you look great . . .") I realize that I am, actually, old enough to be Hunter's mom. My grandmother had my mother when she was twenty, and if I'd had Hunter when I was twenty, he'd be fourteen now. Which is exactly how old he is.

Hunter comes back to join Nate and me, wedging himself between us. The older gentleman he was speaking with walks over to us, too.

"Did you know that it's a myth that female black widows always kill their mates?" he asks. His white hair shines in the light coming off the dance floor.

"I did know that," I say, smiling in Hunter's direction. "Thanks to Hunter Kensington, the fourth."

"Ah, well, he learned it from his old man," he says, extending a hand. "I'm Hunter Kensington, the third. You can call me Trip."

"Very nice to meet you."

"Nice to meet you, too," he says. I can see where Hunter gets his smile. "Well, Hunter here told me that he met the most beautiful woman in the room, and he was right."

"Thank you," I say.

"Besides your grandmother," the elder Kensington adds with a smile. I can't help but smile back. I'm sure when Hunter meets her, he'll be smitten, too. It is practically impossible to avoid falling in love with my grandmother.

"Your grandmother is quite something," Nate adds. I don't know what to make of the statement—is it a compliment?

"Well," I say, putting my hand on Nate's arm. "I don't want to monopolize you all evening. It was so nice talking with you."

"That's it?" Nate says, suppressing a laugh.

"It was really nice talking with you," I parrot back. My grandmother specifically told me that if I ended with the "nice to meet you" part, I could easily extricate myself.

"You can't get rid of me that easily," he says. "Isn't that right, Hunter?"

"Are you leaving?" Hunter asks me. His little face looks so innocent as he looks up at me. There is no way I could walk away now.

"Of course not," I say, and Hunter smiles.

"Want to dance?" Hunter asks.

He puts his hand out for me to take and leads me toward the dance floor. As we walk like that, me following Hunter's lead, I can feel Nate's eyes on me. I turn my head around and he is, in fact, staring at me. He's got an amused smile on his face.

Hunter spins around and puts his arms around me to dance. It's obvious that Hunter's had dance lessons; he's got perfect form. It's equally obvious that I have not had dance lessons. I have no idea where to put my hands or arms, but Hunter takes the lead and makes it easy for me.

"This is a waltz," he informs me.

"I don't know how to waltz," I say.

"Just follow my lead," he says with a smile.

He uses subtle pressure on my hands to guide me along, to show me where I should go.

"Isn't this fun?" Hunter asks.

"It's not as hard as I thought."

"Just think, one, two, three, one, two, three," he explains.

"That doesn't seem too hard," I say, and concentrate on my

steps. I look across the dance floor and see my grandmother dancing with someone, too. Her form is perfect, and they glide across the dance floor as if they were professional dancers.

I look back down to Hunter to make some comment about the waltz, but his head is tilted up toward mine. If I didn't know any better, I'd say he was getting ready to kiss me. Luckily, I've got about a foot in height on him, so it's going to be pretty hard for him to make a move on me without my consent.

I have no idea what to do. Should I pretend this isn't really happening, or is it better to tackle it head on, and just explain to Hunter that I'm too old for him?

I don't have time to figure it out because in the next instant, there is a loud crash at the other side of the dance floor. We all turn around to see what's happened, but a crowd forms around the source of the noise. All we can hear is the sound of gasps coming from the crowd, and I break away to see what's happened.

Eleanor comes fighting through the crowd—against the flow of traffic—and grabs my arm.

"Hannah," she says breathlessly, "it's your grandmother. She's fainted."

I rush to my grandmother's side, through the throngs of concerned partygoers, to find that she is already regaining consciousness. A waiter leans down from nowhere and hands me a towel soaked in cold water. I motion with my arms for everyone to disperse. Some of the people listen, others stay to see what's going on.

"What happened?" my grandmother says, pulling herself up to her elbows. I grab her hand and press the cold compress to her head.

"You fainted," I say. "Just stay still. An ambulance is coming."

"Oh," she says as she looks out into the crowd of concerned partygoers.

"Just relax," I say. "Maybe you should lean back down."

But she stays exactly where she is. And she doesn't move her head one inch. She's looking at something. Someone in the crowd. I turn my head to see what she's looking at and I see a man. A man who looks like Rhett Butler.

Nineteen

"Why do I always get here just in time for the hospital part?" Priya asks me.

"You could have stayed at the party," I say, but I don't mean it.

"I get to your grandmother's house and they are loading her into an ambulance. Stay at the party? I don't think so."

"Thank you," I say without picking my head up off her shoulder.

The ER doctor comes out not long after going in to examine my grandmother—the hospital in Southampton is so small that there's really no wait for an emergency. "Your grandmother is fine," he says as he walks out to the waiting room. I know that he's speaking to me, but he says it out loud to the entire emergency room—the waiting room is so small that it's practically overflowing with concerned party guests. Nate is here, as are the Hunter Kensingtons, and the man who looks like Rhett Butler. He's tried to speak to me a few times, but I've been avoiding him so far.

I cannot bring myself to find out if he is who I think he is. I need to concentrate on more important problems first, like making sure my grandmother's okay.

"Hannah," the doctor says, "would you like to see your grandmother?"

"Yes," I say, standing up. Priya stands up next to me and grabs my hand.

Out of nowhere, Hunter comes to my other side and grabs my other hand.

"Do you want me to come in with you?" he asks, looking up at me. The earnestness of his expression nearly breaks my heart.

"No, thank you, honey," I say. "She's fine. I can go in there myself."

"My mother was at New York Presb," he says. "It was a lot bigger than this hospital. Sometimes I got lost."

I look into his eyes and suddenly he looks so much older than fourteen.

"I'm so sorry about your mom, Hunter," I say.

"It's okay," he says, looking away. And then, looking at me: "Thanks."

"Will you sit out here with my friend, Priya, until I get back?"

Hunter nods and he and Priya sit down.

"Nothing's broken?" I ask the doctor as he walks me back to my grandmother.

"Nothing at all," he says. "She's really quite amazing for a woman her age. I've never seen anything like her before."

"Tell me about it," I say as we continue down the hallway. The emergency room is crowded, but it's easy to spot my grandmother—she's the one surrounded by all the young doctors. And it's not just male doctors. Men, women, children, it makes no difference, they are all equally charmed by her.

"Grandma?" I say, and the crowd of doctors parts for me to get close to her hospital bed.

"Are you all right? How are you feeling?"

"She's fine," one of the doctors says, "she was just telling us about France."

She must have thought she was close to death. My grandmother almost never talks about her childhood. In fact, I barely know anything about it.

But in a moment, it hits me. She wasn't talking about her childhood. What she was talking about is the man who looks like Rhett Butler. Her first husband. The one she ran away with and married when she was just sixteen. The only one who didn't widow her. The one who broke her heart.

"So, that's him?" I ask. "The one who looks like Rhett Butler?"

"That's him," she says. "I had no idea he was even in the country. I couldn't believe my eyes."

"Apparently," I say. "Are you feeling okay now?"

"Perfectly fine," she says. "The doctors say I can go home."

"They don't want to keep you overnight?"

"Well, I think the one with the patch of gray in his hair wouldn't mind seeing me overnight, but no. The doctors say I can go." She smiles at me, and I realize she's made this little joke for my benefit.

"Then let's get you home," I say, and eyeball the paperwork that needs to be filled out for discharge. "You know, it's funny. With all this talk of me coming out here and meeting someone, I just knew you'd find someone first."

My grandmother smiles.

"I saw you talking to a very nice-looking young man," my grandmother says.

"He's fourteen."

"Not him, dear, the other one. The one who came for lunch."

"Nate Sugarman?" I ask, and my grandmother smiles back in response. "I've told you a million times already. I'm not interested."

"I saw you blushing, darling," she says. "Am I to believe you hate him so much that he made you blush?"

I look down, pretending to finish up the hospital paperwork.

"And while we're on the topic of bad news," she casually says, "your mother is flying in as we speak."

"Why?" I ask, and instantly regret it. It's not that I don't want my mother to come stay with us. It's just that I don't want my mother to come stay with us.

"Because I fell and lost consciousness for a few minutes. So the hospital called her," she says, sliding her legs off the hospital bed and standing up. She smoothes out her dress, and then walks over to a medicine cabinet to check her reflection in the glass. "And now that I'm fine, it's too late, because she's already on a private jet on her way."

"I was sitting right there," I say. "I had the situation perfectly under control."

"Maybe they didn't trust a thirty-something-year-old woman who has a fourteen-year-old as her date," my grandmother says, her blue eyes twinkling. Tonight they look ice blue.

"Very funny," I say. "Men don't like funny."

"You're learning," she says, pointing a perfectly manicured nail in my direction with a wink.

"I realized tonight that I'm actually old enough to be Hunter's mom."

"Would that be so bad?" she asks.

"For Hunter to be my kid?"

"To be a mom," she says.

"No," I say. "It wouldn't be bad at all. Actually, I think I'd be a great mom. I certainly couldn't be any worse than my own mother."

"Here we go again," my grandmother says, looking over her shoulder to face me. "You hate your mother. Old news."

"I don't *hate* her," I explain. "She's just not very motherly."

"You know," she says, "I like to think that you spend time with me not to spite your mother, but because I'm so wonderful that you like to be with me."

"I'm not here to spite my mother," I say, sounding more like a petulant child than I mean to. "I spend time with you because I love you. I love being with you."

"Then give your mother a break, would you?" she says. "For me. She's doing the best she can. When did you become so hard on people?"

"I'm not hard on people," I say, and my grandmother laughs in response. She turns and floats down the hallway. I follow close behind, pausing only briefly to hand the paperwork back to one of the nurses. My grandmother walks into the waiting room, where dozens of anxious eyes look up at her. The crowd instantly goes silent.

"The band is paid up until one a.m.," my grandmother says, hands on her hips. "Let's get back to the party. I'll be damned if I let those noise permits go to waste."

Twenty

"I didn't *eat* them, darling," my grandmother says to Hunter, "I simply outlived them."

We are in Rhett Butler's car, on our way to the Islip airport to pick up my mother. It's actually a limo, but I've learned that in Southampton, everyone calls anything on four wheels a car. Even a chauffeured limousine.

When Rhett came to the house this morning, my grandmother casually introduced him to me as "my first husband." He took my hand and kissed it gently. I resisted the urge to roll my eyes at the theatrics and instead took the opportunity to look at his hands: pale and soft, without a hangnail in sight.

Hunter ran up our driveway at the last minute, so he ended up coming along for the ride, too. He's now regaling my grandmother with his knowledge of black widow spiders.

"That's actually a myth," Hunter says. "But there was a movie in the eighties where the Black Widow character killed all of her husbands."

"I hope you're not saying that I *killed* all of my husbands," she says, amused by this back and forth with Hunter.

"No," he says, "I'm just pointing out that there are lots of misconceptions about black widows. Some perpetuated by Hollywood."

"You're a very interesting young man, Hunter," my grand-mother says. "Did anyone ever tell you that?"

"Yes," Hunter says. That he answers her so seriously and so unself-consciously makes the edges of my mouth turn up. And then, turning to me, he says: "I have an idea for a movie, you know."

"You do?" I ask. "Let's hear it."

"Well, I don't actually have the whole thing worked out," he explains, and my grandmother and Rhett have already lost inter-est in the conversation. They are leaning into each other, whis-pering. They are so transfixed by their conversation that they don't even notice me glaring at them. None of this dulls Hunter's excitement for his story, though. "And then, it turns out that she didn't know it, but Chloe is actually her daughter."

"What?" I say, pretending I'd been listening all along.

"The leading lady finds out that the baby is hers. That's the hook—the big catch of the whole story—turns out the baby was hers all along. I'm really into Hitchcock right now."

"How could she not know the baby was hers?" I ask.

"Whaddya mean how could she not know?" Hunter says. "That's the catch ending."

"Yes," I say, "but the woman's the one who actually gives birth. How could she not know she had a child?"

"Oh. Right," Hunter says, and looks out the window. He taps his fingers on the glass. "We're here."

The limo pulls up onto the tarmac. Limos aren't allowed on the tarmac, but my grandmother pulled down her window and batted her eyelashes at the appropriate person, so we get to sit in the car while my mother makes her dramatic entrance.

Gray Goodman always makes a dramatic entrance.

She's caught a ride on a private plane and three other people get off before her. She walks down the steps and onto the tarmac slowly, as if she's taking everything in. I've given up on trying to get my mother to move more quickly—when she gets like this, it's best to just let her take her time. She's probably framing shots in her head as she walks toward us. As much as I complain about the Hamptons, one thing I'll say about eastern Long Island is that it really is beautiful.

I see annoyed passengers behind her, but Gray doesn't even notice. Far be it from her to act like a normal person and acknowledge that other people want to get off the plane. She's too busy being an artist to realize that actual life is going on around her. But no one complains. It's as if once you breathe in some of the Long Island air, your manners go into hyperdrive. It happens to everyone. Except my mother.

Rhett jumps out of the car to help my mother with her bag. It disturbs me when I see that I've learned how to pack from my mother—she, too, has all of her worldly possessions packed into a tiny little tote, even though she presumably has no idea how long she'll be staying. I guess that's something I learned from her: always be ready to pick up and go in a moment's notice. Don't take too much baggage, don't gather too many things that you'll miss when you leave them behind.

"Grace," my grandmother says, and kisses my mother hello on both cheeks. "It's so wonderful to have you here, darling. This is Adan Brushard."

"Charmed," he says, and takes my mother's hand. His accent is much thicker than my grandmother's, which at this point could only be referred to as a trace, and I can see how a woman could find it quite dazzling. From the look on my mother's face, it is clear that she is not one of those women.

She doesn't say a word. Far be it for my mother to participate in the small talk that other people take for granted. My mother refuses to follow societal norms, and instead prefers to simply stare at people when she should just be saying something on autopilot.

In striking contrast to my grandmother, who lives her life by a code of good manners. She always knows the right thing to say and the right way to act in any situation, a fact that has always comforted me. My grandmother believes that graciousness is next to godliness. My mother does not.

"Adan," my grandmother says, filling the silence, "this is my daughter, Grace."

Surely at the mention of his name, my mother knows who she's being introduced to, that she is staring into the face of her mother's first husband. The only man who came before her father, my grandfather. But her face stays expressionless. I suppose a lifetime of photographing wars and public figures has taught her never to let her emotions betray her.

"I'm a Gray, not a Grace," my mother says. "Call me Gray." ("I was never a Grace," my mother once told me. "Even as a baby, that name never quite fit me.")

"Both beautiful names," Rhett says, and guides my mother to the car.

My mother looks back at Rhett, smiles tightly at him, and then makes sure to sit on the other side of the limo, near Hunter and me. Hunter begins telling her about his movie idea. Trying to impress the mother. Seems Hunter the third taught his son well.

"But Hannah said there'd be no way she wouldn't know that the kid is hers, so I've got to rework that part."

"Hannah said that?" my mother asks, eyeing me disapprovingly. "Don't let anyone ever tell you that you can't do what you want to do. And don't ever change your art just to please others."

"Already?" I say. "Here we go."

"Already what?" my mother says. "Already you are slaying this poor child's artist within? Yes."

"I'm fourteen," Hunter says. "Anyway, I think I can still make it work."

"Of *course* it can work," my mother says.

"How would a woman be unaware that she'd had a baby?" I say. "You can't *not* know that you had a baby."

"Of course you could not know," my mother says. "Maybe she has amnesia, or short-term memory loss, or . . . or she was brainwashed."

"I like brainwashed," Hunter says.

"Or maybe the doctors told her that her baby died," my mother continues, "but that was a lie."

"I like brainwashed," Hunter says.

"Interesting," I say.

"I'm just saying that you should grow a child's creativity," my mother says later that evening, after an extravagant five-course dinner, dumping the contents of her tote bag on the bed and then sorting everything out. "It wasn't an indictment of you. You always take everything as such an attack."

"It *was* an attack," I say, fluffing a pillow on the bed. "You were telling me that I was crushing his spirit."

"I was just pointing out the fact that it's important to inspire creativity in children."

"He's not a child," I say. "He's fourteen."

"You don't think fourteen is a child?" she asks, furrowing her brow.

"Since when are you so big on teaching others how to be a good mother?" I ask.

"You love pointing out what a bad mom I was," she says, putting down the shirt she was folding and regarding me. "I wasn't a bad mom. I just wasn't what most mothers were."

"You weren't what *any* mothers were," I point out.

"I'd say that depends on who you're comparing me to," she says.

"The other mothers," I say. "That's what I'm comparing you to. The norm."

What I wanted to say, what I should have said, was that she had no idea how difficult my childhood was for me. I wanted so desperately to be like everyone else. To have a life like everyone else. A place to go at the end of the day that was home. Somewhere with family pictures on the wall and laughter in the halls and food warming up in the oven for dinner. A mother who was there waiting for me. A dad.

"What other person do you know as well traveled as you? Has seen as much of the world? Of other cultures? Does *average* get you any of that? Any of the good stuff?"

"Well, maybe that's not what a little girl needs when she's growing up."

"And what *does* a little girl need?"

"Normal," I say. "To be like everyone around her. To have what everyone else has."

"I tried to teach you that there was a big, wonderful world out there," she says. "And I showed it to you. I taught you that you didn't have to be average. You were special."

"But all I ever really wanted was a more conventional life."

"You think your grandmother is conventional?" my mother asks with a throaty laugh. "Is that why you're always clinging to her?"

"I'm not clinging to her," I say, "but yes, she is like everybody else."

"No, she is not. And she's not at all grandmotherly, so I don't want to hear a speech about how wonderful she is. About how ordinary she is."

"She may not have been sitting around her kitchen baking cookies from scratch for me, but she is very grandmotherly in other ways."

"I just don't understand this obsession you have with being average. There's nothing wrong with being different."

"Of course you'd say that," I say.

"Tell me one thing, Hannah," she says, looking me dead in the eye. "What's so great about being average?"

"Why are you so allergic to being normal?" I ask. I walk out of her room and down the hall to mine, but I can swear that I feel her glaring at me through the walls. This house, all six thousand square feet of it, is apparently too small for the two of us. I decide to spend the night at the guest house.

Once I walk into the guest house, I realize that in my rush, I forgot to bring anything with me. Even as lightly as I tend to pack, there are still a few things that I'll need if I'm going to sleep here. A toothbrush, for one, and also the special face soap that my grandmother has gotten me addicted to. ("Never underestimate the power of a clear complexion," my grandmother says.) There's no way that I'm going back to the house—my mother will see that as a tiny but glorious victory over me. So I forget the toothbrush and just go upstairs to choose my bedroom for the night.

The master seems too large, so I decide between the other two guest rooms. I end up in the pink room, the one with a bathroom attached to it. Not only is the bed bigger in the pink room, but it's also got a claw-foot tub in its bathroom, and I just can't resist.

I open the medicine cabinet in the pink room's bathroom—an antique piece with a delicately painted mirror—and see that there is a spare toothbrush, still in its wrapping, toothpaste, and that soap I've become addicted to. Another life skill my grandmother considers crucial for a woman to have: the ability to make a comfortable home.

I peel off my long-sleeve T-shirt and walk toward the closet. Opening the double doors with a slight *whoosh*, I find just what you'd expect given the state of the bathroom: nightshirts, a robe, a spare bathing suit and also a pair of fuzzy slippers, all lined up neatly in a row.

I hear a gentle knock on the window. It's so quiet out here that it was almost distracting to me the first night I was here. I'd gotten so accustomed to how loud New York City was that I'd nearly forgotten that some people actually need peace and quiet to go to sleep.

I hear another rap on the window and look out to see that small stones are being thrown at it.

Hunter. It can only be Hunter. The teacher who undoubtedly forced him to read *Romeo and Juliet* against his will would be proud.

I'm really not in the mood for Hunter right now. I think that, earlier in the day, I might have thought it was sweet of him to be visiting me at the guest house, but after dealing with my mother, I'm just not in the right state of mind. And I don't want to end up saying something that I'll regret—despite myself, I sort of like him hanging around me.

I throw on the bathrobe and walk over to the window. I have to duck to miss a stray pebble as it careens toward my head when I get the window open. I look down to tell Hunter that it's really too late for him to be visiting me, but it's not Hunter I see down by the pool.

It's Nate.

"Is it too late?" he asks in a half-whisper, half-shout.

"What are you doing here?" I ask, pulling the edges of the bathrobe tightly around my body without even realizing it.

"I can come back if you want," he says. "Do you want me to come back? It's just that I saw you walking out here—I can see your pool from my bedroom—and I thought I'd stop by to say hi."

"You stopped by to say hello at ten at night?"

"Yeah," he says. "No good?"

I have no idea how to respond to this. Of course it's no good, I don't want to see him during the day, much less ten at night. I pull myself back in from the window and shut it. I walk back to the closet and put on a pair of slippers. I make my way back toward the bathroom and I hear someone calling my name. I walk over to the landing and Nate Sugarman is standing in the entranceway of the guest house.

"You're in the house," I say.

"When you ducked back from the window, I thought you were telling me to come in."

I want to say "I wasn't," because that's what I would normally say if someone who I didn't particularly care for was standing in my house. But instead I try to think of what my grandmother would do in this situation. She would be a gracious hostess, regardless of the time of night. My grandmother thinks it is important always to be gracious. "Do you want something to drink?" I ask.

Nate agrees and we walk over to the kitchen. I recall from the two-hour tour of the property my grandmother gave me on my first day here that the guest house has a fully stocked bar. There are no thirsty people at the Mattress King's estate. In addition to the oversized kitchen in the main house, the guest house has its own little kitchen complete with every appliance a chef

could possibly want, along with fully stocked cupboards and cabinets, thanks to my grandmother.

I open the fridge and survey what we've got.

"There's a bottle of sparkling rosé," I offer. I wonder if Nate
knows that sparkling rosé is big in the Hamptons. "But maybe
you want something a little stronger?"

"Rosé's fine," Nate says. "I'll grab the glasses."

As he stands up to find the glasses and I open a drawer to
find the napkins, we bump into each other and self-consciously
apologize. After a brief dance where we get the glasses, open the
bottle, and pour, Nate walks over to the couch to sit down. I suddenly feel uncomfortable with him, so I opt to stay at the kitchen
counter. I perch myself on a bar stool and act as if it's not at all
strange that we're the only ones here, yet sitting more than twenty
feet away from each other.

"So," he begins, "you went to your firm right after law school."

"Yup," I say. "Did you go immediately to the DA's office?"

"That was pretty much the plan," he says. "It's the reason I
went to law school."

"Well, I guess when you don't have to worry about money,
you can do what you want," I say, with the attendant superiority
one feels when one's mother constantly tells her, "*We* aren't like
those people."

"What's that supposed to mean?" Nate asks, furrowing his
brow, and then takes a big swig of his wine.

"Just that you obviously don't have to work," I say, "so it's
nice that you're doing public interest work."

"Nice?"

"Yes, nice," I say, my eyes down in my rosé.

"Nice," he mutters under his breath. And then louder: "You
say this all as if it's a bad thing." Nate laughs under his breath and

gets up from the couch. He downs the rest of his wine and puts the glass into the kitchen sink. "You say 'nice' like it's a curse word. I thought I was being nice by coming over here, but you don't seem to do nice, do you?"

"I do nice," I say, my voice a bit smaller.

"You know," he says, "I was happy to see you out here, to bump into you at that party the other day. Each summer, it's the same people out here, the same crowd. It was refreshing to see you—find someone different. And I really like your grandmother a lot, my whole family does, so even though we weren't friends in law school, I figured that if your grandmother is so cool, you must be pretty cool yourself. But you really seem to have some sort of a problem. I don't know if it's with me in particular, or just the world in general, but I think I should go."

I sit frozen on my bar stool—I'm just so taken aback by how upfront he is. In my experience, the only people you can actually expect to be honest with you are the ones who are related to you. Everyone else is just pretending they're something they're not. But not Nate, apparently.

"I'll see you around," he says.

And with that, he turns on his heel and walks out.

Twenty-one

Vivien Leigh famously complained of Clark Gable's bad breath over the course of filming *Gone With the Wind*. My grandmother does not seem to have any such objections to *her* Rhett Butler. They are sitting so close at today's lunch that it's almost indecent. I'm reconsidering whether or not I should have invited Hunter to this little luncheon, but as I steal a glance at my mother, sitting next to me, I remember why I asked him over: I wanted to have at least one person to talk to.

Today we're dining out on the backyard patio, just off the kitchen. There's a beautiful view of the pool from here, and Rhett insisted on sitting on the side of the table that looks in at the house, so that my grandmother, mother, and I could all have the better view. Hunter did Rhett one better by not only sitting on the far side of the table, next to him, but also by pulling my chair out for me as we went to sit down.

My grandmother's chef has prepared a banquet for today's lunch—two different salads, homemade guacamole, tuna tartar prepared three different ways, bruschetta, an entire roasted chicken, an antipasto platter overflowing with Italian meats and grilled vegetables, freshly baked rolls, and my grandmother's favorite chicken salad from The Sweet Apple, a tiny luncheonette in town. Jean-Marie made her own sangria and steeped a pitcher of iced tea just for the occasion. I tried to help her bring all of the food outside, but was laughed out of the kitchen by her and the housekeeper.

"Your grandmother is only fifteen years old here," Rhett says, reaching over the table to hand me an old photograph. I'm amazed that he's kept this photo for so long—it's so old the edges have yellowed and curled up, but when I look at the woman in the picture, there's no mistaking that it's my grandmother. Her hair is jet black and her eyes look almost clear in the grainy black-and-white. I look from the photo up at my grandmother, and see that not much has changed. Her eyes still sparkle, even when she's not trying.

"And when did you two get married?" I ask. I'm trying to be gracious, but I'm finding it difficult. Earlier this morning, my grandmother asked me to make an effort to get to know Rhett. He clearly has been given the same missive, because he's trying so hard with my mother and me that it's bordering on painful.

"We ran away together about six months after this photo was taken," he says, smiling at my grandmother conspiratorially. It's as if they have an inside joke that no one else knows.

My mother and I smile back at him tightly. "Lemme see," Hunter says, and reaches over the chicken salad to take the photo from me.

"You look like her, Hannah," Hunter says, smiling, and I thank him. I know it's a compliment because my grandmother was beautiful, especially in that picture. Hunter smiles at me and takes a bite of his roll.

"This is the picture I carried with me to America after the war," Rhett says. "It's how I found your grandmother."

"I never knew that you two saw each other after the war," my mother says, even though the comment wasn't directed at her.

"There are plenty of things you don't know about me, dear," my grandmother answers. Then, looking at me, my grandmother says, "It's important for a woman to hold on to some things just for herself."

"By the time I found her," Rhett continues, with a forlorn sigh, "she was already married to your grandfather."

Hunter asks Rhett for a detailed analysis on how, exactly, he was able to find my grandmother, while my grandmother asks me to help her with something in the house.

We go upstairs to her bedroom to her trunk of photographs.

"Don't tell anyone that I have this," she says. "Especially your mother. Let's just take out an album or two to show Adanet."

Her fingers seem to know exactly where to go. She reaches into the trunk and pulls out the first album that she grabs. She opens it to a random page in the middle and nods her head.

"This is the one." I glance over her shoulder and see that it is full of baby pictures of my mother. My grandmother looks like a movie star in each and every one of the shots, even the ones taken right after my mother was born. In each photograph, her hair is immaculate, her face made up, her waistline tiny. I sometimes forget that my grandmother is European until I see something like this. Of course, she wouldn't let a little thing like childbirth ruin her figure or cause her to stop wearing fitted dresses and three-inch heels. I know that my grandmother has grabbed this album because she thinks she looked more beautiful when she was younger, but she's just as beautiful now. I tell her so, and she kisses me on the cheek.

We walk back out to the lunch table and Hunter and Rhett are still chatting animatedly. My mother sits across from them looking a bit green in the face.

"Are you okay?" I ask her.

"Fine," she says, tearing a piece of a roll. "What took you so long?"

"I thought you might like to see this," my grandmother says to Rhett, handing him the photo album.

"Wow," Hunter says, looking on with Rhett. "Mrs. Morgan-felder, is this you?"

"Yes, sweetheart," she says.

I look at my mother and she still looks green—I see her take a sip of water, and then put the glass against her forehead.

"Would you like to take a look, Hannah?" Rhett asks me, and I tell him that I've already seen the album. I know I'm sup-posed to be making an effort with Rhett, but I don't want to have to walk across the table and look at the photographs over his shoulder.

I'm not sure why I dislike Rhett so much. Is it because there's something about him that I inherently don't like? Am I annoyed that I came out to the Hamptons for the summer and my grand-mother found a man before I did? Or is it because I think he'll take up my grandmother's time, time that could be better spent with me?

"Would you all please excuse me?" my mother says, and dashes from the table. I jump up and follow my mother—but she's run so quickly into the house that she's already in the bathroom by the time I get there. From the hallway I can hear her inside getting sick, and I go to the kitchen and get her a cold glass of water.

"I think the chicken salad's been left out in the sun too long," she says as she walks out of the bathroom. I hand her the glass of water, and steer her over to the living room couches so she can sit down.

"It tasted fine to me," I say. "Maybe it was the tuna?"

"I didn't have the tuna," she says, and takes another sip of water. "You don't look so good. Did you have the chicken salad?"

"I feel fine," I say, just as I feel my stomach lurch. All of the sudden, my head feels heavy and a wave of nausea washes over me. I jump up and run to the other bathroom down the hall.

Minutes later, I emerge and Martine is waiting for me with a cold washcloth. I thank her and walk back to the couch. My mother is already splayed out on the couch with a cold washcloth on her head. I walk over to the other couch and lie down.

"We don't have to go back out there now," my mother says. "Right?"

Finally. Something we can agree on.

Twenty-two

Hunter pulls up to the driveway in an enormous red convertible.

"What are you doing?" I say as I walk out to the driveway. The gravel under my feet makes more noise than the car. As I approach the driver's side window, I can smell Hunter's cologne wafting through the warm summer air.

"Picking you up," Hunter says matter-of-factly. "We're going out on date."

"You're fourteen."

"So?" Hunter says.

"I'm . . . not fourteen," I say.

"Are you afraid you can't keep up with me?" he asks.

"I'm afraid I'll get arrested."

"Okay, fine," he says, throwing his hands in the air dramatically. "I give up. Then, it's not a date. But I'm taking you to a bonfire on the beach."

"I'm afraid *you'll* get arrested."

"Why?" he asks.

"Because you're fourteen," I repeat. "You can't drive."

"My dad said it was okay," he says. "Anyway, everyone drives in the Hamptons. I'll wait inside while you grab a sweater. It gets cold on the beach at night."

Apparently, Monday is *the* night to go out in the Hamptons. I assume this is because no kid whose parents have a house in the Hamptons actually has to work for the summer, so they can go out any night of the week that they'd like. It's as if they've subconsciously chosen Monday as the "it" night to party so as to remind the rest of the world, the ones who actually have to work for a living, just how rich they really are.

The beach is packed with people, and there's a bar and DJ set up, out on the bluff. Hunter and I grab drinks and walk toward the bonfire. He was right—it's quite chilly, and I'm glad I put my sweater on.

I spot a group of kids who look to be Hunter's age, so I suggest we walk over and socialize.

"No, let's hang here," Hunter says.

"Don't you want to meet some people your own age?" I say, careful not to call the people his age kids, even though that's exactly what they are to me.

"I know those guys," he says. "They all suck."

"Oh, I'm sorry," I say. "Do you go to school with them or something?"

"Yeah," he says, and sits down on a log next to the bonfire. Hunter usually can't keep his mouth shut, but suddenly, he's monosyllabic.

"Maybe if you got to know them, they wouldn't be so bad," I say, and it strikes me how much I sound like my grandmother. What do I care if Hunter hangs out with kids his own age or not?

"I already know them," he says, downing his cup of beer. "Look, no one will talk to me, okay? I don't really have any friends."

"I'm sorry, Hunter," I say. "I didn't know." I feel awful . . . how could I have not figured that out by the way Hunter's been hanging on to me all weekend? I flattered myself into thinking that he had a crush on me, but maybe he just didn't have anyone else to hang out with.

"I *had* friends. I'm not like a freak or something. Those people were my friends, actually. But it's like since I came back to school after my mom died no one wants to talk to me." I look at Hunter and he's looking out at the ocean, acting like he doesn't care. But I know that he does. I know just how he feels.

"Oh, honey," I say, "that's because no one knows what to say to you."

"What do you mean they don't know what to say to me?" he says. "It's just me. I'm not any different now."

"I know," I say. "It's just really hard for people to know what to say in these situations. Even for adults, you know."

"How hard is it to say, 'I'm sorry about your mom'?"

"It's not," I say. "But for some reason, people get really awkward and uncomfortable when someone young dies. They're afraid to say the wrong thing to you."

"I think it would be better for them to say anything, even the wrong thing," he says. "It totally sucks when people don't say anything at all."

"I know exactly how you feel."

"No, you don't," Hunter says, turning to me and looking me dead in the eye. His face is flushed, his cheeks a flaming red. "Fuck you. No, you do not. Don't fucking say that to me."

"Hunter, I—" I try to speak, but Hunter is not even listening to me.

"Your mother is alive. I met her this afternoon. Your *grandmother* is even alive. You're older than me and you still have a grandmother. I don't have any grandparents or my mother and I'm only fourteen. What the fuck, Hannah?"

With that, Hunter gets up and walks to the bar. I get up and follow him, but I can't walk as fast as he can in the sand. I feel like I'm in one of those dreams where you try to move quickly, but your feet just won't carry you fast enough. I'm still thinking about how angry Hunter is when someone grabs my arm. I turn and see two of the girls that were standing in the group of Hunter's old friends.

"Are you Hunter's date or something?" the one with strawberry blond hair asks me. At first, all I can think is that, if she thinks I'm young enough to be dating Hunter, then this face soap my grandmother's been pushing on me must be really good.

"No," I say, "we're just friends."

She turns to the other girl, who has lighter blond hair and says, "Told you so."

"Are you friends of Hunter's?" I ask them carefully.

"Yeah," they say in unison. The one with the lighter hair self-consciously flips her hair back.

"All you have to say to him," I explain, "is: 'I'm sorry about your mom.' That's all."

Both girls look at me for a moment as if they don't know what I'm talking about. "It's weird," the one with lighter hair says.

"I know," I say.

"What the fuck is this?" Hunter says, appearing out of nowhere, and the two girls scatter. And then to me: "Can't you find someone your own age to hang out with?"

"My husband died," I blurt out. "I'm a widow, just like my grandmother. That's why I said that I know how you feel. I didn't lose my mother, but I did lose the love of my life."

"Oh," Hunter says and looks down at his feet. "I'm sorry."

"Thanks," I say. "It was years ago. I thought I would die at the time. I mean, I really didn't know how I'd survive, but I did."

"Did you just forget about him after a while?" he asks.

"No," I say. "I'll never forget him. And you'll never forget your mom. You'll think about her every day. But at some point, you'll begin to move on. You'll realize that you're allowed to be happy. That she'd want you to be happy."

Hunter wipes his eye under the guise of "sand getting in his eye," and asks me if I want another drink.

"I've been irresponsible enough in letting you drive," I say, taking the cup from his hands. "I'm not going to be letting you drink and drive."

"Fair enough," he says.

"Now, I'd like to meet your friends."

Twenty-three

I thought I had it all figured out. I had graduated law school, started working at my law firm, and gotten married to the man of my dreams. Everything was perfect. Now I can't even bring myself to ever say his name.

We met on the first day of law school and he proposed on the day of our graduation. He showed up to law school with dreadlocks, fresh off a stint in the Peace Corps, and believed in making the world a better place. Gazing into his enormous brown eyes, he made me believe it, too.

He introduced me to a whole new world. I wasn't just seeing the world the way my mother photographed it, I was seeing the real world, real people. Real problems. I was seeing the ways I could help make things different. How I could change the world. It was exciting—helping people was a high I'd never experienced before. I finally felt like I belonged somewhere, to someone. Arm in arm, I felt like we were invincible. There was nothing we couldn't accomplish together.

We planned to work in large law firms just long enough to make enough money to start a not-for-profit that would help children in developing countries: he would pay off his law school loans and I would save up the seed money. The idea of having my grandmother help us out was out of the question for him—he believed in making it on your own, doing things on your own. It was the way he'd been raised, on a farm two hours north of the city. Hard work and an eye toward helping your fellow man. His hands were rough to the touch.

My mother adored him, but she was still very vocal about the fact that I was making a huge mistake in getting married so young. She refused to allow me my romantic fantasy of life.

But my grandmother did. She threw us a small beachside wedding at the Mattress King's estate, charmed the pants off each and every guest, and joined me for long walks on the beach to tell me how my life was going to change, and how to be a good wife. All the things that she'd learned by being married so many times. She walked me down the aisle in the absence of my mother, who was stuck on assignment in Somalia, and my father, who I'd never met. Truth is, I wouldn't have wanted it any other way.

We decided to wait to have children—we both wanted to concentrate on our careers before beginning a family. Then, one day, he simply didn't wake up. He lay beside me, motionless. I knew from looking at him that he was gone, the color drained from his face like a papier-mâché doll, but I refused to believe it.

I didn't yell. I didn't cry. I didn't even say a word. I was utterly, completely, numb. It took me over half an hour to actually register the fact that he was dead, and that my perfect life was over.

I didn't realize that happiness was something that can be measured, that it's not always there to stay. That you should enjoy every second of it, because you're mere minutes from it disappearing into thin air.

My grandmother was the first person I called. She told me to call 911 while she woke her driver up and was driven to my apartment.

My mother flew in for the funeral. She managed to keep herself from saying anything even approaching *I told you so*, but I could see it on her bedraggled face. My grandmother was the one who stayed with me in my apartment for the entire month after he died. She was the one who helped me wake up every morning and get dressed; was waiting in a chauffered car for me on Monday, Tuesday, and Thursday nights, ready to take me to my therapist; and then out to dinner after the appointment.

My grandmother was the only one I could relate to, the only one who could understand.

I quickly got sick of friends trying to make me feel better. As they told me over warm platters of chicken parmesan, "I know how you feel," it took all the energy I could muster not to scream at them: "Oh really? Did your husband wake up today?"

I stayed in touch with his family for a long time. But every time we got together, it inevitably ended up with his mother crying hysterically and locking herself in a bathroom, so after a while, my therapist instructed me to stop going for my own mental health.

Now his mother runs a twenty-four-hour bereavement hotline for mothers who have lost their children. I used to go there to volunteer, but the evenings always inevitably ended up with me crying hysterically and then locking myself in a bathroom.

I don't see her much anymore.

I threw myself into my work from the moment my bereavement leave ended (just one month—a policy clearly created by someone who's never had something to mourn), only taking breaks to see my shrink and my grandmother on her frequent visits to the city. Somewhere in there I met Jaime and decided to give relationships another try, but a love affair should not end with a New York City detective visiting your apartment.

And now I'm out here, hiding from the world. But at least I'm with the one person in the world I love the most. My mother's gone back to wherever she was before she came out here and now it's just my grandmother and me again.

"So, how was your date?" my grandmother asks me. We're laying poolside, waiting for Jean-Marie to set up lunch.

"I don't think you could really call it a date," I say. "I was more like his chaperone."

"Well, I'm glad that you see the difference."

"Please tell me that's not something you were really worried about."

"I just wonder why you'd prefer to spend your time with a youngster when you have your pick of men out here."

"I wouldn't say that I have my pick of men."

"That sommelier was very interested in you, and so is Nate."

"I'm not really interested in either of them."

"But maybe if you took the time to go out with them, you might actually find yourself having a nice time."

"I had fun with Hunter last night," I say, and my grand-mother shakes her head.

"How's he doing without his mom?" she asks.

"Fine," I say. "He seems to be doing as well as you could expect."

"Such a tragedy to lose a parent so young," my grandmother says.

"I told him that I'm a widow," I blurt out.

My grandmother doesn't respond for a moment. She sits still, staring out at the beach.

"Ah," my grandmother finally says. "So, now he knows your big, dark secret."

"It's not a secret, exactly," I say. "It's simply something that I'd rather not talk about."

"I think you're embarrassed about it."

"I'm not embarrassed."

"It's something you don't want people to know," she says.

"Well, I also don't want people to know that my ex-boyfriend's mother is having me investigated for attempted murder, but you seem to have no problem telling people that."

"Yes, dear," she says, "but that I can't help. It's just so funny."

"Is my being a widow also funny?"

"No," my grandmother says, suddenly serious. "It wasn't funny when it happened to me, it wasn't funny when it happened to you."

That brings the conversation to a halt. I feel a tear coming to my eye and quickly brush it away. My grandmother puts her hand over mine as she says: "I'd like for you to be more like me in a number of ways, but not that one."

Under normal circumstances, I'd love to be compared to my grandmother, but I don't think that being a widow once over puts me into the same category as her: professional black widow. I tell her as much.

"I don't think that's fair," I say, taking my hat off and letting the sun hit my face. "I didn't actually kill the last one."

"I didn't kill *any* of my ex-husbands," she says, pale blue eyes widening. "But, with those nuts, darling, *you* certainly tried."

We share a laugh as Jean-Marie comes out with lunch. We decide to stay by the pool and Jean-Marie sets down the tray and leaves us to enjoy our meal. Eating in a lounge chair is an art—you need to position your legs and plate just so in order to avoid a mess. It's just one of the many important life skills I've acquired since being out here.

I lay back in my lounge chair and pick up my chicken salad sandwich, minding my back and legs. Jean-Marie picked up a new batch of chicken salad this morning, so I know we won't be having a repeat of Sunday's debacle. I take a bite, take a sip of iced tea, and then the phone rings. My grandmother passes the telephone to me.

"Do you still have food poisoning from the weekend?" my mother asks. I tell her that I was sick the next morning, too, and a little this morning, but I wasn't too concerned about it. My grandmother furrows her brow, looking over at me. I know she'll want me to relay this entire conversation to her once I hang up the phone, and she's getting impatient waiting to hear.

"Make an appointment with a doctor," she says. "I think we may have caught something out there." My mother never goes to doctors, so I find it curious that she's telling me that I need to see one. She was always the one who would forgo the yearly physical and put off going to the doctor until she was so sick she could barely function. I, on the other hand, make my yearly appointments like clockwork, always going in August, a pattern I established back in high school.

"You went to a doctor?" I ask.

"I haven't been feeling well since I left the Hamptons," she says. "I went to a doctor and he's concerned."

"Concerned?" I ask. The news makes me sit up in my lounge chair. My grandmother does the same, trying to glean what we're talking about from my body language and my responses to the conversation.

"Yes," she continues. "He's run a few tests."

"What kind of tests?" I ask.

"I don't know," she says. "Tests. Don't worry. I'll let you know as soon as I hear something. Promise me you'll see a doctor, though?

If we caught some strange bacterial thing, I want to make sure you get something for it."

Even though it makes no sense—I know the chicken salad is innocent in all this—I can't help but put it down.

Twenty-four

Things are buzzing again in Southampton by Thursday, but the Sugarmans don't make it out to the beach until Friday afternoon. It takes me until Saturday morning to walk over to his house.

I'm nervous once I get to the door. And not just because of Nate. It's because I've built this house up in my head. In my mind, it's decorated traditionally, with a touch of whimsy. Warm colors abound, and it has furniture that's beautiful but also comfortable. It's the sort of place you want to sit down and kick your shoes off in—take a drink in front of the fireplace and read for hours.

And the family. The family is everything I've always dreamed a family could be. Loving, kind, intact. There's a father and a mother, grandparents and siblings. They all know the intimate details of one another's lives. They love to spend time together. They share private jokes. I've walked by this house countless times, and always imagine what it's like inside. Can the reality possibly live up to my imagination?

Apparently, yes. The house is even more beautiful than I imagined. The Sugarmans have retained a lot of the original detailing, and the decorating revolves around enhancing the house's original beauty, not trying to cover it up. The wood floors are refinished, but don't look new, and the windows are original.

Nate's mother lets me into the house, and as I walk past the kitchen on my way up the stairs, I notice it's done as a country kitchen, with couches set up right next to the dining table, and an enormous farmhouse sink. Above the couch, there's a gigantic photograph of the entire family. Even from far away, I can see their smiling faces as they all hold hands, posing, as the sun hits their faces.

We walk up the steps and there are more family photographs. As I look at each one—Nate as he's being sworn into the New York State bar, his brother and sister-in-law on their wedding day, his little sister at her college graduation—I'm hit with a familiar feeling. One that I haven't felt since I was in high school.

Envy.

The photographs tell the story of a perfect family, the sort of family I always longed for. The sort of family that was always just slightly out of my grasp.

"Nate's door is right there," his mother says, and I remember what I'm there to do.

"Thank you," I say to his mother as she walks back downstairs.

"I'm sorry," I say to Nate, barging into his upstairs bedroom. My tone is angrier than I intended when I first mapped this conversation out in my head.

"Nice to see you, too," Nate says, and lies down on his bed. He tucks his hands behind his head.

"I said I'm sorry," I say. He shakes his head and swats at the wind, as if he's telling me to forget about it. But I continue: "About the way I acted."

"I was so sorry to hear about Adam," he says. "I wanted to tell you that I was sorry when I heard."

My throat closes up at the mere mention of my husband's

name and I have to sit down on the window seat. I don't even realize I'm crying until Nate has sat down next to me, asking me if I'd like a tissue.

I don't know why I'm crying. After years of therapy, I've dealt with the pain. I've come to terms with what happened. With how I have to live my life now. I'm a widow. That's the box I have to check off now—no longer single, no longer married, widowed. And that's okay, because there will be many more chapters in my life.

But still the mention of his name does it to me. I'm only human. And now the floodgates are open, and I'm sitting here weeping in front of a man I don't even like.

"I'm sorry," Nate says again. "I didn't mean to upset you. I just wanted you to know that I understand. I know you've been having a tough time."

I wipe my nose on the edge of my bathing suit cover-up and look down at the floor. The floor is a very light-colored wood. I wonder if it's original to the house, too.

"I was at the funeral, you know," he says. "It was just so crowded, and I didn't push through all the people quickly enough to tell you how sorry I was."

I remember what my mother told me that day: when someone young dies, there are lots of people at the funeral. She told me that she hopes there's only a handful of people at hers. That she's so old by the time she dies that the only ones there are the few she's outlived in the natural order of things. Me, a few work colleagues, and maybe a few fans of her work.

"Thank you," I say to Nate once I've stopped crying. "I never knew that you were there."

"I didn't mean to make you cry," he says, handing me a tissue.

"I know that," I say, wiping my nose. I look over at him but it's hard to hold his gaze. "I guess I just got a little emotional."

"That's allowed," Nate says, and smiles. I never really noticed before how nice his smile is. I see that tiny chip on one of his front teeth again and I can't help wondering where he got it.

"It's just hard thinking about him sometimes," I say.

"You don't ever say his name," Nate says. "You should say his name."

"Okay, I think this was enough," I say, and jump up from the window seat to leave Nate's room. I walk down the stairs, but barely make it halfway down before Nate is right behind me.

"Hannah, wait," Nate says, and I see him come flying down the steps. "Come back. Stay for lunch."

"I can't," I murmur as I continue down the stairs. "My grandmother is waiting for me."

"Wait."

I turn to face him and there's a look on his face that I can't decipher. His face is so open, so honest that I can't seem to recall why it is that I hate him so much.

I stay for lunch.

Apparently, Saturday lunch is a big deal for the Sugarmans, and everyone comes home for it. Nate mentions something about a family tradition left over from his grandfather's generation, when they would all stay in and observe the Sabbath. They're not religious anymore but they still do the big Saturday lunch. Nate's older brother drives over, wife and three children in tow, from his own summer house, just fifteen minutes away in Water Mill. His younger sister arrives late, still in her tennis whites, with her college roommate, whose parents' house she'd been visiting all morning.

"Who won?" Nate's brother asks his sister.

She and her college roommate laugh. "It was a tie," they say in unison.

"A tie?" Nate's sister-in-law says. "The Sugarmans don't believe in ties."

"We're going back to Rachel's house after lunch to fix that," Nate's father chimes in, carrying out a tray of food.

"Can I help with anything?" I ask, and Nate shakes his head and motions for me to sit down next to him.

"How sweet of you to ask, dear," Nate's mother says. And then, to Nate: "Your last date never offered to help."

Embarrassed, Nate shrugs his shoulders. I smile at him and he moves his chair a little closer to mine.

"Do you play tennis?" Nate's sister asks me.

"No, I don't," I say.

"Nate will change that," she says.

"Are you Nate's *girl*friend?" Nate's five-year-old nephew asks me. The nieces break into hysterical laughter.

"Would you all leave the poor girl alone?" Nate's brother bellows over the din. "At the rate we're going, she's going to sneak out of here before dessert."

"Don't be ridiculous," Nate's mother says. And then, to me: "You're not going to leave before dessert, dear, are you?"

"I don't plan to," I say. Being with Nate's family is like getting a giant, warm hug.

"Okay, enough chattering," Nate's dad says. "Let's eat."

I steer clear of the chicken salad, seafood salad, and tuna salad, and I don't get sick after lunch, thankfully—more a product of the fact that I can barely eat, but I'll take what I can get.

The Sugarmans scatter after lunch—Nate's brother's family and his mom go into town for a walk, and his father and sister head back to her college roommate's house to play a round of father-daughter doubles on their grass court. Nate and I go for a swim.

The Sugarmans' pool is like a little island of its own, far away from the ocean. It's only when you walk to the end of the backyard that you see the tiny walkway that leads you out onto the beach.

The pool is all stone and granite, and the hot tub is inside a little grotto, off the shallow end of the pool. On the edge of the grotto is an outside bar, and Nate is mixing margaritas.

"Salt?" he asks, and I catch a glimpse of that chipped front tooth.

Maybe this is the recipe for a happy life—not thinking about anything too hard, just going where the day takes you, trying to enjoy yourself, instead of analyzing every second.

"No, thanks," I say, and Nate reaches down under the counter to pull out two margarita glasses.

"This is very festive," I say.

"I'm hoping that if I get you liquored up on tequila, you won't start a fight with me."

I can't help but laugh. Why had I been so intent on fighting with him?

"Cheers," I say, and we touch our glasses. Since the margarita glasses are plastic, they barely make a sound. I take a sip, but instantly feel my stomach lurch from the smell of the tequila, so I place my glass back onto the bar.

"Last one in's a rotten egg," I call out as I walk to the pool, and dive in. Nate jumps in right behind me.

"That shouldn't count," he says, swimming up toward me. "I didn't have fair warning."

"It still counts," I say, smiling. I smooth out my hair with a wet hand. We're about five feet away from each other, treading water.

"So, if I try to apologize again, will you start crying?"

"No," I say. "But I'd like to apologize, too. You're not at all what I thought you were."

"I'm not even going to ask."

"I thought you were a rich, entitled brat, but I think I may have been wrong."

"So," Nate says, swimming closer, "you've changed your opinion of me?"

"No," I say, splashing some water in his direction, "I still think you're rich and entitled. Just not a brat. You're not as bad as I thought."

"And you're worse than I thought," he says. His voice is deeper, stronger.

And then he's kissing me. And I'm kissing him back. We're laughing and kissing and trying to stay afloat in the pool. Nate motions to the shallow end of the pool and we swim over, grabbing for each other as we swim. We get to the edge of the shallow end, where we can stand, and Nate grabs me and presses me against the wall. He grabs my face and then slides his hands through my hair, and then down my shoulders. His hands are rough. I love the way they feel on my skin.

"When's your family coming home?" I ask in between kisses, and we both laugh. He leads me over to the grotto, which can't be seen from the house, and we resume kissing. This time with more urgency. I don't want him to stop.

He kisses me all over, taking my bikini top off, and I throw a quick glance at the house, to make sure no one is coming. Nate catches me and laughs. He promises me that no one will be home for hours.

We're acting like children, like two teenagers afraid of getting caught. It is exactly what I need. I lean back and enjoy Nate's hands, lips, all over my body. In one sweeping motion, he grabs me and picks me up, one arm below my shoulder blades, the other below my knees, and brings me over to a couch that's set up inside the grotto. It feels good to give in, to be in the moment.

"Do you want to . . . um," Nate begins to stammer. I look up at his face and smile. I cannot believe that I am out here making out shamelessly with Nate Sugarman. "Should we go up to my bedroom?" And that I'm about to do a lot more with Nate Sugarman.

We're laughing and kissing all the way through the house, and when we get to his room, tumble into bed. We're still soaking wet, and it's difficult to peel the rest of our wet clothes off, but we manage.

His lips are all over my body, his hands, and I don't want him to stop. I try to memorize this moment, his every freckle, the way his lips feel when they brush my skin, the roughness of his hands. I run my hands down his arms, over his back, and pull him tighter.

His breath is warm on my skin. Everywhere his hands touch, I'm set on fire. All I can think is: more.

"Hannah," he whispers. He cups my face in his hands, and I know what he's asking me.

"Yes," I say.

Then we're making love, and he's gentle and passionate and sweet and fervent and it's everything I want it to be. We fall asleep in each other's arms and I can't remember the last time I felt so comfortable. So at home.

It's around six o'clock when we hear stirring in the house.

"Do you hear that?" I say, shaking Nate's shoulder to wake him up. He opens his eyes and smiles broadly at me.

"Everyone's home to get ready for their dinner plans," Nate whispers. I jump out of his bed and cover myself with a sheet.

"We're thirty-four years old, Hannah," he says. "We're allowed to do whatever we want."

I laugh, but can't help wondering what Nate's mother would think of my being upstairs alone with her son.

Why do I care what she thinks all of the sudden? Yesterday, I hated Nate Sugarman. Now I'm thinking about impressing his mom. A lot happens in a day in the Hamptons.

"So, speaking of dinner . . ." Nate begins.

"Yes, of course," I say, "I should let you get ready. I'm sure you have plans. And I'm sure my grandmother is wondering where I've been all day." I go to give him a peck on the lips and make my hasty exit, but he grabs me around my waist and I fall into him.

"You're not getting rid of me that easily," he whispers into my ear. "How about you go home and change and I pick you up in half an hour?"

I'm powerless to say anything but yes. It wasn't really a question, anyway.

Twenty-five

My grandmother can see it on my face the moment I walk in the door.

"You're gone, aren't you?" she says.

My bathing suit and cover-up have dried, but now they're itchy from the chlorine. I stand there like a little girl, squirming around while my grandmother chastises me.

"Now you don't like Nate Sugarman?" I ask.

"I like Nate Sugarman just fine," she says. "More than fine. But he's besides the point. This is about you. Don't fall too hard for just one."

"What if I don't want to date anyone else right now?" I'm trying hard not to think about sex. I'm sure that if I'm thinking about sex, my grandmother will be able to see that on my face, too. But how can you date someone else when you're sleeping with one person? As I wait for my grandmother's response, I think about whether or not she has this same issue. Does she sleep with each person she dates? As I think about this, I realize I can no longer look my grandmother in the eye.

"You should be meeting all different types of men. Dating all different types of men. You can't really do that if you're smitten with just one."

"I'm not smitten," I say, trying not to smile.

"Oh please."

When I hear the doorbell ring twenty minutes later, I fly down the stairs to meet Nate. My grandmother beats me to the punch and I hear Nate say to her: "Mrs. Morganfelder, may I take your granddaughter out to dinner this evening?"

I stifle a giggle. I think it's completely adorable, but I have a feeling that my grandmother may not agree.

Half an hour later, we're on Route 27, in Nate's windowless, doorless Jeep. I have no idea where we're going. I lean back and take a deep breath. I enjoy the view and try to enjoy the not knowing. When Nate sees my wet hair flopping around in the wind, he leans over and opens the glove compartment. He takes out a baseball cap.

"Thanks," I say as we head further east on Route 27.

We pull off the road, into a driveway that looks like every other driveway on Route 27. I have no idea where we are.

The Jeep glides down the driveway and stops outside a little bungalow with Chinese lanterns strung from every tree in sight. I don't know quite what to expect, but when Nate grabs my hand I realize I don't really care where we are going.

We walk into the bungalow, which is completely empty, except for a small bar without any bar stools. "Where are we?" I ask. Nate smiles, leading me out the back door, and I see what we came all this way for. There are a dozen or so tables right there in the sand. Tiki torches light up the perimeter, and more Chinese lanterns twinkle above. The sun has just about set, and it casts an orange-pink glow on the beach.

"Nate, this is—"

"I know," he says, and puts his hand on the small of my back.

"How did you know what I was going to say?" I ask, smiling. The wind picks up and I catch the scent of his aftershave: lemon, mint, and verbena.

"What were you going to say?" he asks, and leans down toward me.

His lips gently touch mine, and I forget all about what I was going to say. A waiter recognizes Nate, and nods his head at a table where the sand meets the water.

I look around at the crowd, and it's so much more laid back than most of the other places in the Hamptons. This is not the type of place you go to if you want to see and be seen. This is the kind of place you go to if you just want to *be*.

"Do you bring all your dates here?" I ask, leaning toward him. It dawns on me that I have no idea how to flirt. I met my husband in law school, where sharing your notes with someone and joining their study group was as flirtatious as you could get. Then I met Jaime at a downtown club where he was performing. He saw me in the crowd, and the next thing I knew, we were together. The point is, I'm not especially good at getting what I want. I'm better at letting things just happen to me.

"I think my line here is: 'Only the special ones, baby,'" Nate says, and I laugh. I realize that I've laughed more today than I have so far this whole summer. In a long time, actually.

We order our dinner—mussels and fries, the house salad, and grilled lobsters—and we kiss shamelessly.

Nate and I talk about our work, I tell him about my firm's gentle brush off, and we move on to talking about our families. The mussels arrive just as Nate is trying to defend my mother's lifestyle, calling it remarkable. I dip a French fry into the pot of mussels to soak up the sauce, and try to change the subject.

Just then, the waves get a bit stronger and creep up toward our table.

"Should we move?" I ask Nate. He shrugs his shoulders and tells me that it's part of the ambience. I take my shoes off.

For the rest of the evening, the water tickles my toes, and Nate leans over and kisses me whenever he feels like it. The music gets louder and our conversations get more intense. I try to memorize every moment of the night: the sound of the water, the music flowing through the speakers, the taste of Nate's kisses, the way he brushes my hair off my face when the wind moves it around, the way Nate's lips curl when he smiles at me.

That night, I fall asleep thinking of him.

Twenty-six

"No, darling," my grandmother tells me, "these photographs are not gems. If you want to see gems, I can show you my jewelry collection."

She eyes her ruby cocktail ring and uses her thumb to roll it around her finger. I show her the photograph I was admiring.

"These old photos *are* gems," I insist. "But, if you're offering, I'd like to take a peek at your jewelry collection, too."

My grandmother laughs and looks at the photograph of the two of us. I've seen this picture before. It's one of my mother's favorites. For a photographer, she didn't have much of a talent for displaying photographs when I was younger, but one of the things she always carried around with her was a small sleeve that held a few of her favorite pictures: the shot that won her the Pulitzer—a photograph of three Nicaraguan contra rebels smoking, guns strapped to their backs, none of whom look older than sixteen; a picture of her with her parents, when she was eleven years old; and this photograph of my grandmother and me, taken when I was three.

"This picture is so old that your clothes are actually back in style again," I tell my grandmother.

"Nothing about me was ever out of style," she says, and gives me a tiny smile.

"I want to do something with these pictures," I say. "You can't just leave them all to die in this trunk."

"They are not dying in this trunk," she says. "They're just fine the way they are."

"There are so many loose ones," I say, picking one up off the bottom of the trunk to show her. "They're getting ruined. Let me put them into albums or something."

"The way you're giving yourself projects to do makes me think you are not adjusting to the life of leisure the way I'd hoped you would."

"I'm not giving myself a project," I say, laughing. "I just don't want you treating these photographs like garbage. They are treasures. We should be treating them as family heirlooms, not discarding them like unimportant trinkets."

I look up to find my grandmother regarding me. I can tell by the way she's batting her eyes that she's about to lay one on me. I look back at her and wait.

"So," she says, slowly smiling. "Speaking of things that were discarded . . . I guess you didn't hate Nate Sugarman *that* much."

"No, I hated him."

"It seemed to me that you didn't really hate him," she says, eyes narrowing. "If you really didn't care for someone, that person would be inconsequential to you. But you *hated* Nate. With a real passion. And he's really not that objectionable, if you ask me. So, that can only mean that what you really hated was yourself for having feelings for him."

"Wow, Grandma," I say. "You're wise, just like Yoda."

My grandmother doesn't seem to get the reference. "So, what should we call this one?"

"Nate," I say, "we can just call him Nate."

"How about 'the one who tried to have me arrested'?" she says, throwing her arms out dramatically.

"That doesn't really have much of a ring to it," I say, and turn my attention back to the photographs. "Besides, he was the one who got me out of that whole mess."

"The one who got you out of jail," she says.

"I wasn't actually ever in jail," I say. "A police detective visited my apartment."

"How about 'the one who lived next door to us'?"

"You know what? How about we just call him Nate?"

My grandmother raises one eyebrow and looks at me. Her eyes are violet.

"Well, you're right," she says. "He doesn't need a nickname. After all, who knows what will happen between the two of you. I never gave a clever little nickname to your grandfather. And Nate *is* the sort of man you should marry."

"With our family's track record, do you really think either of us should be getting married again?" I ask with a laugh.

"What do you mean?"

"The curse," I say back in a stage whisper.

"I beg your pardon?" My grandmother does not find this line of reasoning funny. Could this mean that she has designs on marrying Rhett Butler? I really hope not. Although, if I'm correct about there being a family curse, that would be one good way to get rid of him.

"It seems to me that anyone we marry ends up dead," I explain sotto voce. I'm still smiling, but my grandmother is not. In fact, she seems deeply annoyed.

"You weren't married to the musician," she says.

"Yeah, and he didn't die."

"Close enough," she says, and examines her nails.

"That's not the point."

"What is the point?" she asks. "That you think there's some silly family curse? Is that why you're so afraid to be happy?"

"I'm not afraid to be happy," I say, and feel my eyes well up with tears. What an awful thing to say to someone. I'm about to say as much to my grandmother when she interrupts me.

"Let's get back to the photographs, shall we?" she asks.

Probably to cheer me up, she begins with a funny one—my grandfather dressed up for Halloween. My mother is young, very young, and she's some sort of princess. My grandfather is playing the part of the evil witch. As I look closer, I realize that my mother is supposed to be Snow White and my grandfather is supposed to be the wench who gives her the poisonous apple. Did my mother hate convention even back then?

Every photograph my grandmother picks up comes with a story attached. I sit, riveted, as she shares each one, complete with descriptions on where each person ended up—the next-door neighbor who died in a plane crash, the school classmate who became famous, the happily married couple whose relationship ended in an acrimonious divorce. I guess when you look at photos twenty and thirty years later, you often know where the story ends. As for me, I'm still trying to figure out my own story.

"So," my grandmother says, "your mother's going to be coming back out to stay with us." She smiles at me with a pained expression and I'm not sure why she's trying so hard to pretend that everything is normal.

"Why?" I don't even try to hide how I really feel about it. And why should I? I'm having a wonderful summer out here, and my mother will only ruin it. I already know she'll just hate Nate—he's way too normal for her. She'll think he's terribly bourgeois.

She won't let me enjoy this. And what I need right now is not to overthink this—whatever *this* is. Maybe if I'm happy for just a moment, if I can just take this snapshot of happiness and try to freeze it, I can figure out the rest of my life. I know that happiness doesn't stick around long, but what's wrong with trying to stretch it out just a bit?

"Enough—I don't want to hear you talking like this," she says, and gets up from the desk strewn with photos.

"Talking like what?" I ask. "The way I always talk?"

"Hannah, I don't know how to tell you this," my grandmother says. She stops at the door, and leans her body against the doorjamb, as if holding the weight of the house on her shoulders.

"Tell me what?" I ask.

She covers her face with her hands and takes a deep breath. I put my hand to her shoulder and her hands fall to her sides. She grabs both of my hands in hers and squeezes them.

"Hannah, your mother is sick."

Twenty-seven

When I was ten years old, I caught pneumonia on a trip to London. I don't remember many details about the trip, other than the fact that I was sick. I couldn't tell you what we were doing in London, for one thing, and I don't remember what hotel we stayed at, or what time of year it was, even. What I do remember is this: my mother being by my side, taking care of me.

I was put on a strict course of antibiotics and told to stay in bed and drink lots of liquids. It being London, my mother had room service bring up a huge assortment of teas that we spent most of my recovery time sampling. We stayed in bed all day together, watching television and talking. And laughing. There was a lot of laughing.

She would put strawberry jam on my toast for me, and force me to drink three cans of ginger ale each day. I would act put-upon and pretend that I didn't want to drink the ginger ale, but the truth was, I loved the attention.

Attention from my mother wasn't exactly something that was lacking in my life, but this sort of attention, what I imagined the care of a real mother was like . . . that was something I ached for. I pretended that the hotel room was my bedroom in our very big house, and my mother stayed with me in my room while I was sick so I didn't have to be alone. I told myself that she prepared with her own two hands everything that room service brought up, that she even boiled the water for the tea herself. And of course, I imagined that she didn't work. That our every day was like this. That she wasn't just home with me because I was sick; she was home with me because that was what she did *every* day.

Ten days later, when the hotel doctor came up to our room to examine me, he told me that my lungs had cleared. I was crushed. My mother went back to working the very next day, and I went back to resenting her. We flew back to New York soon after, and I spent the rest of the semester hoping, praying that I would get whatever virus was going around.

I would leave the house with a wet head on cold days, cozy up to kids who were coughing. I even took extra science labs, certain that whatever was in those petri dishes would give me something. Anything. But I didn't get sick again.

"What do you mean sick?" I say.

"Why don't we sit down and talk for a bit?" my grandmother says, trying to motion me over to a chair.

"I don't want to sit down," I say. "I want to know what you are talking about. Gray Goodman doesn't get sick," I say, parroting back one of my mother's famous lines.

"I'm so sorry, Hannah," she says.

"Sick how?" I say. "What does that mean?"

"Well, it means—"

"Really sick?"

"I'm afraid so," she says.

"What is it?" I say, my voice getting smaller and smaller with each question I ask.

"It's cancer," my grandmother says. "I'm so sorry."

"Well, cancer can be curable," I say. "Which kind does she have?" I know that Priya's mother had ovarian cancer and after a very long year filled with treatment and hospital stays, made a full recovery. I now find myself in the strange position of rooting for ovarian cancer.

"Pancreatic."

"Is that one of the better ones?"

"It's not good," my grandmother says.

"I know cancer's not good, but is it curable?"

"There is no cure," she says. "At most, they'll try to keep her comfortable for the next few months, but it will continue to grow."

"Then why's she coming out here?" I ask. "Shouldn't we all go into the city to get her the best treatment we can?"

"Your mother is declining treatment," my grandmother says, her head nodding downward just the tiniest bit. "She doesn't want to spend her last few months on earth getting painful treatments if they won't cure her. She'd rather just live out the rest of her life in peace. With us."

"She's declining treatment?" I ask. "Who declines treatment?"

We both answer at the same time: "Gray Goodman."

"Sweetheart," my grandmother says, "you have to understand. Cancer treatment is just miserable. I went through it with my sixth husband. It is extremely unpleasant and if your prognosis is either six months of misery as you go through treatment or two months if you just live your life, some people would choose to just live their days out more peacefully. Without the needles and doctors."

"She only has two months to live?" I ask. My voice is barely a whisper.

"Darling," she says, pulling me toward her for a hug. "I'm so sorry. It's about two months, if she's lucky."

"Two months?" I say, and burst into tears. We may not get along, but she is still, after everything, my mother.

But the emotion I feel most is guilt. Guilt that I was never close to my mother. Guilt that I hadn't spoken to her in months before she last came out here. Guilt that she's dying alone.

"It's going to be okay," my grandmother murmurs into my ear, as she holds me tight in a hug. "It's going to be all right."

My mind goes to what my grandmother said about all of her husbands. About husband number six dying in the "best possible way to die," as if there were a "best possible way." You get to make peace with everyone you care about, you get to say good-bye.

That's why she's coming out here; that's what she plans to do. And if that is what she wants, then I'm on board. Happiness will have to wait.

Twenty-eight

"Do you have a minute to talk?"

"I always have time to talk to you, Hannah," Nate says. It feels so good to hear his voice. I take a deep breath and my shoulders begin to relax. After three hours, my grandmother and I are pretty much talked out about the whole thing, but it seems I still have more to say.

"Were you in court or something?" I ask, realizing that I'm about to embark on a conversation that may not be appropriate for the telephone. "I'm sure you're busy. It's only Tuesday."

"It's okay," he says. "I'm not too busy."

"You know what? This can wait until next weekend," I say. I tell myself that I don't want to occupy his mind with my problems if he's about to go argue a big case. But maybe I just don't want to taint what we have going so far with reality. "Let's wait until you're out here and I'll talk to you then."

"No, you should tell me now. You seem upset. Let me just close my office door for a second."

"My mother is sick," I blurt out, but the second I say it, I realize that he probably didn't hear me, since I can hear the office door slam shut, and then Nate shuffling back to his desk.

"Hannah, I'm so sorry," he says. "I didn't hear that. Did you say that your grandmother is sick?"

"My grandmother?" I ask, and can't help but laugh. "No, she's like a cockroach. She's going to outlive us all. My mother, on the other hand, is a mere human."

"Your mother?" he asks, and I can hear something in his voice. I don't know what it is. In that split second, I realize we're at that point in the relationship—the one where you know you're crazy about the other person, but that's all you really know. You can't stop thinking about him, but things come up that make you realize you really don't know much about him just yet. You still don't know what his favorite flavor ice cream is. Or if he prefers to rent a movie or go out. What his favorite book is. Or if he's ever lost someone he really loved.

What do I really know about Nate?

I know that he works for the DA, that he lives on the Upper West Side, eight blocks from the brownstone where he grew up, that he keeps in touch with almost all of his friends from college, but none of his friends from law school. I know that he loves the beach, hates the snow, and doesn't like to drink beer. I still don't know how he chipped that tooth.

"She has pancreatic cancer," I say. The words hang in front of me. I can't believe I've said them out loud. Once you say it out loud, it's true.

"My god, Hannah. I'm so sorry. What can I do?"

"Nothing," I say. "There's nothing anyone can do, actually. They can treat it, but it would mean living the last few months of her life in a doctor's office, going through painful treatments, and my mother doesn't want to live out the last days of her life like that. That's what my grandmother told me."

"I'm so sorry," Nate says. "There has to be something I can do. Has she gotten a second opinion yet?"

"She's already gotten four, actually," I say. "My mother isn't big on listening to authority."

Nate laughs. "I'm coming out there right now. Stay put."

"No," I say. "You don't have to come out here. I'll see you on Friday."

"Friday?" he says. "I can't wait until Friday to see you."

"I'm fine now," I say. "I think I'm still processing the shock of it. But I have a feeling I'll need you by Friday. I'll need you a lot."

I call Priya next. It's easier to get the words out now that I've said them already. She offers to cancel her weekend plans to come and see me—she was planning to go to Fire Island with Detective Moretti, who she began dating the day after my interrogation—but I insist she keep her plans and just promise to call me every day.

After hanging up the phone, I don't really know what to do with myself. What do you do on the day you find out your mother is suffering from a terminal illness? I think about what my grandmother would do in the face of such morbid news. That one's easy: she'd go shopping for pearls. I look out the kitchen window and see that I'm not that far off. She's out by the pool, on a chaise longue, talking on the phone.

I cannot sit on a chaise longue and talk on the phone the day I find out my mother has cancer.

I sit down on a kitchen stool and take a deep breath. All at once, the room seems small and I have the overwhelming desire to run. I take another deep breath and put my hands onto the bottom of the stool. *You are not like your mother*, I remind myself. *You are not the type of person who runs away.*

But all I can think about is getting out of this house. The

walls are practically closing in on me. I have no idea where I'd go. It would be silly to go back into the city when my mother is coming out here to spend her last weeks with us, but I have to do something. I have to go somewhere. I settle on a drive into town to go to the bookstore. Reading up on my mother's condition will make me feel more in control.

I walk out to the driveway and see Hunter walking up. What am I going to say to him? He just lost his own mother and now I have to tell him about mine. I don't want to bring back painful memories he's trying to get over. I just want to grab him and hug him tight—tell him that everything is okay, and then will it to be so.

"Hunter," I say, and reach out to touch his arm without realizing it.

"Hannah, we need to talk," he says. He motions to the front porch, and we sit down on the swinging bench. I kick my feet and the bench begins to swing, but Hunter puts his feet down on the ground and stops it from swinging, saying: "This is serious."

"It's a serious kind of day," I say, looking at Hunter.

"I don't know how to tell you this," Hunter says, "but I've met someone."

"That's wonderful!"

"No," he says, furrowing his brow. "I mean there's someone else. Another woman. I can't see you anymore."

"Another woman?" I ask. "Please don't tell me you've found another thirty-four-year-old."

"You're thirty-four?" he asks.

"Don't look so surprised," I say. "Why don't you tell me about her?"

"Oh," he says. "Is that okay to talk to you about her?"

"Of course, honey," I say. "I'm so happy that you're happy."

"Okay," he says, still unsure of my motives. "Well, you actually met her."

"It's one of the girls from the beach?"

"Yeah," he says, looking down at his feet.

"That's so great," I say. "Those girls seemed really sweet. Is she staying out here all summer, too?"

"Yeah," he says. "So, I guess I won't see that much of you now."

"Don't be silly," I say. "You two are welcome over here to swim, or have lunch, or hang out whenever you want. And I expect to be invited to the next bonfire."

"But won't that be weird?" he asks. He clears his throat. "You know, given our history?"

"I think it'll be okay," I say. "I actually went out with Nate on Saturday night."

"Nate Sugarman?" Hunter asks. "I didn't think he was your type."

"I didn't either," I say. I'm smiling despite myself.

"Well, then, that's great," Hunter says, and then gets up to leave. "Maybe the four of us can get together for a double date or something."

"We'd love that," I say. I really have no idea what Nate would think of a double date with a couple of fourteen-year-olds, but I get the sense that he finds Hunter just as charming as I do.

"Oh, and Hunter," I say, as he begins walking down the driveway. He stops and turns around. "*We'll* drive."

I never make it to the bookstore. In fact, I don't make it off the bench. I kick my foot and start to swing. All I can think about is Hunter and his mom. What she was like, what their relationship was like. How she died. How a fourteen-year-old kid can deal with losing his mother. How a mother can handle the knowledge she's leaving a child behind.

Then my thoughts float to Nate. What will he think of my relationship with my mother? What will he do if I fall apart? Why did I insist that he not come out here until Friday? But I don't have to think about that last one for very long.

Three hours later, Nate's Jeep is pulling into my driveway.

Twenty-nine

The Hamptons are quiet during the week. No crowds. No week-end refugees. No reservations. Best of all, no traffic. Nate has in-sisted that we take advantage of this, so today—the day before my mother comes out to spend the rest of the summer in the Hamptons with us—we're taking a leisurely drive out to the tip of Long Island. Out to Montauk. He tells me that the drive will clear my mind and prepare me for my mother's arrival.

It's one of those perfect summer days, the kind of day when the sun is out, but it's not too hot. A breeze is coming off the ocean, and there's hardly any humidity in the air. Nate is wearing a T-shirt with a pair of khaki cargo shorts. He's even got on a baseball cap. I love that he's forgone the usual Hamptons summer uniform of collared polo shirt and pressed khakis. I, myself, am wearing one of my Vivienne-approved outfits, a white halter sun-dress with flats. Nate comes to the door and rings the bell, ever the gentleman. My grandmother loves the fact that he doesn't stay in his car and merely honk his horn at me. I have to admit, I like it, too.

He grabs me around the waist and kisses me. I wasn't expect-ing it, so I lose my breath for a moment. I give in to the kiss and he tangles his hands in my hair. It sends chills down my spine. Every time he presses his lips to mine, I feel like I'm in junior high, being kissed for the first time. He looks at me, and brushes his hand across my right shoulder.

"Ready to go?" he asks. I look outside and see that he's taken the windows and doors off his Jeep.

"I'm just going to let my grandmother know that we'll be out for the day," I say, and Nate nods. He grabs my tote bag and brings it out to the car.

I walk through the kitchen and then outside to find my grandmother. From the patio, I have a clear view of the pool, but she's not on her usual lounge chair. I hear voices near the pool, so I head in that direction.

"After all these years, Viv," I overhear Rhett saying to my grandmother. "You have a lot of nerve."

"But you're here now, Adanet," she pleads, in a voice I've never heard before. "Isn't that what's important? Right now?"

I try to walk over to them quickly, so I don't overhear any more of their private conversation, but I can't find them. Seconds later, I see them emerging from the outdoor shower. I retreat immediately—the sight of Rhett and my grandmother walking out of the shower together is really too much for me to bear—but my grandmother sees me first.

"Hannah?" she calls out to me. Reluctantly, I turn to face her. Thank goodness, she's already wrapped herself up in a bath-robe. Rhett is tailing behind her, a towel around his waist.

"Hey," I say, "just wanted to let you know that Nate and I will be spending the day together."

"Okay, darling," my grandmother says. "Have fun." She's smiling, but I can tell she's upset.

"Unless you'd rather I stay here," I say under my breath, walking back toward her. My grandmother keeps the smile on her face and assures me that everything is fine and that I should go. I ask her if there's anything I can help her with before my mother comes out to stay with us, but she laughs and reminds me that everything's completely under control. Silly me. When you have an in-house staff of five, things generally are under control.

"What you can help me with is enjoying your date with your beau," she says. "That is what I would like you to do today."

I practically skip back to Nate's car. He's already got it running, radio blasting, but he still jumps out of the driver's seat to help me in.

"I would open the door for you, but . . ." he says, motioning to the space where the door should be, and we both laugh. I love that he refuses to drive out of the driveway until I'm snug in my seat belt.

The drive out east to Montauk is beautiful and it's easy to enjoy the drive. The only way to describe it is "peaceful." The air is fresher, warmer, and as I take it in, I feel my breaths getting deeper, slower. Each time the road twists or turns there's something new to see. A windmill, a tiny lake, even a family of deer. After about twenty minutes, we drive through the town of East Hampton. It's much larger than the town of Southampton, but otherwise very similar. Many of the same stores are here, but each shop is a bit bigger. Everything in East Hampton is bigger. In South, we have hedge-fund millionaires and trust-fund babies. In East, they have movie stars.

"That place looks good," I say, pointing out a restaurant filled with diners at outside tables. "Should we stop there?"

"I've got something even better planned," Nate says, smiling to himself. I can't help but smile back.

We drive a bit further east on Route 27 and then pull off the road when we get to Amagansett. It looks like we're pulling off into a dusty parking lot, but as Nate parks the Jeep, I see that we're at a roadside oyster bar. Yet again, he's shown me a side of the Hamptons I wouldn't have expected. Yet again, I'm pleasantly surprised.

We order way too much—a veritable feast of fried foods. The sun begins to burn my shoulders and I wish I could freeze time. Just take a photograph of this very moment and save it for all of eternity. Be able to look back on it fondly, like my grandmother does with her photographs, and remember how blissfully happy I was on this day. I feel Nate's eyes on me, and I turn to find him smiling at me. I wonder what he's thinking.

"I just want to memorize this moment," I say.

"Well, yes," he says. "These clams are pretty perfect."

"You know what I mean," I say, laughing.

"There will be lots more times like this to look forward to," he says matter-of-factly. "And lots more clams, of course," he adds, popping one into his mouth.

"What if there's not?" I ask, and I'm surprised at myself for saying the precise thing I feel. "What if happiness doesn't last?"

"I'm not going anywhere," Nate says, and gently takes my hand.

"Everything's going to be so different tomorrow," I say, looking off at the street. I can see the ocean over the houses on the other side of the street.

"But we can still be happy," he says. "Maybe this time will be good for you and your mother. Maybe you'll find something deeper than what you had. Everything happens for a reason."

I don't think everything happens for a reason, but I don't tell Nate that. Is there a reason my mother lost her father when she was only twelve years old? Why I'm a widow? What's the reason why Hunter lost his mom, I want to ask.

Instead I say: "You're right."

It's still quite a drive to Montauk, but I can see why Nate said that it would be worth it. It's breathtakingly beautiful, but there's more to it than that. The beach out here seems slightly more natural, more untouched than the beaches further west. I lie down on the blanket we've set out and Nate sits beside me. He takes my hand and kisses it gently.

I think about what he said earlier—that we can be happy. Even with everything going on in my life right now, Nate thinks we can be happy together.

My mother is dying. My strong-willed, passionate, impossible-to-talk-to mother is dying. And now I no longer have the luxury of being mad at her for things she cannot change. I can either try to talk to her, carve out some kind of relationship, or regret it for the rest of my life. But the time is now. Find a way to be happy now. Deal with the issues I've got with my mother now. I vow to make the time I spend with my mother count.

And what has she done that's really so bad, anyway? She didn't give me a conventional life. But lots of mothers give their kids more conventional ones, and they're still screwed up. She's difficult to get along with, impossible really. But I can be difficult, too. She is artistic, and she resents me for not being more like her. But I resent her for not being more like me. Nate turns to me and smiles and I tell myself that yes, we can be happy.

"Go for a swim?" he asks, and I nod my head yes. As he takes off his shirt and I start to take off my dress, I think about the last time we went for a swim together, and I blush. He wraps a towel around his waist and then takes his shorts off and puts a bathing suit on like a kid would do at the beach. I can't help but find it adorable.

He grabs my hand and we run toward the water and jump

right in. It's colder than I expect, and I back away, releasing Nate's hand.

"You can't get away from me that easily," he says, and grabs me around the waist and picks me up. It's so unexpected that I let out a half-laugh half-scream, which only makes Nate forge deeper into the water.

"Okay, I give up! Put me down!"

"Never," Nate says, and pulls me tighter. He goes further into the water, and the waves crash against us.

"I surrender," I say.

"Me too."

Nate sets me down gently and we descend into the water. He gets closer to me and I put my arms around his neck. He puts his lips to mine. He tastes salty sweet. We're tangled in each other, and the outside world is a blur. So much so that we don't even realize when a huge wave is coming. We're kissing and kissing as it knocks us both over and we go under the water. We both pop back up at the same time and begin laughing hysterically. Nate's hair is going in fourteen different directions, and mine has released itself from the baseball cap and is all over my face.

The baseball cap is soaked and it begins leaking water from its bill. I take if off, ring it out, then put it right back on my head.

I'm about to suggest we head back to our beach blanket when Nate says, "Let's jump over the waves." And that's how we spend the remainder of the afternoon. Holding hands like little children, jumping over the waves, not thinking about tomorrow.

Thirty

Even though I'm thirty-four years old, I still feel odd about waking up in my grandmother's house with a boy in my bed. Even if that boy is a thirty-four-year-old man. But my grandmother doesn't seem to mind. After all, she's got a man at the breakfast table the following morning, too. I imagine she won't lecture me about putting all of my eggs into one basket as Rhett and Nate talk golf, politics, and wine. I'm surprised to learn that Nate has such a strong opinion about the wines coming out of Australia. Rhett, of course, refuses to drink anything that does not come out of France.

After breakfast, Nate still refuses to leave. He's there when my mother arrives, entourage in tow. Which, I now realize, was his plan all along. To be there for me. To make sure I'm okay. To be my rock, should I need it.

My mother looks thinner than the last time I saw her, but I've only noticed it because I'm looking for it. I want to tell myself she's not that sick, that she will recover. I'm looking for signs, grasping at straws.

The hospice worker was here yesterday when I was out with Nate and set up a bunch of rooms on the opposite end of the house from where my grandmother's room is. I've decided to move my things back into the main house from the guest house, and my room is somewhere in the middle, just down the hall from my mother, a little closer to my grandmother's.

"Who are you?" my mother asks Nate.

"Mom, this is Nate Sugarman," I say.

"Nice to meet you," Nate says, and my mother nods, sizing him up. In lieu of small talk, she simply stares at Nate, taking in every inch of him. It's times like these when I pray that my mother won't act like she usually does, and just follow societal norms. But she doesn't. She would never tell someone "nice to meet you" unless she really did find it nice to meet that other person. Clearly, she does not find it nice to meet Nate.

"I'm Gray's assistant," a young girl says to me. "You must be Hannah."

I shake her hand and introduce her to Nate. She won't be staying with us, but she's here today to get my mother all set up in her rooms. Nate offers to help her move some of my mother's equipment to the basement—one of the rooms down there has been converted to a dark room—and my grandmother supervises the movers as they cart my mother's things in, box by box.

"Tea?" my mother asks, and I nod my head yes and follow her into the kitchen. "I brought this tea back from China last time I was there."

"Okay, great," I say, smiling. I am turning over a new leaf with my mother. I will get along with her if it kills me. "Let me get the kettle for you."

I walk to the stove to grab the kettle from her, but she blocks my path with her body.

"Oh no," she says. "You're not doing this."

"It's just tea," I say, laughing self-consciously.

"It's not just tea," she says. "You know, I told Vivienne that if I was going to come out here, you were not allowed to do this."

"Do what?" I say, and walk back to the island. I pull out a stool and sit down on it.

"Treat me like I'm dying," she says.

I have no response to this. I resist the temptation of explaining to her that my behavior is justified. She *is* dying.

"Let's just talk the way we normally talk," she says, lighting the stove and walking over to me at the counter. "For all these years, we've agreed to disagree. Let's not walk on eggshells now. Don't talk down to me. Don't act any differently."

"Well," I say, "I'm doing this thing where I try to make the most of my time with you."

My mother laughs heartily. "That doesn't mean that you can't be yourself. So what if I'm dying? Everyone dies, eventually."

I have no idea how she can be so cavalier. Unless she's still processing the shock of her diagnosis. Or maybe it's because, after a lifetime of covering people dying in wars, you come to accept that everyone dies eventually, and that your time will come, too.

"So how about this?" she asks me. "We just act the way we normally do—no special efforts, nothing different from the usual. And then you can tell your future kids stories about how we spent this summer together even though I was such an awful mother."

"I don't really think you were an awful mother," I say under my breath. I can tell that she's heard me by the sly smile playing on her lips.

The kettle begins to whistle. My mother is about to remove it from the burner just as Nate comes back upstairs from the basement.

"Let me help you with that," he says, and slides in next to my mother. Before she has a chance to object, before she even knows what's going on, he puts the kettle onto a trivet and smiles at my mother.

"So, you're Nate Sugarman," she says, hand on one hip.

"It's so nice to meet you, too," Nate says, and tries to hug her. My mother doesn't respond to his hug, so Nate eventually releases his grip and just stands there smiling. My mother regards him.

Finally, after what seems like hours, she says: "I can't wait to get my claws into you."

Thirty-one

"That's how you know he's a keeper," I tell Priya, but she's distracted.

"Who's a keeper?"

"Detective Moretti," I say. "Because he insisted you cancel your plans and instead come out to see me this weekend."

We're walking through town with ice-cream cones from the Fudge Company. Priya's is dripping down her arm and she doesn't seem to notice.

"Oh, Vince," she says.

"I can't call him that," I say, and hand Priya a napkin.

"Should we go into this store?" she asks, pointing to the window of a boutique. "It looks cute."

"You can't go into any of the stores here with ice cream," I say. She's trying so hard to distract me that it's almost difficult to have a conversation.

"We can talk about it, you know," I say. "You don't have to try to keep my mind occupied."

"I'm sorry, honey," she says. Tears are streaming down her face. "I'm just so sorry."

"I know," I say, and motion to a nearby bench so we can sit down.

"I don't know what to say," she says. "I certainly don't want to compare it to what I went through with my mother because—"

"I know," I say, and we are both silent for a minute. I know that we're thinking the same thing: this is different from when Priya's mom got sick because her mom got better and mine is going to die.

"Okay," Priya says, breaking the silence. "Here's the deal. I love you, so I don't want to say the wrong thing and upset you even more."

"Thanks," I say. "I appreciate that."

"I'm not trying to be weird. I'm trying to be awesome, but no awesomeness is coming."

"You are awesome, I assure you."

"I miss you," she says.

"I miss you, too," I say.

"So, is there something I could say to make you feel better?" she asks. "Since the whole distracting-you thing isn't working out?"

"No," I say. "Just having you here is making me feel better. I'm glad you didn't listen to me."

"I'm really glad, too," she says. We both smile.

We sit on the bench for a while. I'm not sure how long, since I don't have a watch on. But it's long enough for our ice cream to melt completely, long enough for the shops to close for the day, long enough for me to feel just the tiniest bit better.

Thirty-two

"So, how are you holding up?" my grandmother asks the following morning.

"I'm fine, thanks," I say, and my grandmother lets me off the hook. I'm not fine, not at all, but I have the feeling that this situation is only going to get harder as we go along, so I think it's important to try to be fine now.

"Well, that's good," she says, a pained smile on her lips. "I'm fine, too."

We're alone at the breakfast table, just the two of us, but it seems different from all the other mornings. Before, we were alone and it was just us. Now, we're alone, and it's not just us. We have a full house with my mother, her nurses, and our respective boyfriends. We're alone, but not alone. I can practically feel the other people through the walls.

"It's going to be another beautiful day," she says.

"Great," I say, stirring some milk into my coffee. "Do you think Gray would be up for a walk on the beach today?"

"I think the sun might be a little too much for her."

"Well, we do have those floppy hats," I say, smiling as I take a sip of my coffee.

"Indeed we do," my grandmother says, eating a piece of fruit.

"So, then, let's do it. When everyone comes downstairs, I'll announce that today we take a walk after breakfast."

"Maybe it should just be the three of us," I say.

"What a lovely idea."

We smile at each other, but it's like two different people have taken over our bodies and are speaking for us. The conversation is stilted. The air around us feels heavy.

We sit like that for a while, smiling at each other, eating fruit, and drinking coffee. I'm mindful not to touch my hair at the table, and my grandmother plays the role of old-fashioned grandma, asking me how I slept and how my breakfast is. I half expect her to start baking oatmeal cookies from scratch.

After what seems like an eternity, I say to my grandmother: "I'm scared."

She barely waits for me to get the words out of my mouth before she says: "I'm scared, too."

Later that afternoon, Nate is finally ready to leave me alone. For the first time since Tuesday, he leaves my grandmother's house, off to play a round of golf with his parents, who have just come out for the weekend.

Before I have a moment to enjoy any time to myself, my mother insists that I go see a doctor for a full workup, since apparently pancreatic cancer runs in families. I'm able to get an early appointment, and so I'm back before eleven.

As I walk into the house, I think about what I should do with my time alone—take a swim, go for a walk on the beach, read a paperback by the pool—but Hunter's got other things in mind. When I get inside, he's sitting in the living room with my mother.

"Your mother is going to teach me to shoot," Hunter announces.

"How lovely," I say, sitting down next to him. I have a strange urge to pull him and hold him close to me. To protect him from my mother. But he seems perfectly all right. Happy, even, to be in her presence.

"How did it go with the doctor?" my mother asks.

"Fine," I say. "He thinks that everything is just fine."

"And the nausea you've had?" she asks.

"That was just bad chicken salad," I say. And then, turning to Hunter, "So, you want to be a photographer?"

"Maybe I should go to the doctor, too," Hunter says. "Good idea, Hannah."

"It was my idea," my mother says. "It's always a good idea to go to the doctor to get checked out."

I resist the temptation to point out that my mother never went to the doctor before she got sick, that maybe if she had, she wouldn't be so sick right now.

"Why would you need to go to the doctor?" I ask Hunter.

"You know," he says, sitting up a bit straighter on the couch. "I'm in a new relationship now. I should get checked out for SDTs and stuff."

"STDs, you mean," I say. Surely the fact that he doesn't know his SDTs from his STDs is a sign that he's too young to be checked out for them, altogether.

"Before Skylar and I do the deed," he whispers conspiratorially.

"Oh, my god," I cry out. "Don't you dare do the deed. Any deed that you may be referring to. Just don't do it."

My mother catches my eye. I can practically see the wheels turning in her head. I look back at her, challenging her, and just wait for her condemnation. Don't tell him what to do. Let him find his own way, Hannah.

"Relax, Hannah," Hunter says. "Isn't that why you went?"

My mother lets out a huge belly laugh.

"No," I say through gritted teeth. "That is not why I went."

"Well," he says matter-of-factly, "Sugar has been around the block once or twice, if you know what I mean, so maybe he should get checked out, too."

My mother laughs even harder. I shoot her the evil eye, but she cannot stop laughing. Tears form at the sides of her eyes as she continues laughing out loud, and she bends over and holds her stomach. It devolves into a cough, so she runs off to the kitchen to get a mug of tea. I want to help her in the kitchen, get the tea for her, but I know that she won't let me.

"Anyway," I say to Hunter, "I'm thirty-four. You're fourteen."

"You don't understand," he says. "Skylar and I have known each other our whole lives. We had this whole thing going on in elementary school and in sixth grade, she was the first girl I kissed. Ever, I mean, not just the first one I kissed in the sixth grade."

"Okay, just the fact that you can remember what happened in elementary school shows that you are not ready to have sex," I explain. "You're too young."

"I know, I know. I've heard this speech before. You were going to say: but, if we're going to do it," he says, "we should at least be responsible, right?"

"That is not what I was going to say. I was going to say: just don't do it. You're too young."

"How old were you the first time you had sex?"

"That has nothing to do with anything," I say. "And, more to the point, it's none of your business."

"Then why shouldn't we have sex?" he says. He's pouting like a little kid and I want to put a mirror to his little fourteen-year-old face and show it to him, since that's the crux of my argument.

Instead, I say: "If Skylar gets pregnant right now, it will ruin your life."

"She's not going to get pregnant," he says.

"That's what everyone says!" I say. "And look at how many people get pregnant!"

"Well, we're in love," he says, and folds his arms across his chest.

"You're fourteen."

"You can still be in love even if you're fourteen," he says, turning to look at me.

"Yes," I explain. "But that's puppy love. You have no idea what real love is."

And it dawns on me that maybe he does know what love is. Who knows what love is, after all? He's suffered a profound loss at such a young age, does that intensify your feelings? Does that make you feel more? Less? Or maybe he just wants to have sex so he can feel close to someone again.

"Skylar knew my mom," he says. Without thinking, I grab him into a huge hug and hold him tight. I feel him take a deep breath and let it out. I kiss him on the top of his head and squeeze him tighter.

"Okay, that's enough," he says, pulling away. "Skylar's going to think I'm cheating on her."

"With her?" my mother says as she walks back into the living room, and laughs out loud again. She's careful not to spill her mug of tea.

I'm about to say something that I now realize is ridiculous—something about how it's perfectly reasonable for Skylar to think that Hunter might be cheating with me—when I'm interrupted by my grandmother.

"You three ready for lunch?" my grandmother asks.

"Yes, Mrs. Morganfelder," Hunter says, and jumps up and heads out to the patio. I excuse myself to go to the ladies' room.

In minutes, I'm outside and I see Rhett and my mother already at the table. From the look on her face, I can tell he's been trying to bend her ear, and already exhausted her patience for the day.

"We're surrounded by such beauty, aren't we, Monsieur Kensington?" Rhett says to Hunter as I make my way to the table.

"Yup," Hunter says, and pops a roll into his mouth.

My grandmother looks at Hunter and smiles.

"So, tell us more about your movie ideas," my mother says to Hunter. It's obvious how much she enjoys Hunter's company, and as I see him talking to my mother ("Actually, my lawyer has advised me not to talk about my films anymore. You know, for trademark and copyright reasons."), I can see why. He's the only one at the table who doesn't treat her like she's sick. While the rest of us fall over one another in an effort to get my mother everything she needs and make sure she's comfortable, Hunter just sits back and acts like today is any other day.

My mother announces that she's going to teach Hunter what she knows about photography, which will undoubtedly help him with his future film career.

"How lovely," my grandmother says.

"I can't wait," Hunter says, beaming.

"It's a shame Peg isn't here," my mother says, thinking out loud, "because we could really use an assistant."

"Oh, Hannah will do it," Hunter says.

"Then it's settled," my mother says.

It happens so fast that I don't have a moment to object, but when I have a second to think about it I realize that at least it will enable me to help my mother get her tea.

The whole thing makes me think of something that my mother's assistant said to me, just as she was leaving the house. She said: "You must feel so lucky to have such a brilliant mother." At the time, all I could think to say back was: "As a matter of fact, I do not," so instead, I just smiled at her and nodded my head.

My whole life, people have told me that I was lucky to be Gray Goodman's daughter. But I never saw it that way. To the outsider, it looks like a glamorous life filled with public accolades, world travel, and proximity to an accomplished public figure. But on the inside, you know the truth. You see what it takes to be a woman like Gray Goodman—the sacrifice, the way you have to live your life. The way your daughter has to live hers. I didn't feel lucky when I missed my eighth-grade graduation dance, the only one that a boy ever asked me to, because we had to travel to Indonesia for a story. I didn't feel lucky at the award ceremony when she won the Pulitzer, where I was mostly ignored for the evening. I didn't feel lucky when she missed the third-grade spelling bee where, after months of studying, I took first place. And I don't feel lucky now.

I wish I could see my mother through her assistant's eyes. Just see her for the brilliant photographer that she is, and not dwell on the mechanics of how much sacrifice it took for her to get the career she's got. How much I missed out on because of her life choices. I bet that her assistant would think that I was lucky to have so many stamps in my passport. That I was lucky just to be Gray Goodman's daughter.

"Hannah doesn't understand that at all," I overhear my

mother say, and it breaks my train of thought. I don't even think to ask what it is that I don't understand. I'm realizing that when it comes to the things that I don't understand, the list is as long as it is varied.

Thirty-three

Nate and I spend another blissful weekend together: Saturday lunch with his family, Saturday night barbecuing with Hunter and his new girlfriend at Hunter's father's house, a lazy Sunday with my grandmother and Rhett by the pool. By Monday, it's just my grandmother and me again.

I find myself back at my grandmother's trunk, intent on spending the day with her, organizing her photos, when my mother marches in. My grandmother smiles and nods her head toward my mom, my signal to go with her. To leave my grandmother and spend the day with my mother. She doesn't have to say a word; I know exactly what she's telling me.

I walk out of the room and my mother tells me it's time to begin the photography lessons. Only, she doesn't say it that way. She could never say something normal like "I want to teach you photography." Instead, Gray Goodman says: "I'd like to teach you to find beauty."

Hunter seems to have no problem finding beauty. As I walk downstairs, I find him on the couch in the living room, arms intertwined with Skylar's. I knew I liked her immediately when I met her at that bonfire on the beach. My feelings were confirmed this past Saturday night, when Nate and I spent the evening with her and Hunter. When we arrived at Hunter's house, she pulled me aside and said: "I hope that this is all okay for you. That this isn't weird or anything." She seemed so genuine, so concerned with hurting my feelings, that I couldn't help but be charmed. I told her that I would be all right, and she seemed relieved.

"Are you ready to learn photography?" I ask them.

"We're going to find beauty," Hunter parrots back to me.

"I'm sure we will," I say as my mother walks into the room.

"The best way to learn something is to just do it," she lectures. "So let's go outside and begin shooting. Then, we'll go back to the dark room, develop our film, and talk about composition."

"Doesn't everyone just use digital these days?" Hunter asks.

I hold my breath as I wait for Gray to jump all over Hunter for questioning her. But she doesn't.

"Yes," she says, smiling. I can see in her face that she's glad that Hunter is thinking, questioning her assumptions. "They do. In fact, I do, myself, quite often when I'm on assignment. It's the direction the world has moved in and you do need to keep up with the times. No one would hire me if I refused to use digital. But if I'm going to teach you about photography, I want to teach you every aspect of photography, so I think it's important to learn about film."

"Makes sense," Hunter says, and shrugs.

"So why do you have a dark room out here?" Skylar asks.

"Because when I'm shooting for myself, I like to use film. It's more real, it's grittier. It's not perfect like digital film, but those imperfections are what make it beautiful."

"I want to shoot something gritty," Skylar says, and it makes Hunter smile.

Hunter and Skylar jump from their seats. I see that my mother has loaned Hunter one of her cameras and I wonder why she's given it to him. Shouldn't she be giving me the things that are most valuable to her? After all, I'm the one who's going to inherit them. Realizing that nothing will cast a pall on the day like the fact that I'm already thinking about what she will leave to me when she dies, I bite my tongue. Instead, I pick up the bags that my mother motions for me to tend to. But then, I remember that she's instructed me not to walk on eggshells with her, so I reconsider.

"Why did you give that camera to Hunter?" I ask. She looks back at me, but doesn't say a word. So, I clarify: "Shouldn't you have given it to me?"

"Why would I give that camera to you?" she finally says. "You're just the assistant."

"Oh, right. Gee thanks," I say.

"Anyway, I always thought you were content just to have the pictures taken of you. I never knew you to want to take the pictures yourself."

I look over at Hunter and Skylar, and they are taking turns using the camera. Even with all of the natural beauty that surrounds us, Hunter only wants to shoot Skylar. It's adorable how he can't keep his eyes off her, both behind the lens and when she's the one holding the camera.

I look out to the beach and think about what I would shoot. If I wasn't the mere assistant today, that is. I see a couple on the beach, walking along the water, holding hands. It reminds me of Nate and I can't help but smile. Friday can't get here soon enough.

My train of thought is disturbed by Hunter—he's still shooting Skylar, only now he seems to be playing director. "You're a tiger!" he calls out. "You're a tiger!" Skylar turns her hands into claws and begins to purr. Gray walks over to them quietly, with a small smile on her face. She puts her hand on Hunter's and begins to make a few adjustments. "Tell a story with your pictures," she says. Hunter nods in response. He shoots a few shots, and then conferences with Skylar to discuss the story they will be telling with their photographs.

My mother walks back to me and begins shooting.

"Don't shoot me," I say, covering my face. She doesn't stop shooting. "My hair is a mess."

"No, it's not. You're losing your light. Look up."

"No," I say, careful to do the exact opposite of what my mother has just suggested, so that she can't get the shot.

"What made you say that?" my mother asks from behind the camera. She stops shooting for a moment, waiting for my response.

"Grandma told me that my hair was a mess this morning," I say.

Gray laughs and I can't help but laugh, too. Before I came out here, I really wouldn't have noticed whether or not my hair was a mess. As long as it was relatively clean, that was usually enough for me. As we continue to laugh, I realize that we are bonding at the expense of my grandmother, and it makes me feel slightly uncomfortable. Is it okay for us to be laughing at her expense? Would my grandmother encourage us to do so because it means that Gray and I are at least getting along? It makes me wonder, what do they say about me when I'm not around? Do they laugh at my expense?

"Okay, let's get a shot of you going this way." My mother gently takes my arm, and tries to position me.

"Why don't I shoot you instead?" I ask.

"What is wrong with you?"

"Nothing," I say. "Why does there have to be something wrong with me if I want to take your picture?"

"Well, I don't want you to take my picture," she says. "I want to take yours."

I reluctantly allow her to begin shooting again, but moments later, she takes the camera down from her face.

"I can't concentrate with all of the teenage angst you've got coming off you. You're worse than those two," she says, motioning over to Hunter and Skylar. "Out with it already."

"I want to shoot you," I say. She furrows her brow, and I can tell that she does not plan on losing this argument. I decide to go for broke, tell her how I really feel. "If you just shoot me all day, all I'll have left of you is a picture of myself."

"No," my mother says, walking over to me and putting her hand onto my cheek. "You'll have a picture of the way you look through my eyes."

Thirty-four

"How are things at the office?"

Priya rolls her eyes at me and shakes her head. I've worked at the firm long enough to know that this will always be her response. Things are the same as usual, which isn't great, but it's not horrible, and she'd rather not talk about it, especially on a day off. I shake my head back at her. The unspoken language of friends—you can have an entire conversation without saying much.

Priya insisted on driving out today to visit the Southampton Historical Museum. She tried to convince me that she simply had to see their exhibit of pottery made by local artisans, but I know she's just checking up on me.

"This is so Southampton," she says, pointing at a yellow bowl.

"So Southampton," I say, but the truth is, I'm just waiting for her to say what she's here to say.

"Your mom looks like she's hanging in there," Priya says, trying to be casual. She's trying to sandwich this observation into the conversation, as if it's not the whole reason she's out here to visit, and I love her for it.

"She's really tough," I say, and I smile, because I know it's true.

"She is," Priya says, looking up at me, "and so are you."

"I used to be tough," I say, "but I'm not sure if that's true anymore."

"This blue is so beautiful," she says, looking at a vase that's painted a faded-out denim blue color.

"It is," I say.

"I think you're still tough," she says, still looking at the vase. "You just don't always show it. You're still you, you know."

"I'm not sure about that."

"Remember when I met you?" Priya asks. "On that tax evasion case? The client saw the two of us and decided that we were way too young. And definitely too female. How did he put it?"

"He complimented our outfits and then asked us what year we graduated law school," I say, remembering the story and smiling.

"So, you thanked him for the compliment, and told him that we'd graduated nine months prior, but then took over the meeting and wowed him with your knowledge of the case."

"I remember," I say. "I was so nervous, but I just wanted him to give a good report back to the partners."

"And when we went out for lunch," she says, "he called the partners to sing your praises."

"Our praises."

"Yours," she said. "You were never afraid of anything, you were always so strong."

"That's not me anymore," I say. "It's like I'm just floating, since . . . well, you know."

"You're still you," she says. "That tough girl who could take on any client, no matter how sexist or ageist, is still there."

"Is she?"

"Yes," Priya says. "You can handle anything. You have handled anything. Give yourself a little credit."

"I just have no idea how I got here."

"We all lose our way from time to time," she says, running her fingers across an oval serving platter. "But you're on your way back. I know it."

"Thanks, Priya," I say. As I let the words sink in, I start to feel that they're true. Maybe I am tougher than I think. Maybe I can handle more than I give myself credit for.

We spend the rest of the day in town, shopping and stopping for lunch. We talk the whole time, but we don't really say anything important, anything meaningful. Priya's already said to me what she came here to say. She heads back to the city around three, and it gives me just enough time to get ready for tea with my mother at four.

As I walk into the house, the phone is ringing. I stop in the living room to answer it and practically walk into my mother, who was rushing to answer it. She waits with me as I answer the phone, just in case it's one of her doctors.

The conversation doesn't take very long.

"You're green," my mother says as I hang up the phone. "What is it? What wrong?"

I turn to face her, but no words come out of my mouth.

Panic lights up my mother's face. "What did the doctor say, Hannah? Do I need to go back to see them?"

"It wasn't your doctor," I manage to eek out. "It was mine."

"Your doctor?" she asks. "Is something wrong with you?"

"I'm pregnant."

Thirty-five

"How can you possibly be pregnant?" my mother asks. But the thing is, judging from how far along the doctor told me I am, I know exactly when it happened. Two months ago, when I was still with Jaime, I'd had walking pneumonia. I remember asking my doctor about whether being on a strong antibiotic would lessen the efficacy of the pill, as I'd heard it could, and him telling me yes, we should probably use a backup. But the thing is, when you're in a long-term relationship and you're used to forgoing the use of condoms, it's kind of hard to go back to them. Especially when you no longer keep any in your apartment.

I tell my mother all of this, and she looks back at me and asks the question I'm not yet ready to hear: "Are you ready to be a mom?"

"I am thirty-four years old," I say.

"What does age have to do with this?" she asks.

"I don't want to lose the chance to have a baby altogether," I say. "Maybe the time is now."

"But you still seem so lost," she says, and in her eyes I can see how much it hurts her to say this to me. I know in my heart of hearts that she wants what's best for me, and tries to help me in her own way, but she just never knows quite how. Which I suppose is the crux of what's wrong with our relationship.

"You and I both know you're just going to do what you think 'normal' is, and normal doesn't include having a baby before you're married—to a man who doesn't want you, much less a baby."

Her words are like a knife going into my heart. Before I can control it, I take a quick breath in and look down at the floor. It's moments like these when I realize why we were never close. Why we can never be close. She doesn't understand me in the way I need her to; she doesn't know that now, what I need most is compassion, not tough love. I need my grandmother.

"What if I want to have this baby?" I ask. The look she gives me is too much to bear. I march right out of the kitchen, through the backyard, and onto the beach. The sand feels hot under my feet. I head toward the ocean, to the point where the water hits the sand, and the sand is cooler from the waves washing over it. Firmer. I stride past Nate's house, and past all the other estates. I walk so far that I can no longer see any of the houses. There's just plain untouched beach, and no one around. My legs begin to ache, so I sit down on the sand and look out to the water. The sun is burning down on me, but I can't go any farther.

I'm pregnant. I keep thinking that it's a dream, that I will wake up and this whole day will have disappeared, but the knot in my stomach tells me that it's true.

How can I be pregnant? Jaime and I haven't spoken since the first week I was out here, and now I'm with Nate. Happy. But I knew that my happiness couldn't last. It's as if I'm being punished for actually thinking it out loud. For daring to think that happiness could stay.

Nate. What am I going to do about Nate? I can't have a relationship with one man while I'm having the baby of another. I can't have a fatherless child. I won't do to my own child what my mother did to me.

I try to think of a way to justify the fact that this child could be Nate's. But there's just no way that seven weeks can become two. I think about what a life with Nate would have been like. What kind of a husband he would have been. What kind of a father he would have been.

And Jaime. How can I tell Jaime? He barely wanted to commit to a relationship, much less bring a child into the world. I don't know what he will say. I don't know what he will do.

Hunter's face pops into my head and it makes me wonder if I would be a good mother. If I could be a good mother. Maybe my own mother is right. Maybe I am too lost to have a baby of my own.

By the time I finally get back to the house, it's hours later. The sun has already begun to set. My face and shoulders are completely sunburned, and as I walk into our backyard, I find my grandmother waiting for me on her favorite chair.

True, she's spent most of this summer on this very lounge chair, but I know she's waiting for me by the look on her face. Not to mention the fact that there's nary a phone, a drink, or book in sight. She's not out here to lounge; she's out here to wait. Her eyes are trained on the little walkway that connects the backyard to the beach, and I wonder how long she's been waiting here for me.

I **walk** over to her lounge chair and without a word, she stands up and gathers me into a hug. She holds me tight and kisses my head and tells me over and over how much she loves me. For some reason, even though she's giving me the kindness that I need, I cry hysterically. The tears just fall from my eyes and there's no way to control it. "It's okay," she tells me, over and over. "This is all going to be okay."

"How is this going to be okay?" I say, through my sobs. "How can this possibly be okay?"

"Because we've got each other and that's all we need," she says. We sit down next to each other on the lounge chair and she rubs my back.

"I'm sorry," I say. "With all that's going on right now, we really don't need this."

"Maybe it's exactly what we need."

Thirty-six

I'm alone in the tub for almost an hour before it dawns on me that I probably shouldn't be taking such a warm bath. The steam is making me feel faint and I get a fleeting image in my mind of my body cooking the baby from the inside out.

I walk into my bedroom and I'm grateful that my grandmother is the type of woman who believes that women should own a few different bathrobes. After my talk with my mother this morning, I'm desperate for warmth, for comfort, and a silk kimono simply won't do. I put on the fluffy white robe and matching slippers that my grandmother bought for me and lie down on my bed.

There's a gentle knock on the door and I can only assume that it's my mother, trying to make peace. I turn over in my bed so that when my mother comes in, she won't see me crying. Gray thinks that crying is a sign of weakness.

"Can I come in?" I hear through the door, only it's my grandmother, not my mother.

"Yes," I call out, but I stay curled on the bed, facing the wall. I don't have the energy to get up.

"How are you feeling?" she asks. "I brought you some decaffeinated tea and cinnamon toast."

I sit up and my grandmother places a tray on the bed. I want to ask her whether she made the cinnamon toast for me or if she had the chef do it, but then I think that maybe it's beside the point.

"I feel okay," I say, taking a bite of the toast. I don't have to ask—I can tell by the taste that she made it herself.

"What are you thinking?" she says. "Do you want to talk things over?"

"I'm a little confused right now," I say, taking a sip of tea. "I don't know what to do."

"Do you want to have a baby?" she asks. I can tell from the look in her eyes that she wants the answer to be yes.

"I really don't know right now."

"Is this about Nate?" she asks quietly.

"I don't know," I say. But then I decide to be honest: "Maybe."

"You can't make major life decisions based on a man you just met."

"I know," I say. "You think I should be dating more."

"This isn't about that," she says. "This is about the fact that the only person you need to worry about is you. What do you want? What's best for you? Make the decision for yourself. Not based on a flirtation you have going on with your next-door neighbor."

"It's more than a flirtation," I say, looking up from my tea.

"It's barely been two weeks."

"We've slept together."

"I know," my grandmother says, without hesitation. "You were in my house."

"I mean, it's more than just dating."

"Just because you've had sex with a man doesn't mean it's anything more than a flirtation. Don't make it more serious than it is. You need to make a decision for yourself, and only for yourself. No one else should be in the equation."

"Well, I want to be with Nate."

"So, then, that's your decision?" she asks, and I feel the muscles in my neck begin to tense. "Do you want to have a baby?" she asks slowly.

"It's not that easy," I say, and my grandmother cuts in before I can say more.

"Yes, it is," she says. "You either want to have a baby or you don't."

"No, it's not," I say. "It's not just whether or not I want to have a baby. This is Jaime's child, and I need to decide if I want to have a child with him. I haven't even spoken to him in weeks."

"Now we're talking about that musician again?" she asks. She won't even say Jaime's name.

"Things change," I say, and marvel at how quickly things do, in fact, change out here in the Hamptons. One day, my grandmother was alone, a widow for the sixth time, and overnight, she reconnected with her first love. In a flash, I discovered something with Nate Sugarman. Just as fast, my mother found out that she was dying.

"Am I understanding you correctly? This decision is all based on which man you want? You either decide to have the baby and get back together with the musician, or you decide to be with Nate and you don't have the baby?" my grandmother asks.

"No," I say. The more I speak with my grandmother, the more my thoughts get all jumbled up inside of my head. "I'm not saying that. But if I'm going to have a baby, the baby's going to have a father."

"Hannah, this decision is as easy as you let it be. All you need to figure out is what you want."

But that's the one thing I've never been able to figure out.

Thirty-seven

"I don't know if I can deal with this," Nate says, and I can't help but feel sorry for him. I want to tell him that I don't know if I can deal with this either, but I know that it is hard enough for him to hear what I have to tell him without me editorializing it.

I take the kettle off the burner—my mother now has me completely obsessed with her tea from China—and pour the water into two mugs. I sit back down at the counter with Nate and give him his tea.

"It was one thing," he says slowly, "when there was one man in your life. I could deal with Adam, but this is a different story."

"I know," I say, stirring the sugar into my tea. Nate hasn't touched his. "And I'm so sorry that I've brought you into this crazy screwed-up situation. You should've stayed away from me."

"I don't want to stay away from you," Nate says, and moves his bar stool a bit closer to me. He puts his hand on my left cheek and I close my eyes and put my own hand over his.

"I'm sorry," I say.

"You don't have to be sorry," he says. "Have you decided what you're going to do?"

"I think so," I say. "I know that I want a child. And you were the one who said the other night that 'everything happens for a reason.' So, maybe I'm supposed to have this baby. But, obviously, I need to talk to Jaime a little more about this, too."

Nate looks down and slides his bar stool back. Under his breath, he says, "This is a lot to deal with."

"That's the thing," I say. "I don't want to make you deal with this. I feel awful about this whole situation. I've been thinking about it, and I think that what would be best here is to take some time off."

"You want to take time off from us?" he asks.

I can't meet his gaze. "What if I never get another chance to have a baby? I'm a widow once over. What if I never get to try again?"

"What if you do?" he asks, and I can see in his eyes what he's saying to me. What if I had a chance to do this right? What if I had the chance to have a baby with him?

"I just think that maybe, for the sake of this baby, I should give it a try again with Jaime. When I told him about it, his first reaction was that we should get back together and I think that . . ."

Nate's face crumbles. Clearly, he had no idea that this was an option. But how could it not be? A child needs to have a father.

"I've got to go," he says, and jumps up from the kitchen counter.

"Wait," I say, grabbing for his arm. "Don't go like this. Hear me out."

But Nate wrestles from my grip and runs out the door.

I find myself running after him, begging him to wait, because there are so many things I never got the chance to tell him.

I didn't get to tell him that I don't want my child to have the same experience I did. I do not want to repeat the mistakes my mother made.

I want to say to him: "Nate, I never knew my own father. I never even met him. He was just my mother's friend, and when she decided that she wanted to have a baby, he agreed to help her, but only if he wouldn't have to actually be my father. She didn't want a husband, so she found someone who didn't want to be a dad and together they made me. But I want so much more for my child."

These are all the things I want to say to Nate. But when I get to the edge of our driveway I hear the front door of his house slam. Maybe it's better this way. Maybe this is how it was meant to end.

Thirty-eight

"When you know the person you're going to spend the rest of your life with, you want it to start immediately," he says, and my stomach turns for two reasons: (a) my rocker ex-boyfriend is quoting rather liberally from *When Harry Met Sally*, and (b) that he's quoting from *When Harry Met Sally* at all.

I met Jaime at a rock club where his band was the headliner. I don't know what I was even doing at a rock club. It certainly wasn't the sort of place I was used to frequenting, but a few of the summer associates at my firm were going, so I just sort of tagged along. It was a strange time in my life. A year and a half after Adam died. All I did all day was talk about my emotions, think about my emotions. I just wanted to go somewhere where it was too loud to talk, too loud to think.

When I saw him on stage, he was lost in the music, playing his heart out. He was so into his bass guitar—sweating, oozing sex from every pore. He caught my eye from the stage and made a beeline over to me the second the set was over. It felt like a movie: we literally saw each other across a crowded room. Priya once asked me what it was that I liked about Jaime so much, but it's hard to say. I was drawn to him. An animal thing, physical, visceral, and he felt it, too. That night, I went home with him, something I'd never done before. But after a year and a half of therapy, I'd had enough of talking. I just wanted to feel.

After that night, we began seeing each other all the time. Usually after his gigs, late at night. We didn't date in the traditional sense; I could count the number of times we went out to dinner together on one hand. More often it was grabbing a slice of pizza here, a falafel sandwich there. We've never gone to a movie together. Never went to a wedding or social event as a couple. But we were a couple. It was understood that we were monogamous, that we were together from the night we met.

We didn't have much in common, didn't have the same types of friends. He called most of my friends "Richie," even to their faces sometimes. He grew up in New York City, too, but in a rough part of Brooklyn that was a far cry from the Manhattan my schoolmates inhabited.

Even though at first he resented all the money I had in my life, eventually he began to enjoy the creature comforts of my apartment. A shower that never leaked, an espresso maker that worked properly, heat in the winter.

"So," I say, "you're coming out here?"

"I'm coming out there," Jaime confirms. I don't know if I'm happy or sad about this. True, I've made my decision, but there's something about getting exactly what you want. It tends to make you wonder whether or not you actually wanted it in the first place.

I think about my mother's warning—that a baby can't be the answer to your problems—and it's haunting me. Is that what I'm trying to do? Solve everything that's wrong with my life by having a child? That's not a reason to bring a kid into the world. But the one thing I've figured out over the last couple of days is that I completely and utterly, with every ounce of my being, want to have a baby. I want to have this baby. So I need to make this work with Jaime.

When I told my grandmother about my decision, I couldn't tell if she was happy about it.

"I thought you'd be happy that I'm considering more than one man at a time," I said to her.

"It seems to me that all you've actually done here is to substitute one beau for another," she replied. I wondered why that was such a bad thing. Isn't that what she'd done her entire life? You don't get to be a widow six times over if you don't substitute one man for another.

"Do you think I should have this baby?"

"Do you think you should have this baby?"

"Yes," I said quietly. "So, is it okay that I've invited Jaime to stay out here with us?"

"Whatever you want is okay with me," she said. "I just want for you to be happy. Are you happy?"

"Yes," I said, responding as quickly as I could. I didn't want my grandmother to know that my actual response was: I don't know. My eyes began to tear up and I took a deep breath to get them to subside.

"Oh, and Jaime," I say, just as we're about to hang up the phone, "there's just one condition."

"What's that?" he says, and I can tell from his tone that he's flirting with me.

"Your mother has to drop the charges," I say. "She's still having me investigated for attempted murder."

"Consider it done," he says. "And just so you know, I wasn't actually planning to break up with you."

Thirty-nine

The second I see him, my heart drops into my stomach. It's as if I've forgotten what he looked like in the few weeks since I've last seen him. But as I watch Jaime coming off the train and onto the platform at the Southampton station, I realize it's more than that. When you're in a long-term relationship with someone, you take them for granted. You forget what made you fall in love with them in the first place. You don't even notice what they look like anymore. I'd forgotten that Jaime's long hair and dark hooded eyes get a reaction from every woman he meets.

Jaime sees me, smiles, and waves, and I can't decide if I should get out of the car, or just let him hop inside. I've driven here today in one of the Mattress King's fleet. My grandmother wanted her driver to take me, but I decided that the shock of the estate alone is going to be enough for Jaime. I didn't need to freak him out with a driver, too.

I open my car door and get up, just as Jaime approaches. He throws down his duffel, grabs me, and kisses me hard. I lose my breath for a moment. I wasn't expecting him to kiss me. I thought we'd have an awkward embrace, and laugh about how we should greet each other, what would be appropriate, given the circumstances. But then I remember something else about Jaime: he doesn't do awkward.

"It's so good to see you," he murmurs, lips still all over mine.

"You, too," I say, and we kiss again. His kisses are so different from Nate's—Jaime's kiss is more animalistic, as if he's about to rip off my clothes and take me right here in the middle of the Southampton train station's parking lot. I break from his embrace and take a deep breath. Jaime walks around to the passenger side of the car and as I watch him walk, I wonder how you can feel something for two people at once.

We get back to the house, and my grandmother gives Jaime the grand tour. ("It is rude for a hostess to be out of the house when a guest arrives," my grandmother explained.) Walking around in his Rolling Stones concert tee and ripped jeans, he's in sharp contrast to the manicured grounds. My grandmother doesn't seem to notice, and it's the sort of thing that I wouldn't have noticed either before I came out here. I can't decide what annoys me more: that I've noticed this at all, or that it sort of bothers me.

After the tour, I show Jaime to my room—our room—and he looks around. I considered having him stay out in the guest house instead of moving into my room, but since I was already pregnant, I wasn't really fooling anyone with the Pollyanna routine. Least of all Jaime, who throws me onto the bed and jumps on top of me. In an instant, he's tearing off my clothes.

"Slow down," I murmur. "Slow down."

"Why?" he whispers, lips all over my neck.

"Don't you want to talk for a second?" I ask.

He laughs. "No."

We make love and it's hurried, rushed, and completely unsatisfying. I tell myself that it will be better once he's settled in, once we've gotten back to normal with each other. I pull the flat sheet up around my shoulders and tell myself to stop thinking about Nate. To stop comparing Jaime to him. Jaime looks at me, and I feel guilty that I'm thinking of another man while I'm in bed with him. Maybe Nate is right. Maybe I just don't do nice.

"Wanna play a quick round of tennis before dinner?" I ask Jaime. He's already back up, unpacking his duffel, naked, while I'm still lying in bed. "We could run over to Hunter's place for a quick game."

"Tennis?" he asks, laughing. "You know sports aren't really my thing. And anyway, I didn't get a chance to go uptown and grab your sneakers."

It was the only thing I'd asked him to do (unless, of course, you count calling off the attempted murder investigation, which I don't), and I'm slightly disappointed that he didn't make a point of doing it.

"No problem," I say, and try to smile. He regards me for a moment—clearly he can tell that it actually is a problem that he didn't do the one thing I'd asked, the one thing he'd agreed to do—but then opts to just let the moment pass and ignore it.

"So, what time did your grandmother say dinner was?"

"We eat at seven," I say, and look over at the clock. It's not even five o'clock yet.

"What should we do?" Jaime asks, with a look in his eye that suggests what he wants to do.

"Let's go have drinks," I say, and pop out of bed. I ignore the fact that Jaime was clearly suggesting sex again. I ignore the fact that I'm pregnant, and can't actually have a drink. I ignore the fact that I can't stop comparing Jaime to Nate. I ignore all of this, and instead get up and get dressed for drinks.

I try to suggest to Jaime that he wear a pair of jeans that isn't ripped, but it turns out that he's only brought the one pair. The one other pair of pants he packed are a pair of army green cargo pants, so I have him throw those on, along with a white button-down shirt that was lurking toward the bottom of his duffel. Judging from the wrinkles, it's not clear to me whether he packed the shirt for this trip, or if it was just left in the duffel from some other trip, and then never unpacked. But it doesn't matter. A wrinkled white button-down is still better than the rest of the options: unwashed concert tees.

We walk out to the patio, and it seems that cocktail hour has already started. My mother's substituted her usual cup of tea for a glass of sparkling rosé, and she's sitting with my grand-mother and Adan, who are munching on homemade guacamole and chips. My grandmother makes the introductions between Jaime and Adan while my mother refreshes her glass of wine.

Gray has always been a big fan of Jaime's. True, she's only met him a handful of times, but I know that she loves the fact that he is an artist. I think she secretly hopes that some of his talent will rub off on me. But I've never really been artistically inclined. The closest I've ever gotten to a creative endeavor is my recent organization of my grandmother's trunk of photographs.

"How's the music going?" my mother asks Jaime, once we've all settled into our chairs. Jaime's sitting next to my mother, looking out at the ocean, and I'm next to Adan, facing the house.

"Great," Jaime says. "Just great. In fact, we've booked a gig out here for Friday."

I'm about to ask Jaime what he's talking about when my grandmother's chef comes outside with a glass of decaffeinated iced tea for me, and the table gets into a heated conversation about whether or not I can still put Sweet'n Low in my tea, given my condition. The consensus is that Splenda might be accept-able, but that plain old sugar is probably best.

By the time the debate over artificial sweeteners is done, I've almost forgotten that Jaime's casually mentioned that he's booked a gig.

But my grandmother has not.

"So, what sort of gig is this?" my grandmother asks. The way she says "gig" with her slight French lilt is nothing short of hilarious. If I wasn't seething at the thought that Jaime already booked work for the third night he'll be out here, I probably would have laughed. My grandmother is smiling, but I see in her eyes that she, too, is disappointed that Jaime's head is not completely with me and the fact that we are having a baby together, that he's already moved on to thinking about other things.

"There's a rock club over in Quogue. Do you know it?" he asks my grandmother, smirking.

My grandmother smiles back sweetly in response. It is a smile that says: "I know that you are trying to make fun of me, but I will have the last laugh. I always do."

Jaime has never really gotten my grandmother. I thought that spending more time with her would make him fall in love with her, the way that everyone else does, but he is seemingly immune to her charms.

"Well," he continues. "It's on Friday night, ten o'clock. My guys are going to drive out for the night. We'll play the gig and then they'll head back to the city."

"Nonsense," my grandmother says. "We have a perfectly good guest house right here. Why don't you have them stay out with us for the weekend?"

"Wow," he says. "That's really generous. I don't know if I can accept." He looks at me, and I nod.

"Of course you can," I say, and take a sip of my iced tea. I know what my grandmother is doing here: she is giving me enough rope to hang myself.

"Thank you," he says. I'm not sure if Jaime's saying this to me or to my grandmother, but she answers, saying that it's nothing. Nothing at all.

Forty

The guest house already smells like boy. Dirty clothes are strewn everywhere, and music is blaring from the living room speakers. I don't know if they've found beer somewhere in the guest house or they brought beer with them, but open cans are everywhere. Quite a feat, considering they've been out here less than an hour. These guys move quickly.

"So, my grandmother's throwing a little cocktail party for you tomorrow night," I tell Jaime. "Your friends are more than welcome to stay the weekend and come."

My grandmother insisted on throwing a small Saturday-night cocktail party to celebrate Jaime's arrival. I didn't want her to do this, but I really couldn't say no. I can never say no to my grandmother.

There are no tents this time, but there is a caterer. And a party planner, who is flitting around the house nervously, trying, in just the seventy-two hours she's been given, to put together a cocktail party that will live up to my grandmother's exacting standards. I almost walked into her on my way out to the guest house, since I couldn't help but look up at Nate's room. I don't know exactly what I was expecting—for him to be up there, staring down?—but I couldn't stop myself from looking up every three seconds, like a nervous tick.

"Sounds great," Jaime says. "I'm sure the guys would love to stay for a party."

"Good," I say. "My grandmother's parties are always a lot of fun."

"Fun is good," he says, and leans in to kiss me. I kiss him back, and before I know it we are kissing, really kissing, and I remember what it's like to be with him. Not the way we've been together these last few days—stilted and unfamiliar—but the way we used to be. Jaime puts his arms around me and lets his right hand meander down my back. He pushes against my lower back and I fall into him. Pressed up against him, I take it all in— his lips, his smell, the way the stubble on his face always rubs against mine, leaving my skin raw.

"Whoa, man, sorry to interrupt," Johnny, the drummer, says, coming down the stairs. "I can come back if you want."

"No, it's cool," Jaime says, pecking me on the lips. Turning to me, he says: "Babe, give us some time to warm up a bit. I'll see you later." We kiss again and I spin on my heel and head toward the door. He pats me on my butt as I walk out and it makes me giggle.

I make my way across the pool area, on my way to the main house, and I just can't resist—I look up at Nate's window again. I expect that I'll see the same thing I've seen each of the other 432 times I've looked up there today, but this time it's different. This time, Nate's standing at his window, looking down at me, refusing to turn away.

Jaime's up on the stage, doing a sound check. When I see him onstage with his band, I get a rush of excitement. It's been so long since I've seen him perform. After a while, there are just so many gigs that you can't go to all of them, so I ended up going to none of them.

The bar is packed with summer-share kids, some of whom came here straight from the train station. You can tell by the bags they are carrying, the work clothes they are still wearing. I managed to get a spot at the bar for my mother and myself by pulling the I'm-pregnant-and-she's-got-cancer card, and we've actually got a pretty decent view of the stage.

My grandmother is nestled in at a tiny table for two in a corner of the club with Adan. She's wearing jeans and an old Beatles concert tee, paired with leopard stilettos with four-inch heels. I love that she's made such an effort to fit in here. She made a special shopping trip just to look, as she put it, "rocker chic." The jeans are from Georges Mandel (and yes, you pay extra for all of the carefully placed rips), and she picked up the concert tee from a boutique in town (pre-aged and studded with tiny little rhinestones). Normally, she wouldn't venture west of Southampton—Southamptonites never set foot in Westhampton or Quogue; they only ever drive west to get back to Manhattan.

When Adan saw her, he told her that she looked like a teenager. Even though that's not really how my grandmother dressed when she actually was a teenager, which he would know. And I've got the photos to prove it. Still, I can't help but think it's adorable that in Adan's eyes, my grandmother is only sixteen years old.

It's ten-thirty already and Jaime's band still has not gone on. He jumps off the stage and walks over to my mom and me.

"You two all set over here?" he asks, running his hands through my hair.

"We're good," I say.

"We're excited for the show," my mother says. "Do you want a drink?"

"I've got a beer with me up on stage," Jaime says. "Give me a kiss for luck."

I oblige, and then Jaime turns and hops back onto the stage.

"So, do you think you can handle raising a child with someone who's out every night?" my mother asks me casually.

"He's not out every night," I say, but then when I think about it, I realize that he is out most nights of the week. Something that didn't make much of a difference when I was working as a lawyer, stuck at the office until nine at night.

"Even so," she says, "do you think you can be with someone who works at night?"

"I thought you loved Jaime," I say.

"I do," she says, taking a sip of her drink. "I think Jaime is wonderful and talented and a very good guy."

"So, then what's the problem?" I ask, annoyed at this whole line of questioning, annoyed that there is a line of questioning. She shrugs. "Just because someone's great doesn't necessarily mean they're great for you."

I don't answer. Instead, I swivel around in my seat so I can have a better view for when the band begins playing, but my mother isn't done yet.

"Why didn't you make partner?" she asks. She is practically screaming in my ear, the noise level of the club getting louder and louder.

"They went with someone else," I say, back still turned to her, and take a sip of my water.

"But when you were a fifth year, they'd told you that you were on partnership track," she says. I'm surprised that she's remembered this. I wasn't aware that she'd been following my career so closely. I'd always thought that since she had such disdain for lawyers, she didn't really care much about how I was doing at my firm. "And then, when you had your reviews, every other year after that, they told you the same thing, didn't they? So, when did you get off course?"

I swivel my chair back to face my mother. "Well, they didn't exactly tell me that I was on course every year after that. Adam died, and there was a lot I was dealing with."

"So they didn't make you partner because you were grieving?" she asks. "Why didn't you just take more bereavement leave? Can't you sue them for that?"

"Well, it wasn't just that," I say, stirring my drink slowly. "I got interested in other things."

"That's great," she says. "I had no idea you were interested in anything but law. What other things were you doing?"

"Um," I say. I'm not accustomed to speaking to my mother about my career. "I just got really involved with pro bono work."

"You mean you were working for free?"

"Yes," I say, "but through the firm. So the firm was fully aware of what I was doing. And it looked really good for the firm to be logging so many pro bono hours."

"Well, that's great, Hannah. What kind of work?"

"Oh," I say, "it started with a few social security cases. Trying to help people get their benefits and stuff."

"That sounds great," my mother says. "And I'm sure that it does look really good for the firm to do a few cases like that each year. Sort of offsets all the work they do for those evil uber-corporations."

"Well, it was more than just a few cases," I say. "I would do anything I could get my hands on. After a while, it gets really contagious. Trying to help people, I mean. Making a difference."

"How many hours were you billing, exactly?"

"I started off slowly, but then it sort of took on a life of its own. I guess when I started, it was only an hour or two a week. Then it became a quarter of my yearly billables, and then half, and then last year I ended up not taking on any client cases at all."

"What do you mean?" she asks, leaning closer to me to hear the answer. She may not know much about the practice of law, but she certainly understood what I was trying to tell her.

"I only did pro bono work." I look ahead at the bar, and stir the lemon into my iced water.

"Did the firm know?" she asks. "Are you allowed to do that?"

"Obviously not," I say, laughing a bit to break the tension.

"Why would you do that?" my mother asks. She puts her hand on my arm to get my attention.

"You know what?" I say, turning to face her. "I don't feel like talking about this anymore."

"Why would you sabotage your own career?"

"I didn't," I say. "I was helping people."

"You were helping other people," she says. "At the expense of your own career."

"I didn't sabotage anything."

"Yes, you did. Are you really so afraid of having something good in your life that you'd rather take on the burdens of others, at your own expense? Well, I'll tell you what happens if you continue doing that. Eventually, you give so much of yourself that you no longer have anything to give. Don't let that happen to you, Hannah."

I swivel my chair back around to face the band. Even though my back is to her, I can feel my mother still staring at me.

The band starts to play and I'm grateful for the timing. Now I can do what I always do. Avoid this conversation and hope that it doesn't get brought up again. Music blares through the club and it's so loud, we don't get a chance to talk again.

Forty-one

"What the fuck is this?"

"It's a dance floor laid over the pool," I explain to Jaime. "Why, did you want to take a dip today? You could always walk out to the ocean, or we can go to Hunter's house."

"No," Jaime says. "There's a setup for a band. And that band's not us."

"What?" I say. "Oh, wait, you wanted to perform at this party?"

Jaime doesn't answer; he just looks at me and shrugs his shoulders in a way that suggests that it's obvious that his band would want to play tonight.

"But it's a party for you," I explain. "Everyone's here for you. You can't be the hired help."

"The hired help?" he asks, furrowing his brow. Clearly, my irony was lost on him. "Hannah, you've been out here a month and already you've changed."

"I was just joking," I say, reaching out to grab his arm.

He jumps back, away from my touch. "I'm an artist," he practically spits out at me.

Jaime stomps back to the guest house, and I let him go. It isn't until later, once the party's already started that I see him again. About forty-five minutes late, he and his bandmates saunter out into the party. They are all drunk. Really drunk.

I'm chatting with Hunter and Skylar about their photography lessons with my mother. They've set up a field trip to shoot out in Montauk the following week, and Hunter wants me to come along. It's not clear yet whether I'll be given a camera or if I'll have to play the part of the assistant again, but still, I tell them that I'm in.

"Why is this kid here again?" Jaime asks, walking over to us. He met Hunter the previous night, at their gig in Quogue, and couldn't understand why he was there. Jaime can't seem to wrap his brain around the fact that I choose to socialize with a fourteen-year-old.

I try to laugh to make Hunter think that Jaime's just kidding around, which only comes out sounding incredibly fake. I begin to wonder how much a tiny little glass of wine will actually harm my baby.

"He's just joking," I say, wrapping my arm around Jaime. For some reason, I think that if I steady him, he'll be less drunk.

"Good to see you again," Hunter says. "You remember Skylar."

"You were great last night," Skylar says, and Jaime just stares at her.

"You must be so excited about the baby," Hunter says. I love that he is trying to salvage this conversation, that he's trying so hard to see the good in Jaime. I think of Hunter's mother, and how proud she'd be to see how well she raised her son; how well-mannered he is, even in the face of an uncomfortable situation. Is it possible that this fourteen-year-old boy is more grown up than my twenty-seven-year-old boyfriend?

"Skylar and I are so excited about the baby," Hunter says, putting an arm around Skylar's shoulder.

"Why are you excited about the baby?" Jaime says to Hunter, a bit too aggressively.

"I think we should get you some water," I say loudly to Jaime, and direct him toward the pasta bar. As we walk away, over my shoulder I mouth the words "I'm sorry" to Hunter and Skylar, and Hunter flashes me a smile. A sad smile. I can tell he is the one who feels sorry for me.

I push ahead to the front of the line ("You can do anything you want, generally, as long as you have a big smile on your face," my grandmother would say), and get Jaime a huge plate of pasta in a thick alfredo sauce. I put a big chunk of bread on the plate, too, and swipe a few pieces of fried calamari from a passing waiter. I'm counting on the carbs and grease to help absorb all of the alcohol that's undoubtedly made Jaime so mean. We find an empty table, just off the bar, and sit down. I command Jaime to start eating, as I get up to fetch him a large glass of water.

"So, here's the happy couple," Hunter Kensington the third says, pulling up the extra chair at our table and sitting down. I suppose that Hunter told his father how excited he was about the baby and that Hunter's dad naturally assumed we were happy about it as well.

"Hi, Mr. Kensington," I say.

"Trip," he corrects.

"Yes, of course. Trip. This is Jaime," I say. Jaime looks up from his dish of pasta and nods.

"I heard that you are quite the musician," Trip says. "What kind of music do you make?" From the corner of my eye, I can see Jaime roll his eyes.

"I hope you're enjoying yourself here," I say. "This is a fun party, isn't it? Hunter and Skylar are having a blast."

"They are," he says. "Great kids, aren't they? I'm glad you've been taking such good care of them. You're going to make a great mother."

"Thank you," I say, and feel a flush come over my cheeks. I'm inexplicably moved by his words.

"So," he says, taking a sip of his champagne, "will the next party your grandmother plans be a wedding?"

"No," Jaime says quickly. He laughs into his bowl of pasta. "No."

"We're just taking things one day at a time," I say, smiling so hard my cheeks hurt.

"I'm sorry," Trip says. "I shouldn't have been so presumptuous. Of course you should take things one day at a time."

Jaime grumbles something about how he thought rich people out in the Hamptons had better manners as Trip excuses himself from the table.

"What is wrong with you?" I say, just as soon as Trip is safely out of earshot.

"What's wrong with me?" Jaime asks incredulously. "What' wrong with you?"

"Nothing is wrong with me," I say. "Is there a reason v since you've been out here, all you've been trying to do is hu ate me?"

"I'm not humiliating you, babe," he says. "You're (pretty good job of that all by yourself."

"Drink more water," I say. "You're still drunk."

Jaime takes a big swig of his water, followed by a pasta. With his mouth completely full, he says, "Wl to get married now?"

"I didn't say that," I mutter.

"Good," he says. "Because the best part of dating you used to be that you never wanted to get married. You've always been pretty adamant about that one. The fact that you're knocked up shouldn't really change things, you know. Because that would make you a really big hypocrite."

"You're an asshole," I say, and get up from the table. Over my shoulder, I can hear Jaime yelling, "I'm just kidding, babe!" but I keep walking. I have no idea where I'm going, but I just walk.

The truth is that I never thought I'd get married again. I don't know if it's the family curse, or that I couldn't bear to again go through the pain I felt when I lost Adam, but marriage was something that was off the table for me.

And Jaime's right, even though I'm now pregnant, it doesn't mean I want to get married. Jaime came out here to see if we could make things work, to see if we could have a baby together. Not to get married. Still, there's something about the way Jaime so adamantly refuses to entertain the thought of marriage that gives me pause.

I may not ever want to get married again, but I do want to be in a committed relationship, and the point of Jaime being out here is to figure out if we could do that for the long haul. To figure out if we can be a family. Can you be with someone who thinks that your best quality is the fact that you don't want to ever get married?

I walk past the dance floor and toward the pool, and recognize an unmistakable aroma. Something that I don't think I've smelled since I was in college. I turn toward the smell, and there's my mother, on a swing, smoking a joint.

"It's legal, counselor," she says as I approach her. "Don't arrest me." She puts her hands up in the air for effect, joint dangling between her teeth.

"I practice civil law," I say.

"But you could still make a citizen's arrest," she says, furrowing her brow in slow motion.

"So," I say, slowly and carefully. I don't want her to think I'm judging. "When did this start?"

"The doctor gave it to me this week," my mother says, taking a long inhale.

"Is the pain that bad?"

"It's getting there," she says. "But I don't want you to worry about me. I am seriously mellow yellow."

"You'll let me know what I can do," I say.

"Take a hit," she says. "It's sad to smoke up alone."

I take the joint between my two fingers and inhale, then remember that I'm pregnant and choke as I rush to exhale. My choking half to death makes my mother laugh uncontrollably. I pass the joint back to her, pouting.

"I'm sorry," she says. "You just looked so cute choking like that. God, I must be the worst grandmother in the world, suggesting that my pregnant daughter smoke up with me."

I shrug my shoulders. After all, we both know that my mother smoked and drank when she was pregnant with me, and I turned out all right.

Sort of.

"I've got bigger problems," I say, and tell her everything that has happened with Jaime since the party started. But before I can finish the story, Jaime comes and finds us by the swings.

"Babe," he says, slurring his words. "I was looking for you. The band's going to take a break and let us do a few songs and I didn't want you to miss it. Sweet! Is that a joint?"

My mother nods her head slowly, and Jaime says: "Gray, you are the coolest."

"I'm going to get some water," I say, and hop up from the swing. My mother tries to stop me, but she's smoked so much that she's moving too slowly to catch up. Jaime plops down on the swing next to her, and grabs the joint.

I walk quickly back to the dance floor, somehow thinking that if I'm in a well-lighted area, I'll be safe. I spot Rhett and decide that now is as good a time as any to get to know him a little better.

"Hannah." I'm stopped by Nate. He looks so handsome in his pressed white shirt and rumpled linen pants that I almost have to look away. "We need to talk."

"I was just on my way to say hello to Adan," I say, looking over Nate's shoulder. "I'm afraid I haven't been very nice to him since he got here."

Nate puts his hand underneath my elbow. "Please. Talk to me."

I look into his eyes and he's got that expression again. The one I can't decipher. The one that draws me in.

"Where did you go to college?" I ask.

"That's not what I meant when I said that we needed to talk," Nate says, laughing despite himself. He looks around the dance floor self-consciously. The bandleader begins a slow song, and the whole dance floor fills up with happy couples, swaying to the beat.

"Do you love him?" Nate asks me. "If you tell me you love him, I'll let you be. I'll go away and I won't bother you anymore."

I don't know what to say. I don't know the answer anymore.

"Hannah?" he says, but I still can't speak. "I get the feeling that you don't love him. I get the feeling that things aren't over between us."

"It's not that simple," I say.

"If you tell me you love him, I'll leave you alone. Do you want me to leave you alone?"

I don't say anything back. It's like I can't speak. I can barely catch my breath.

Nate pulls me close and whispers into my ear. We are on the dance floor, arms around each other, dancing slowly. "Listen, we could still make this work, you and I."

"No," I say, pulling back. "We can't. I've decided that I want to keep this baby."

"But do you love him?" Nate asks.

"We're having a baby," I say.

"What does that have to do with us?" Nate asks, putting his face close to mine again. "I know I freaked out at first, I know I said that I couldn't handle it, but the things you have to work for the hardest usually end up being the most worth it."

"What would we tell our child?" I ask.

"The truth," he says. "That we're in love. That's the truth, isn't it?"

"How screwed up would our child be?" I say, pulling back again. For a second, I get a fleeting image of the microfiche machine at the New York Public Library, spending a day searching for my father's bylines. "I have to try to make this work with Jaime."

"Tell me that you love him and I'll go away," he says.

Nate pulls me tight and I don't want to pull away. He bows his head down toward mine, our faces only inches apart. "Hannah, I love you."

"I don't even know where you went to college," I say, closing my eyes. "There are so many things I don't even know about you. Where did you go to college?"

"I went to Michigan," he says.

I open my eyes and let out a deep breath. "Okay," I say. "I went to Cornell."

"Oh no," he says, feigning upset, "how will we ever make it work?"

The song ends and all of the couples part to applaud the band. Nate and I continue dancing, our faces still only inches apart. I can tell he's about to kiss me, and I'm about to let him. Even though this is a party for my boyfriend, Jaime. Even though I'm pregnant with Jaime's child. Even though everyone here knows that, and is staring at me, with their jaws on the ground.

"Can I please have your attention?" a voice slurs from the microphone. I immediately recognize Jaime's drunken voice and I jump away from Nate like a kid who's been caught with her hand in the cookie jar. "I'd like your attention, please," Jaime continues.

"My band and I are going to play a few songs for you tonight," he says as his various band members, who are all in different states of drunkenness, take the stage. "But first, I've got an announcement to make. Hannah, where are you, Hannah?" He puts his hand over his eyes, as if the lights are blinding him somehow and he can't find me. I raise my hand and try to smile. Nate is still standing right next to me. I can't help but think that if the roles had been reversed, Jaime would have skulked off the dance floor and out into the night.

"There you are, Hannah!" Jaime continues.

I see my mother step from out of the darkness toward my grandmother, who motions to a waiter to refill her champagne glass. He fills up her glass and I see my grandmother staring at me. She's not smiling and neither is my mother. They both stand there, side by side, just looking at me.

Jaime continues his drunken speech: "I'm so happy to let all of you know that Hannah and I are engaged!"

The crowd erupts into happy cheers and I'm enveloped into hugs from a million different strangers. I steal a look over in my grandmother and mother's direction and they are frozen, still looking at me with furrowed brows. The crowd takes me farther and farther away from Nate. Each time I get a glimpse of him, through the crowd, he's just standing there, not moving, staring at me.

"To celebrate this happy occasion," Jaime yells into the mike, "we'd like to sing a song for you."

Jaime switches places with the lead singer, who takes the mike. Jaime leans down to pick up his bass, stands back up, and throws up all over the stage.

Forty-two

It's not that I object to people getting drunk and stoned at my grandmother's parties and then throwing up all over the bandstand. It's more that I'm beginning to see that Jaime is merely going through the motions of doing the right thing. Maybe he feels some sort of Cuban-Catholic guilt. Or sense of responsibility. Either way, we need to talk.

At the end of the night, Jaime passed out in the guest house with his bandmates, and I think it says a lot about our relationship that I wasn't angry about the fact that he never came to bed last night. I was just happy that I wouldn't have to clean up after him.

I brush my hair back into a ponytail, ready to make my way out to the guest house when I hear yelling down in the kitchen. Screaming. Blood-curdling cries. I abandon my brush and run down the stairs.

"You weren't going to tell me this?" my mother screams. "You're only telling me this because I'm dying?"

"I was going to tell you," my grandmother says, in a voice I've never heard from her before. "I just thought if we had more time, it might be easier for all of you."

"Well, there's no more time," my mother yells just as I walk into the room. "There's no more time!"

"What's going on here?" I ask.

My mother is standing right against the back door. It looks as if she's about to run at any second. My grandmother is curled up, hunched over, sitting at the kitchen table. She's quietly crying. Adan is next to her, rubbing her back. He looks as if he's about to cry, too.

"Will somebody tell me what the hell is going on here?" I ask. I can hear my voice begin to shake, but I take a deep breath and I'm okay.

"You think she's so fabulous," my mother says to me, "go ask her."

She walks out the back door into the backyard. Adan excuses himself and I'm left alone in the kitchen with my grandmother.

"What's going on?" I ask, my voice barely a whisper.

"Sit down," my grandmother says. Her voice is so tiny, so weak, that I barely recognize her.

"Tell me what's going on," I say, grabbing my grandmother's hand. "Is it my mother's health?"

"No, it's not," she says, giving my hand a squeeze. "It's about me."

"Are you sick?"

"No," my grandmother says. "This isn't about health. It's about a lie I told. A lie I told many, many years ago, that's now come to light."

"What is it?" I ask. "You can tell me anything." As the words come out of my mouth, I think to myself: Do I really mean it? Can my grandmother truly tell me anything?

"Adan is your grandfather," she says. She says it quietly, emotionlessly, as if she is trying to be strong for me. Or perhaps it's that all of her emotions are drained from admitting this to my mother.

"I don't understand," I say, even though I understand perfectly. My grandmother explains herself to me. The story Adan told about coming to find my grandmother after the war, how she fainted when she first saw him at the beginning of the summer, how desperately she wanted my mother and me to connect with Adan.

"What about my grandfather?" I ask. Even though I never really knew him, I feel as if someone needs to be looking out for him about now.

"He knew," she said. "He always knew."

"You told him?"

"Your grandfather knew," my grandmother says, taking my hand once again. I'm not sure when I dropped my hand from hers, but she grabs it now, and looks me in the eye. "He knew, and he forgave me."

"How could he forgive you?" I ask, my voice barely a whisper. I hate that I'm judging my grandmother. I know that if the roles were reversed, she would grab me and hold me and tell me that everything is okay, that everything works out the way it's supposed to, and that what I'd done wasn't so horrible. But I can't help but think that what she's done is horrible.

If you've done awful things in your life, does that make you a less judgmental person? Maybe once you've done the unthinkable, you lose the right to look down your nose at someone. Maybe I've lost that right myself. Thinking of one man while pregnant with another's child . . . maybe I really am my grandmother's granddaughter after all.

"Love is complicated," my grandmother says, getting up from the table and putting a kettle up for tea.

I have to hold my tongue—the only time I've truly been in love was with Adam, and it wasn't complicated at all. It was just entirely too short. But her statement gets me thinking. If Adam were still alive today, if our relationship hadn't been cut short, would I, too, think that love is complicated?

"It's the nature of love," my grandmother continues, not even noticing that I'm lost in my own thoughts. "Forgiveness. Love's not the sum of what you do. Well, it is, of course it is. I shouldn't say that. I should say that love isn't only the sum of what you do. It's more than that. Love is two people trying to make a life together. It's not easy. It's messy. What's important, at the end of the day, is the sum of who you are." She takes two teacups out of the cabinet, and when she turns back to face me I can see that she's crying. I put my arms around her and hug her.

I don't really want to hug her—the anger over what she's just told me is building in my chest—but I know that's what she would do for me if the roles were reversed. I think that's what she would do, anyway. Perhaps I don't know anymore. My grandmother isn't the woman I thought she was.

"I should go and talk to Gray," I say, and my grandmother nods her head yes.

I walk out into the backyard to find my mother. She shouldn't be alone right now, and the truth is, I don't want to be alone either. For the first time in my life, I don't want to be with my grandmother.

I walk around the backyard, past the pool, onto the beach, looking for Gray. The boys are all still asleep in the guest house, so they wouldn't know where she could have gone. I check the garage, and then the main house. But my mother's nowhere to be found.

Forty-three

Growing up, my mother and I lived in hotels and didn't even have a phone. If you wanted to find us, you'd have to figure out what city we were in, guess what hotel we'd be staying at, and then call the front desk. They'd take a message and give it to us when we waltzed in. Then we'd have to find an empty phone booth and call you back.

It's not so difficult to find someone these days. Now, we've all got cell phones that we carry around with us. Emails, Facebook, and Twitter. Instant access whenever you want it. But not if the person you're looking for doesn't want to be found.

I've called my mother fifteen times so far on her cell phone, and she hasn't picked up once. I also sent her thirteen text messages, and seven emails, all of which have been ignored. I know she's upset about my grandmother's announcement, but surely even she can understand that we need each other now more than ever?

I drive over to Hunter's house. I know it's a long shot, but she's been enjoying teaching him so much, and if I were having a really bad day, one of the first people I'd turn to would be Hunter, so I give it a shot.

"You've lost your mother?" Hunter asks me.

"I didn't lose her," I say. "She's just really upset and ran off somewhere."

"I did that once when I was seven," Hunter says. "I got so upset that I grabbed a blanket and left our apartment. I only got as far as Fifth Avenue, but my plan was to move to Central Park."

"I don't think she actually ran away from home," I say. "She just needed to get away to clear her head."

"I know the feeling," Hunter says, nodding. "No offense but you're not a very good assistant if you don't even know where your boss is."

I'm about to explain to Hunter that I don't actually work for my mother on a day-to-day basis when it hits me: there's someone who does. I get back on my cell and call Gray's assistant.

At first, she doesn't want to tell me where my mother is. She says something about assistant-boss confidentiality, but then I pull the I'm-pregnant-and-she's-got-cancer card (an amazingly effective one-two punch, I've discovered), and I've got the information I need to find my mother.

This whole process has taken me two hours, so by the time I hit the road, I'm sure that my mom's already back in the city, hunkering down in the one place I don't want to be right now. The one place that will make me remember all of the things that I think are wrong with my mother and the way she raised me.

The Hotel Chelsea.

The front desk gives me a key, assuming "I don't want any visitors" doesn't extend to one's offspring. As I stand in the lobby, waiting for them to locate the second set of keys to the room, I stare at a huge photograph that my mother used as rent one month when she couldn't pay our bill.

It's a picture of me, taken when I was ten or eleven. I'm

running through the Parque del Buen Retiro in Madrid, wearing a white dress. I vaguely remember when my mother took the photo—he was finishing up a day of shooting in the park, and I was enjoying the last shreds of sunlight—but I've never looked at it that closely before. In all the years I'd lived here, I'd always just walked right by, dismissing it as part of the scenery.

My mother's done something with the light and the tilt of my head—it looks as if a halo of light is all around my bushel of big brown curls. My arms are in front of me and my hands are reaching up. Was I chasing a butterfly? A ladybug? Whatever it was, the photograph is ethereal and beautiful and gives me a feeling of happiness and utter calm. My mother's so well known for her photos of war and destruction that I often forget that she has the ability to make something really beautiful, too.

"Here you go," the desk clerk says, and it takes me a second to respond.

"Thanks."

The elevators are all broken, so I have to trudge up four flights of stairs to get to the room.

"You know how much I hate it here," I say as I walk in. My mother is sitting on a chair by the window, barely moving.

"They weren't supposed to let you in," she says, staring out the window. "And I can't believe Peg caved and told you I was here. You just can't get a good assistant nowadays."

When I sit down on the bed I realize that she's not moving because she's in pain.

"What can I do?" I ask.

"If you want to do something for me . . . I mean, really do something for me," she says, "you'll leave so that I can smoke some pot."

"You can smoke pot when I'm here," I say. "I think we're already established that I'm not going to arrest you for it."

"The baby," she says, and I feel like it's a big step that she's looking out for her grandchild.

I jump off the bed and open the door. There's a tiny Juliet balcony, not even as big as a fire escape, but we both step onto it, and, at the same time, put our arms on the railings and look down at Twenty-Third Street.

My mother and I often did this when I was younger—step outside of our room at the Chelsea and just stare down, watching the city go by. She'd always marvel at how amazing it was to watch the world going on with their day-to-day lives, while we were up here, just taking it all in. I remember she would tell me that there are a million things happening to a million different people out there at this very moment. Someone down there is having the best day of their life. Someone is having the worst.

We stay like this for a moment, and then I remember the point of our being out here, and ask my mother where her marijuana is. She tries to light up the joint far away from me, and let the breeze take it away from my pregnant body, but the city is sweltering, and the air just hangs.

"I'm sorry," I say. "I'm so sorry you have to deal with all of this right now."

"Just because you like her better than you do me," my mother says, "doesn't mean you have to feel sorry. It doesn't mean you're responsible for what she's done."

"I don't feel responsible for what she's done," I say. "I'm sorry that with everything you've got going on, you now have this to deal with."

"That's how he figured it out, you know," she says.

"Who? What?"

"Adan," she says, and then takes a long drag of her joint. "Pancreatic cancer runs in his family. He started asking questions."

"I'm so sorry," I say.

"Your grandmother is a real piece of work, you know."

"That's one way to put it," I say. I look down and I see a young couple. They're having a quarrel. The man grabs her arm. The woman wrangles herself free and rushes off away from him in a huff. "When we get back out there, we should just all sit down and talk."

"I'm not going back out there," my mother says, and I turn to face her.

"You have to."

"No, I don't," she says. "I'm dying. I can do whatever the hell I want."

"Please," I say, and then turn to look back down at the street. I don't know what I'm looking for exactly, but I quickly find it: it's the quarreling couple. The man's caught up to the woman, and they're kissing in the middle of the street.

"Give me one good reason why," my mother says, bringing my attention back up to the balcony.

"I need you," I say, and I really mean it. Before the words were out of my mouth, I didn't quite know what I was going to say to her, but suddenly I realize it's true. I need her.

"No you don't," my mother says. "You have never needed me a day in your life. You just don't want to feel guilty about me dying."

"That's not true," I say. "I need you. I need to feel close to you. I need for you to understand who I am, who I've become, and be okay with it. I need your advice. I need you to tell me how you're feeling about everything and I need to tell you how I feel. I may not have needed you before, and you may not think that I need you now, but I do. I really do."

My mother doesn't respond; she doesn't say anything at all. We stay there, out on the balcony, for a long time, looking out into the street. We stand there long after she's finished her joint, long after the sun has set over the Hudson River. We do not say anything inane to each other, like "Isn't the sunset beautiful?" We just stand, side by side, looking out into the city, and we don't say a word.

Forty-four

"Feel any better?" I ask my mom as we walk down Sixth Avenue, on our way to get something for dinner. I don't know who spoke first, who broke the silence, but it doesn't matter.

"You know, I think I always knew," my mother says, looking out into the evening sky, barely watching where she's going on the busy street. "I just always knew something was missing."

I nod my head in agreement, waiting for her to say more. All of my years of therapy have taught me that it's good to talk, good to let things out, so I let my mother do that. If I were to actually tell her that she should talk it out, she'd probably laugh at me, so I just stand next to her, nodding, not saying a word.

"I mean, maybe that's why I've always been traveling the world. It was never a desire to travel. It was a need. It was like, if I didn't travel, if I wasn't always moving, I'd die. So, maybe I've just always been looking for something."

I nod and my mother continues talking.

"Now I've found it and the only way I know how to deal with it is to run away from it."

We get to the diner, the one we always went to when I was a kid, and walk inside. The manager recognizes us and ushers us over to our favorite booth, the one next to the window that has eighties songs on the mini-jukebox. We don't even need to look at menus.

"You know," I say, "I always want to run, too, but I force myself to stay."

"Well, then, maybe I can learn something from you," she says.

"I think we can probably learn something from each other."

She smiles at me and I look at the selection on the jukebox. The songs haven't changed—Donna Summer's "I Feel Love," Simon and Garfunkel's "Bridge over Troubled Water," Pete Townshend's "Let My Love Open the Door"—and I'm comforted to see that some things stay the same, always.

"You have to come back with me," I say as my mother puts a quarter into the jukebox. The Eagles's "I Can't Tell You Why" plays softly.

"Why don't we talk about this in the morning?" my mother says.

"I think we should talk about it now."

"I don't really want to see your grandmother," she says, shrugging her shoulders. "And we've already established that I don't have to do anything I don't want to do. Not now."

"You should talk to her."

"What could she possibly have to say to me?"

"That's what you should find out," I say. "That's what I plan to find out when I go back there."

"You're just angry that you found out she's not perfect," my mother says.

"That's ridiculous," I say. "I'm worried about you right now."

"Yes," she continues, "you're upset that the normal childhood you think she gave me was a lie."

"No, that's what you're angry about," I say, looking at her.

"As much as you preached to me about the merits of my extraordinary childhood, you're angry that she took away your normal one."

My mother opens her mouth to say something back to me, but then puts a finger to her lips instead.

"Just admit that," I say. "Admit it." As I hear the words coming out of my mouth, they sound harsher than I mean them to, but it's like I can't stop. I want to treat her more gently because she's sick, but we seem to have moved past that.

"Maybe," she says.

"Maybe," I say back.

"Well, counselor," my mother says, "you've made such a good argument, I think I will go back."

"Thank you," I say. "I really appreciate that."

"But there's just one condition."

"What is it?" I ask. I was about to say "sure," but it's my mother I'm dealing with, and although we've taken a big step forward today, I still don't entirely trust her.

"Let's stay here in the city tonight," she says. "For old time's sake."

"All right," I say. "For old time's sake. I was supposed to talk to Jaime about last night, but I guess it can wait."

"Oh please," my mother says. "As if he's even still there. When he woke up and saw you were gone, he probably thanked his lucky stars and took the first jitney back into town."

"Thanks, Mom."

"What?" my mom says, feigning innocence. "You don't really want him. You want that other one, the one who looks like he belongs out there. Only you don't want to admit it to yourself yet. I'm just saying that the work's probably been done for you, so we're clear to stay here tonight. There's nothing to worry about."

She smiles like a little girl. I can't remember the last time I've seen that smile.

"I guess you're right," I say. "One good way to get rid of Jaime is to leave him alone for twenty-four hours."

"Or you could always just try to kill him," my mother says with a little smirk, just as the French fries and vanilla milkshakes are being brought to the table. "Oh, wait, you already tried that."

I toss a fry across the table at my mother and we both dissolve into a fit of laughter.

Forty-five

The drive back to the beach feels shorter than when I was headed into the city to find my mother. Along the way, we stop for coffees, stop for water, and we talk the whole time. There's more laughter, and I think I may have even convinced my mother that when she gives her next photography lesson to Hunter, I should be more than an assistant; I should be a student, too.

Somewhere around exit 65, my mother says: "I'm glad you convinced me to stop running away." She smiles at me—I can see her from the corner of my eye—but it just makes me think. I've been fooling myself into thinking that I no longer run. True, when I heard about my mother's illness, the first thing I wanted to do was flee, but I stayed. And I'm really proud about that.

But isn't this whole summer just one big escape from reality? Running away from the trouble I got myself into in the city. I realize that's probably the real reason I didn't want to go back to New York yesterday. The scene of the crime. And maybe I'm the one who should grow up and start acting like an adult. Especially since I'm about to become a mother.

I silently vow to call my law firm the following day and tell them that I'll be back. I will immediately then mention the fact that I'm pregnant, so that they can't fire me. The one thing big law firms hate more than associates who take all twelve weeks of their amassed vacation at once are big discrimination lawsuits.

I will follow my own advice. I will stop running away. I will cut my never-ending summer vacation short and go back to my old life. I will work during the week, come out to see my mother and grandmother on weekends. I will face problems like an adult, by talking them out, not by running away from them.

Forty-five minutes later, my mother and I pull into the Mattress King's estate. Every time I pass through the majestic gates, I notice something new. This time, I've noticed that the gates have tiny red hourglasses on either side. They glisten in the light from my headlights, probably because they are encased in tiny red crystals. Viuda Negra, indeed. The Mattress King really did have a great sense of humor—it was what I liked most about him. I wonder for a moment what he would think about what's been going on this summer. I wonder if he knew my grandmother's secret.

After depositing the car safely into the garage, we march back upstairs and hear laughter coming from my grandmother's bedroom. I call out a loud "we're home!" so that we don't catch my grandmother and Adan in the middle of anything.

"In here," my grandmother calls out. My mother and I walk into the bedroom, where we find my grandmother, Adan, and Jaime sitting around the trunk of photographs. The picture of domestic bliss makes me feel uncomfortable.

"Hey, babe!" Jaime says as my mother and I walk into the room. He jumps up from where he was seated and gives me a peck on the lips.

"Look at the three of you, all together," I say. I look at my grandmother and Adan, and they gaze back at me with happy expressions, as if they are my parents and it's prom night.

"Of course we're all together!" he says. "Why wouldn't we be? I proposed to you, didn't I?"

"Not really," I say. "You just sort of announced to the world that we were getting married after telling me that the best thing about our relationship was the fact that I never wanted to get married."

Jaime launches into a grand speech about how perfect our life will be, the gist of which is this: now that he's gotten his ambivalent feelings out, he's ready to start fresh. Everything is clear. He knows what he needs to do. He's ready to be a dad.

"I'm in love with someone else," I blurt out. Shock registers on everyone's face. Everyone's but Jaime's.

"With who?" he says, a sly smile playing at his lips. Does he think this is a joke? Step one of acting like a grown-up: come clean to those that are close to me.

"Nate Sugarman," I say. "You met him at the party."

"That tool?" Jaime asks, laughing. "Are you fucking kidding me?" And then, looking at my grandmother and Adan: "Pardon my French."

Does he see the irony in saying "Pardon my French" to a couple of French nationals?

"You know what," Jaime says, "I don't care about any of that. All I care about is you and me. And our baby. And the life we're going to have together." He puts his hand over my abdomen, and I instinctively shy away from his touch.

"We're going to have a life together?" I ask.

"We can have the perfect life: I'll be home with the kid all day when you're at work, and then you'll come home from work and I'll run my gigs."

And when he says it like that, it does sound like a perfect life. We'd have a happy child who was always in the care of a parent and Jaime and I could both continue to work, so money wouldn't be much of an issue. I have nothing to say in response. I suppose I do owe it to Jaime to give things one more try. I owe it to our unborn child.

"We should let the two of you talk," my grandmother says, and she and Adan leave their own bedroom so that Jaime and I can be alone. "You and I need to talk, too," she says to my mother on her way out of the room.

"Let's go to our room," Jaime says, and grabs my hand, as if nothing has changed, as if I hadn't just been gone for twenty-four hours, as if he hadn't just found out that I was in love with another man.

I let Jaime grab my hand and lead me back to my room. Our room. I do it as if it's the most natural thing in the world.

Forty-six

"And what did he say?" my mother asks me. We're down in the basement in her dark room, getting ready for today's photography lesson. She's taking down Hunter and Skylar's photos from the drying line so she can give them their pictures.

"He said that I should take my time out here, that they've got my cases covered for now and that I should come back when I'm ready."

"Your job will just be waiting there for you?" my mother asks. "After not coming in to work for weeks, and getting other people to pick up the slack, your job is still going to be there for you?"

"That's what they said," I tell my mother. "Anyway, I was taking my accrued vacation." We then have a debate on whether this is the nature of big firms in general—that they can always use little worker bees, especially worker bees who do not expect to make partner—or if this is because I immediately dropped my pregnancy into the conversation with Tim.

"Or maybe Tim's just a decent guy," I tell my mother.

"Well, I've never met him, so I wouldn't know," she says. She thinks for a second, and then asks: "What do his hands look like?"

"Prep-school-boy perfect."

My mother wrinkles her nose and we both laugh.

"I think you did the right thing, you know," she says, grabbing a few cameras. I smile back at her, but she sees right through it. "What? You don't think that going back to your job is the right thing to do?"

"I guess it is," I say. "Of course it is. But Grandma offered to let me stay out here full-time, on her dime, so that's pretty tempting, too."

"You have to work," my mother says, taking a few test shots out of her camera. "You can't rely on your grandmother's money. That's not how I raised you."

"Why would that have to be an indictment on you?" I say. "On how you raised me? Can't I just make a choice for myself?"

"Of course you can make a choice for yourself," she says, looking up at me. "I just never thought you'd choose her way of life."

"Just because you're mad at her—" I begin, only to be cut off.

"I'm not mad at her anymore," my mother says, quickly. "I told her that I forgive her. And I do. But this has nothing to do with her and me. This has to do with you and the kind of life you want to live."

"I don't know what kind of life I want to live," I say, and I don't. I have no idea what I want. I'm no closer in discovering the recipe for a happy life than I was when I first came out here this summer.

"I didn't raise you to be dependent on other people," my mother says.

"I'm beginning to think that maybe depending on other people isn't such a bad thing," I say.

I turn around to gauge my mother's reaction to what I've just said and she's silent. She's perched herself on a stool and is bent over slightly in the stomach. Her eyes are closed. This can only mean one thing: the return of debilitating pain. I know that she decided to forgo the marijuana this morning since we'd be seeing Hunter and Skylar, but I rush over to her stash and grab a joint and lighter.

"No," my mother says as I try to force the joint into her hand.

"Yes," I say. "If you want, I'll leave so that I don't breathe any of it in. But, yes. Take it."

She does as I say, and then waves me off so that she can smoke without worrying about my baby. I refrain from making a comment about how the smoke is no match for the fumes from the dark room, and walk upstairs without saying a word. My mother comes up to the kitchen fifteen minutes later, and I've already got a cup of hot tea ready for her.

"Thank you," she says, taking the mug from my hands.

"No problem," I say. "Feel any better?"

"It takes the edge off," she says. "But we're not done talking about you and your job."

"What else is there to discuss?" I ask, taking a sip of my water. "You want me to be miserable at a job I hate."

"I don't want you to be miserable. Of course I don't want you to be miserable," she says. "But you have a profession, for chrissakes. You're really telling me that you don't have any other options? It can't just be either a job you hate or you don't work at all."

"I don't know," I say. "But even if I did have options, I have no idea who would hire a pregnant woman."

"They can't not hire you because you're pregnant," Hunter says in lieu of "hello" as he and Skylar come into the kitchen. Skylar gives my mother and me each a kiss on the cheek and a big hug. "That's discrimination."

"Now you want to be a lawyer?" my mother asks Hunter with a smile. "I thought you were going into movies."

"There are a lot of great legal thrillers, Gray," Hunter responds gravely. "It's good to be well-rounded."

"You're right," my mother says. "Then I guess we should start today's lesson."

"If the pictures should tell a story," Hunter says, "then I need Mrs. Morganfelder out here."

"I really don't see why you should need my mother," my mom says to Hunter. She claims she's not angry with my grandmother anymore, but she goes out of her way to not see her. I'm in no position to judge, since, lately, I've been doing pretty much the same thing.

"I'm telling a story about love through the ages. So, I'll shoot Mrs. Morganfelder and Adan, and they'll represent old love, then I'll have Hannah and we'll get Sugar out here, and they can represent middle-aged love, and then you'll shoot Skylar and me. We represent young love."

I'm not sure which of these statements to address first: that Hunter thinks I'm middle-aged, or that he wants me to do a photo shoot with Nate. I decide to tackle the easiest first:

"Why don't you shoot Jaime and me?"

"Jaime doesn't like us," Skylar says. "He's mean."

Both statements are true.

"I think it's a great idea," my mother says. "Why don't the two of you go into the house and grab my mother and Adan. First, think about wardrobe, and then think about setting. Don't forget what we've been discussing about use of light. How will you use light to help tell your story?"

"Okay," Hunter and Skylar say in unison, and rush off to the main house.

"So, what story should we try to tell?" I ask, sitting down on my grandmother's favorite chaise longue. "One about a thirty-four-year-old who becomes middle aged?"

My mother puts her camera up to her face. She gives me no direction, just shoots, so I stare into the lens, expressionless.

"Did I ever tell you why I named you Hannah?" she asks, camera still up to her face.

"No," I say, and she takes a shot.

"Because the name Hannah means 'grace.' You are a part of me," she says. I furrow my brow, and she takes a shot. "I know you hated the way I had you, but you have to understand. I wanted you more than anything in the world. You are the love of my life. You're a part of me."

I'm so taken aback by this that I don't know what to say. Why didn't my mother ever tell me that before? It's the sort of thing I would have loved to hear when I was younger. Why did she wait until now to tell me?

There's so much I want to say to her, but I don't know where to begin. As I formulate the words, she continues to shoot me, in rapid succession.

"Thank you," I say, since I don't know what else to say.

"For what?" she asks, and takes the camera down from her face.

"For telling me that."

Later in the day, when we develop the photographs, I'll think about what my mother said to me and smile. For the first time, I will hold on to a photograph my mother took of me and treasure it.

Forty-seven

My mother still hasn't forgiven my grandmother. She claims she's not angry anymore, but her eyes betray her. She refuses to look at my grandmother when she speaks to her, and she can barely stand to be in the same room with Adan.

When I try to broach the topic with my grandmother, she, too, pretends that everything is okay, that all is forgiven.

"Why would anything be wrong?" my grandmother asks with a slight smile, as if she hadn't revealed her deepest, darkest secret just days earlier. We're lying poolside together, just the two of us. Adan is off playing golf. Jaime is practicing his music. My mother is inside her room, getting checked out by her doctor.

"No reason," I say to my grandmother. Two can play this game. I can pretend everything is perfect, too. But I'll still get it out of her. I am a lawyer, after all. I've had witnesses who were far more difficult than my grandmother, and I always got them to tell me what I wanted to know. "Feel like taking a walk?"

"Sure," my grandmother says, and in minutes we're out on the beach, both in wide-brimmed hats and wearing liberal amounts of sunscreen. My grandmother's advice is infectious. Once I began following it, I just couldn't stop. I wonder, for a brief instant, just what else of my grandmother has rubbed off on me.

As we hit the sand, my grandmother walks toward Nate's

house. I think about objecting, but then remember that in order to get my grandmother to tell me what I want to know, I have to play her game.

"It's been quite a summer," I say. It takes all of my energy not to look up at Nate's room as we pass his house.

"It most certainly has," my grandmother says.

"I spoke to the firm," I say. "I'll be headed back to the city sometime soon. I think it's time for me to get back to work."

"How are you feeling?" my grandmother asks.

"Okay, I guess. The nausea seems to have passed."

"No," she says, turning to face me. Her eyes are a faint blue. I can just make them out from behind her sunglasses. "I meant, how are you feeling? How do you feel about everything?"

I pause for a moment, unsure how to respond. Then, I let loose.

"About what, exactly? My mother, who I never really got along with, is dying. I'm pregnant with Jaime's child, and our relationship is falling apart. And then, I find out that the one person I've looked up to my entire life has been living a lie. So which part do you want to discuss?"

"All of it," my grandmother says, taking a deep breath of salty ocean air.

"I'm angry with you," I say, practically under my breath. And then, a bit louder: "I'm so angry with you."

"I know," my grandmother says. Her voice breaks slightly, and when I look at her, I can see tears forming at her eyes. "I'm so sorry."

"It's okay," I say, and we stop walking. We're just standing there, on the beach, looking at each other. My grandmother begins to cry and I don't do anything to comfort her.

"I'm so sorry," she says again. "I'm sorry for everything."

"It's okay," I parrot back, but the more she cries, the angrier I get. "Actually, it's not okay. I'm so, so angry at you. It's like I don't even know you anymore. Who are you?"

"I'm still the same person," my grandmother says, wiping her tears away with her hand. "You know who I am."

"I don't," I say. "Not anymore. Let's just go back to the house. I'm too angry for a walk on the beach."

"I know you're angry," my grandmother says. "You should be angry. But hopefully, once that subsides a bit, you'll come to realize that I thought I was doing the right thing."

"Hiding such a huge secret from my mom? How can that be the right thing? How can lying to someone you love ever be the right thing?"

"I just wanted her to be normal. To have a happy, normal life with a mother and father. Under one roof."

"Maybe normal isn't so great," I say, channeling my mother. Which is weird, because I never agree with my mother. And normal is what I've been striving for my entire life. Why am I fighting my grandmother on it now? Would I hide something from my child if I thought it would protect her? Probably.

My grandmother barely notices that I've cut off her train of thought. She continues speaking as if I'd never interrupted. "And your grandfather was a great man. A great father. Your mother had a very happy childhood with him, you know. Until he was taken from us, of course. But he was a wonderful father."

I don't respond, I just look out to the ocean. I think about the way my mother used to speak of her father, about what a kind, gentle man he was, and how he always made her laugh. Always protected her. Made her feel safe.

"I think that what you need to know is that I always tried to do what I thought was the right thing at the time," my grandmother says.

"Do you think I'm doing the right thing now?" I ask. "With the choices I'm making?"

"There's no right or wrong," my grandmother says. "There's only what you do and what you don't do. You'll never know what the path not taken might have held for you, so you should just try to make the decision you think is right. That's what I did."

"I need to sit down," I say. Suddenly, I feel faint. I'm not sure if it's the walking or the sun, but I need to sit immediately.

My grandmother ushers me to the edge of the beach, where the waves lick the sand, and we sit down together. The cool water makes me feel better, and once I no longer feel like I'm about to pass out, my grandmother pulls two bottles of water from her beach tote.

My grandmother puts her hands into the cold ocean water and presses them against my forehead, my back, and my neck as I drink the bottle of water.

"Any better?" she asks. I nod my head yes.

"So maybe I should do the same? Stay with Jaime so my child can have a normal life?"

"Is that what you want to do?"

"Isn't that what you did? You sacrificed the man you loved so your child could live a normal life." I ask.

"Adan was my first love, the love I never fully got over, but that doesn't mean I didn't love your grandfather. I never saw it as a sacrifice."

"So what are you going to do about Mom?" I ask.

"Your mother came back. She has forgiven me," she says, but

we both know that it's not true. Gray may have come back, but she's a long way from forgiving my grandmother.

"What are you going to do?" I ask. I'll continue to ask until she tells me what is really on her mind.

"She's forgiven me, so there's really nothing else to do," she quietly says.

"What are you going to do?"

My grandmother puts her hands into the water and presses them to the back of my neck and my forehead. Then she dips her hands in the water again and does the same to herself. Quietly, she says, "I don't know."

The walk back to the house is lovely. Late afternoon—my favorite time of day. The heat is gone, but the cool breeze from the evening hasn't yet set in. The sky is breathtakingly beautiful, and the wind coming off the ocean is just wonderful, like that first burst of spring air after a freezing cold winter.

As we near the house, we pass by Nate's family's home again. This time, I look up at his window. And I don't hide it either—no sly glance out of the corner of my eye. No, this time I just turn my head and look. But he's not there.

He's standing right in front of us, out on the beach.

"Fancy meeting you here," he says, and smiles.

"Nate," I say.

"I'll see you at the house, darling," my grandmother says, and walks off before I have a chance to protest.

"Nate," I say. I'm not sure of what else to say.

"I've been wanting to come by, but I just never know when it's the right moment," Nate says. He's tracing something in the sand with his right foot. "You still haven't told me that you love him. If you tell me you love him, I'll leave you alone."

"You could've come by," I say, crossing my hands in front of my chest. "Jaime knows about us, and he's okay with it."

"What's that supposed to mean?" Nate asks, looking up from the sand, right into my eyes.

Now it's my turn to look down. "He knows that we had something, but he doesn't feel threatened. He's okay with it," I say. "We're going to try to make a go of it. For the baby," I quickly add.

"Is that what you want?" he asks. "Do you love him?"

I hesitate for a moment, and Nate seizes on my uncertainty.

"I didn't think so," he says, his eyes never leaving my face. "Then why be unhappy?"

"I'm trying to do the right thing here," I say.

"Who says that being with Jaime is the right thing?"

"This baby is his." I'm suddenly very aware of my body. From my chest that's beginning to burn in the low afternoon sun, to my belly, which is beginning to poke out just the tiniest bit.

"I want to see you," Nate says, putting his hand on my arm.

"I don't know if that would be such a good idea," I say, wriggling from his grip. I wonder if Jaime will be able to tell that Nate has touched my arm. If it will somehow leave an invisible mark.

"Please," Nate says. "I want to see you."

I look back at my grandmother's house for an instant. I'm not sure exactly what I'm looking for, but I feel like a teenager out past curfew. "Jaime has a gig tonight. We could meet up at around eight. I think he's leaving at seven."

"Okay," Nate says. "Then tonight it is." He leans over to kiss me, but I give him my cheek.

I feel shivers run up and down my spine as I race back to my grandmother's house.

Forty-eight

It's a beautiful night for a date. Not a trace of humidity in the air, the sun still high in the sky at eight o'clock. You couldn't ask for a better evening. Surely it can't be wrong to be going out with Nate on a night like this? If I were doing the wrong thing by seeing Nate while Jaime's at his gig, the air would be colder, the wind would be sharper, and the temperature would have dropped. But we've got the sort of night that's just meant for going out.

Nate has created a pregnancy-friendly plan for our evening by consulting with his older brother's wife. His thoughtfulness tickles me pink, and I find myself giggling nonstop as he tells me what he has in mind.

"So, sushi was out," he tells me, "that much I could figure out on my own, but my sister-in-law also told me that we should stay away from things like bowling, because you wouldn't want to strain your tummy muscles."

"You were going to take me bowling?" I ask, a smile playing on my lips.

"Yes," he says, looking very serious. "That was on my list of things."

"Well, maybe we could go to the drive-in instead," I say. "And save bowling for next time. And then after that, we can share a milk shake." It dawns on me that I seem to have learned how to flirt.

Nate has made reservations at a seafood restaurant, reporting that white flaky fish is really good for my developing fetus, but I have other ideas about what's good for me and my pregnant body. We end up at La Parm, ready to gorge ourselves on pizza and pasta.

We grab a table in the back, behind the deli, and order. The place is packed, with various share house kids, straight off the beach, picking up pizza pies to enjoy before they hit the clubs. Our salads arrive, and out of the corner of my eye I can see a guy with a baseball cap in the front of the restaurant. He's exactly the sort of guy I thought Nate was before I got to know him this summer: a rich, entitled brat who still thinks he's in college. I'm so glad I was wrong about Nate. I turn and look over at him. He's mixing up his salad, reaching for the olive oil, and he catches my eye.

"What?" he says.

"Nothing," I say, suddenly embarrassed for staring at him.

"You were looking at me," he says.

"I'm not allowed to look at you now?" I ask, trying to be playful.

"You can look at me all you want," Nate says, taking a sip of his soda. (He refused to order wine, since I couldn't have any.) "Looking at me is good. Look at me all you like."

He begins to lean into me, slowly, and I lean into him, too. We meet in the middle and he gives me a peck on the lips. When I open my eyes, I see the guy with the baseball cap again.

"That's the sort of person I thought you were," I say, motioning to the guy in the baseball cap. "The type of guy I went to school with."

"Who? Him?" Nate says, looking at the guy in the baseball cap, who is looking toward our table. "He looks awful."

"Sugar!" the baseball cap guy calls out in our general direction. And then I realize he's coming toward us. "Hey Shuge!"

Nate gives the guy a wave.

"Hannah, this is Todd. One of my fraternity brothers."

Todd reaches over the table and gives Nate a huge bear hug. He then turns to me and shakes my hand.

"Really nice to meet you, Hannah," he says, looking me in the eye when he does. "Any friend of Sugar's is a friend of mine."

"Nice to meet you, too," I say, but my voice is a bit smaller than it was before.

"Hannah thinks you remind her of someone she went to high school with," Nate says, smiling, trying to hide the laughter in his voice.

"I went to Fieldston," Todd says. "Are you from the city?"

"I went to Pearce," I say.

"So, we're practically related," Todd says, and we all laugh.

"See that, Hannah," Nate says. "We're all practically related here."

"Yeah," I say, and just have to giggle despite myself.

Nate and Todd catch up for a few moments, and I smile as I listen to them speak. What strikes me about the whole thing is that I don't even mind Todd coming over to the table, screaming out "Shuge" like, well, a fraternity boy. I can't help but think, how did I get here? How did I get to this place? When I came out to the Hamptons for the summer, that sort of thing would have driven me crazy. Would have proved to me that my feelings about Nate were one hundred percent dead on. When I came out here, I hated Nate. And now, not only am I sneaking around with him behind Jaime's back, I'm actually enjoying a conversation between Nate and one of his old fraternity brothers.

Our food arrives and Todd excuses himself after promising to call and make plans with Nate.

"Man, that guy was terrible," Nate says.

"You're terrible," I say, and Nate gives me a peck on the lips.

"So," Nate says, "what do you want to do after dinner? Go to the beach to relax? Or we could catch a movie. Or rent one, if you'd be more comfortable hanging out at home. I just don't want to exhaust you too much. My sister-in-law told me that when she was pregnant, she used to go to bed at nine o'clock, so I want to make sure we don't overexert you in any way."

"Thank you," I say. "That is so incredibly thoughtful."

"I try," Nate says, the sides of his lips curling into a shy smile. "So, what'll it be?"

"Let's go dancing."

An hour later, we pull up to an old boathouse somewhere between North Sea and Sag Harbor. We valet park the car—Nate's taken his mother's SUV in lieu of his usual Jeep, which is "too bumpy for a pregnant person"—and walk right in. There's no bouncer, a rarity for a Hamptons club. This place is so hard to find, so hidden in the woods, that I guess they figure that if you're able to actually find the place, you should get to go in.

We walk through a crowded living room into the main part of the boathouse. The entire inside is just like a big barn—no walls, incredibly high ceiling—and the back door to the outside is swung open. Nate and I grab a table, and from it, we can see the people sitting outside, on oversized couches, just looking at the water. But we came here to dance, so we stay inside.

A waiter comes over to our table and Nate asks him for one milk shake, two straws. The waiter's a bit confused, but I smile, thinking about how I teased Nate before. Most people don't really listen to what you say to them, but Nate does. He listens to everything I say.

I haven't heard much dance music this summer—anything that doesn't entail a twelve-piece orchestra isn't really my grandmother's speed—and I feel it pulse through me. It's loud, really loud, and it takes me out of my head. I can barely hear Nate as he asks me to dance, but I let him take my hand and lead me out to the center of the dance floor.

The room is crowded and sweaty, but there's a cool breeze coming in from off the water, so Nate and I gravitate toward the edge of the dance floor.

The breeze blows in, and Nate grabs me close. We're dancing as if it's a slow song, even though it's fast, but I don't care that everyone's staring at us. I don't think about what will happen later when I get back to my grandmother's house and have to face Jaime. I'm living in the moment. Living in this moment.

Nate pulls back and spins me around, and my dress twirls as I twirl. The song changes and now we're dancing fast, in time with the music. Nate's still holding my hand, and I feel myself getting hotter the more we dance.

I see our waiter set sodas and bottled water onto our table, but I don't want to leave the dance floor. I just want to keep dancing. I want to dance harder. I want to dance until my feet hurt and the sun comes up and it's tomorrow.

And then I feel it. It comes on suddenly, and I don't know what's hit me at first. One moment I'm dancing along to the music, and the next, I've got a sharp pain just below my belly. I'm not really showing yet—my stomach's a bit rounder than it normally is, but no one would know I'm pregnant just from looking at me. Still, I'm very aware of where the pain is. My hand instinctively flies to my stomach, and I pause for a moment.

"Are you all right?" Nate asks, leaning in so he's right by my ear.

"I'm fine," I say, straightening up. The pain goes away just as quickly as it came, and I smile at Nate. He grabs my hand and we continue dancing. I take a deep breath and look out the window to the water. Nate grabs my hand and I turn to face him. We're dancing, holding hands, and I can't stop smiling.

Seconds later, the pain is back. Only now, it's sharper, stronger.

"I think I need to sit down."

Nate ushers me over to an empty table and we sit down. Nate motions to a waiter, who brings over a pitcher of water. I feel better for a moment, but as I reach to grab the glass of water Nate has poured for me, the pain hits me again.

"I don't know what's wrong with me," I say.

"What does it feel like?" Nate asks. His voice tells me he's trying to be calm, but I can see panic forming in his eyes.

"My stomach," I say. "It's sharp pains in my stomach."

"Okay," Nate says. "I think we should go and maybe swing by the hospital. Get you checked out. I'm sure nothing's wrong, but just to be on the safe side." He says it like he's suggesting we stop in town for some ice cream at the Fudge Company.

The valet picks up Nate's car quickly—more people are coming into the club than leaving—and Nate opens the passenger door for me.

"Is it better when you sit up, or do you think you should lie down?" he asks.

"I guess I should lie down," I say. Nate opens the back door without a pause, and helps me in.

I climb into the backseat and curl up into the fetal position. Nate gets into the driver's seat and asks, "Should I call Jaime?"

"Yes, please," I say. And then: "I'm sorry."

"You have nothing to be sorry for," Nate says as I call out the number. "He's the father of this baby. If it was me, I'd want to know."

I can hear the ringing on the car's speaker phone, and Jaime's cell phone just rings and rings until it finally goes to voice mail.

"Do you know the numbers of any of his bandmates?" Nate asks.

"No," I say.

Nate calls information to get the number for the club where Jaime's performing.

"Are you feeling any better?" he asks while the operator gets the number for us.

"The sharp pains have become dull aches," I say.

"That's good," Nate says. "Dull is better than sharp, right?"

Information connects us to the bar where Jaime's playing, and the bartender asks us to hold on while he goes to look for Jaime.

"I can't find him anywhere, mate," the bartender reports back a few minutes later.

"Okay, thanks for checking," Nate says. And then, to me: "We're here."

We pull into the hospital parking lot and all I can think is that God is punishing me. And why shouldn't God punish me? I'm pregnant with one man's child and out with another.

The next call Nate makes is to my grandmother and mother. They're both at home. My grandmother tells Nate that they will meet us at the hospital. And then, under her breath: "We are spending an inordinate amount of time at the hospital this summer."

Forty-nine

The one advantage to going to the emergency room is that it seems to have brought my mother and grandmother together. When there's an emergency, you hardly have time to entertain the various grievances you have with someone. When there's an emergency, you just get into the car and go.

My grandmother and mother gather around the emergency room bed where I'm stationed, and Adan grabs my hand without saying a word. I squeeze his hand and see a smile play on his lips. In his eyes, I can see that I am his granddaughter. He loves me as if he's been my grandfather all along.

"Are you all right?" my grandmother asks, putting her hand on my cheek.

I look across the small hallway at Nate, who's seated in a chair directly across from my emergency room bed. I'm certain he can hear every word we're saying to one another, but I say it anyway.

"I think God is punishing me," I say, my voice almost a whisper. "I was out with Nate while Jaime was out at a gig."

"Thinking like that is not the recipe for a happy life," my grandmother says. "What's next? God will then punish Jaime because he was at a gig when something happened to you and couldn't be here at the hospital? The cycle would never end."

"I really don't believe God has quite as much time on his hands as you think," my mother says. I wonder for an instant whether my way of thinking has angered my mother, as if she thinks that I'm suggesting God is punishing her for something by making her sick.

My grandmother and Adan go to find the doctor on call and I'm left with my mother at my side.

"Everything's going to be okay, you know," she says matter-of-factly. "And if it isn't—which it will be, but just in case it isn't—then it wasn't meant to be, and this is the way it was meant to happen. No one's punishing you, least of all God. No amount of worrying is going to change it, so for now, we're going to sit tight, and breathe, and just know that whatever happens now will be the right thing."

I regard my mother.

"What?" she asks. "Why are you staring at me like that?"

"It's just that you're actually giving me good advice," I say.

"You're surprised?" she says.

"Giving me appropriate advice?" I say with a slight chuckle. "Yeah, I'm a bit surprised."

"Appropriate?" she says, feigning insult. "I've always just tried to be honest with you."

"But sometimes a kid doesn't need complete honesty," I say. "Sometimes a kid needs sugar coating. Hugs. Support."

"So, now I didn't hug you enough?"

"Sometimes you just need a mom to be a mom."

"I think you're going to be just fine," my mother says, and pushes back the hair that's fallen onto my forehead.

Over my mother's shoulder, I see my grandmother walking with Adan and the doctor. I explain the pain to the doctor, and he has a nurse begin to take my blood pressure.

"Has there been any blood?" the doctor asks. "Cramping?"

"No," I say.

"What were you doing when the pain started?" the doctor asks.

"Well, I feel really guilty about this," I explain.

"Why is that?" he asks calmly as he tells the nurse to draw some blood.

"I was dancing," I say.

"This isn't *Footloose*," the doctor says, smiling. "You can dance in the Hamptons."

I force a weak smile.

"Look, don't be so hard on yourself. Let's just take a peek at your baby, okay?"

Another nurse wheels over a large machine. The doctor adjusts my gown so that my belly sticks out, and he squirts some gel onto my stomach.

And there it is on the screen. My baby. I hear a loud, fast swooshing noise, which the doctor explains is the heartbeat. Then, he shows me the baby's head, body, and limbs, which are beginning to form.

"We have got a perfectly healthy baby here," he says, looking at the screen. Nate gets up from his chair across the hall and walks toward me. He stops once he's halfway across the hallway, and I motion for him to come closer, to take a look at the sonogram.

I look up and see my mother with tears in her eyes. My grandmother reaches for her hand, slowly, gingerly, and my mother grabs it and gives it a squeeze. Moments later, she grabs her for a hug.

Before I know it, my eyes are tearing as well.

"Everything is perfectly okay," the doctor explains. "What you were likely experiencing is called round ligament pain, and it's very common. I know it's early into your pregnancy, but already your body is expanding and changing to accommodate the growing baby. The sharp pains you were feeling were actually your ligaments making way for your growing uterus."

"So a sharp pain is okay?"

"Yes," the doctor says. "In fact, you'll often feel it when you exert yourself, like if you take a vigorous walk, or go dancing. But you might also feel it if you turn over in bed, or reach down for something. It's nothing to worry about at all. Next time you feel it, just sit down and relax until it passes."

"So everything's okay?" I ask. I know the doctor has told me that everything's all right a few times already, but I can't hear it enough.

"It's actually a good sign. It means that things are all moving in the right direction."

"Everything's moving in the right direction," I repeat. I look at Nate and see him staring down at me. Everything's moving in the right direction.

I couldn't agree more.

Fifty

"Excuse me, Hannah?" a nurse says, walking over to me just as the doctor is finishing up with us in the emergency room.

"Yes?" I say. I'm still beaming from ear to ear from the fact that everything's okay with the baby. And everything's falling into place in my world. My mother and grandmother are on their way to a reconciliation, I'm starting to see how Adan might have a place in my life, and I've got Nate standing right here by my side.

"The baby's father is here?" the nurse says. She does that twenty-something thing where she says it like it's a question, and I don't know how to respond.

"Let me give the two of you some space," Nate says, and walks back across the hallway, to sit back down on the chair to wait for me.

I turn toward the nurse and see Jaime trailing behind her.

"Babe," he says, and reaches down and gives me a hug as I'm still in the hospital bed.

"Thanks for coming," I say, and immediately regret it. I'm treating this as if it's a cocktail party—why am I thanking him for coming? He's the father! I'm incredibly aware of the fact that Nate is sitting across from us.

"What's he doing here?" Jaime says as he catches a glimpse of Nate out of the corner of his eye.

"He brought me to the hospital," I say.

"Oh," Jaime says. And then to Nate: "Well, thanks, man."

"No problem," Nate says.

"So," Jaime says to me. "Are you okay? What happened?"

I begin to tell Jaime what happened—how I was feeling sharp pains and I feared that something was wrong with the baby—but I can tell he's not really listening. Not listening in the way that someone who was worried about me would be. I can't help but picture the expression that was on his face when he walked into the hospital. There was something on his face that really shouldn't have been there. It wasn't sadness, or nervousness, or concern.

It was relief.

As I finish up the story, explaining how everything is okay now, I realize that Jaime was actually glad that there might have been something wrong with the baby. He was glad to have an out.

"Well," he says, "then, that's all great."

"You know you don't have to do this," I say. "I don't want you to feel like you have to stay out here with me or that you have to try to make things work just because I'm pregnant."

"That's not what I'm doing," he says, and he brushes something nonexistent off his nose. "That's not why I'm out here."

"I know that your mother is really religious and—"

"This isn't about my mother," Jaime says, cutting me off.

"I just mean . . . you don't have to be here for your family. I know how religious they are."

"This isn't about my family," Jaime says. "They don't even know I'm out here."

"Your family doesn't know you're here?"

"No," Jaime says back quietly. "I'm here because I decided to be."

I know he's claiming this as a moral victory, that he's proud of doing something outside of the prying eyes of his mother, but that doesn't mean he's separated himself from her. It means he was afraid to tell her.

"Your mother doesn't know I'm pregnant?" I ask.

"No," he says. "I thought that would make you happy. I know you can't stand her."

"It's not a question of whether or not I like your mother," I say. "Were you ashamed to tell them what happened?"

"It's no one's business," Jaime says, his voice barely a whisper. I know he's trying to make sure that Nate can't hear what he's saying, but at the rate we're going, I'm just going to repeat the whole conversation to Nate later, so it's really a moot point. "What we do, what we're doing, is no one's business but our own."

"I think you need to tell your mother," I say.

"Now that Gray is back in town, you're suddenly an expert on mothers?"

"I think you don't really want me to have this baby," I say. I think, but don't say: and you're hoping that I'll lose the baby or decide to terminate the pregnancy before you have to tell your mother. "You don't, do you?"

"So what if I don't?" Jaime says. "You made your decision and you don't really care what I think anyway."

"Well, I'm giving you an out here. I made my decision, and now you can make yours. You can walk away if you want. It's okay. I won't think less of you. No one will."

Jaime stands and looks at me for a long time. Finally, the doctor comes over to tell me that my grandmother has taken care of all my paperwork, so I can leave. Jaime's driven one of the Mattress King's cars to the hospital, so he decides to drive home on his own, telling me I should be with my mother and grandmother for the ride. But I know what he's really saying. I know he just wants a few minutes to himself. I know he needs it. I can see it on his face.

He walks away from me, and I watch him as he gets smaller and smaller, walking down the long corridor. I watch him walk away from me, and this time I know it is for good.

Fifty-one

"We heard you were in the hospital last night, so I came by to bring you these," Hunter says as he hands me a giant basket of flowers. There's a card tucked inside that says "Get Well Soon, Love and Hugs, Skylar and Hunter." It's written in the kind of loopy script that all girls in their early teens use. "Skylar picked them out. She loves hydrangeas and lilies."

"I love them, too," I say, and smile at Hunter. We grab iced teas and walk out toward the pool.

"So, you must be really happy that nothing's wrong with the baby," Hunter says. "Your grandmother told my dad that you were scared you were going to lose him. Or her. You know, the baby, whatever it is."

"I was," I say. "I was really scared. And now I'm just scared because I'm actually having a baby." I laugh nervously and Hunter raises an eyebrow at me.

"Are you scared because that guy left? Because Skylar and I didn't like him."

"I didn't really like him either," I say. "Well, toward the end, anyway. But now I think I'm just scared that I'm having a baby and I'm alone."

It occurs to me that I'm doing to Hunter the exact thing that

I resented my mother for my entire life: speaking to him as if he's my age, not his. I'm saying things that are inappropriate for his age. I'm about to try to change the subject, but Hunter persists.

"You're not alone," he says. "You've got Sugar now. And Skylar and I really like Sugar. So you don't have anything to worry about."

"Well, I don't really have him. Yes, we're going to try and make a go of things, but there's no knowing where that will lead. Anyway, we really shouldn't be talking about this at all. You're fourteen."

"Your mother says I have an old soul."

"My mother has no idea how to talk to children."

"Then it's a good thing I'm not a child," Hunter says. "I'm fourteen."

"Exactly," I say. "You're fourteen."

"Exactly." I may be a New York City attorney, but I am losing an argument with a fourteen-year-old. But I guess if he's a fourteen-year-old with a very old soul, I shouldn't beat myself up too much.

"Look, Hunter. I may not be alone, but I am this child's parent. And I'm scared."

"What are you scared of?"

"A million different things," I say, and look out at the ocean. The waves are rough today, and there's a red flag up, telling swimmers that it's not safe to go into the water.

"Tell me one," Hunter says.

I look at Hunter and remember that first night we met. How charmed I was by Hunter Kensington the fourth. How did a fourteen-year-old turn out to be one of my best friends in the Hamptons?

"I'm scared that I'll do a bad job," I say.

"You won't," Hunter says. "And Skylar and I will babysit for you whenever you want. She has two little sisters, so she's practically a baby nurse. She knows everything there is to know about babies."

"I'm scared that I'll mess up this human being's life irrevocably. I mean, that I'll screw it up in a way that can't be undone."

"I know what irrevocably means," he says.

"Of course you do."

"Go on."

"Can I tell you a secret?" I ask.

"Something that no one else knows?"

"Something that no one else knows," I confirm. "Something that I probably shouldn't say out loud."

"Then maybe you shouldn't say it out loud."

"You're right," I say, and take a sip of my iced tea.

"No, just say it," Hunter says, shaking his head, almost as if he's trying to screw up the courage to hear whatever awful dirty secret I've got to tell. "Whatever it is, you can say it to me."

"Okay," I say. "I'll tell you. When I was little I used to wish that my grandmother was my mother. When my mother was on shoots, I'd spend time with my grandmother and we always had the best time together. We'd go to amazing places, and she'd tell me these wonderful stories. She just led this totally unbelievable life, you know?"

"So did your mom," Hunter says. "I looked her up online. Did you know she won a Pulitzer?"

"Yes, Hunter. I knew that."

"Well, are you upset that you haven't lived the kind of life your mom and your grandmother lived?"

"No," I say, slowly, dragging out the *o*. I think, but don't say: Well, not until now, I wasn't.

"I always thought I had my grandmother as a role model,

that she was the perfect model of how to live your life and be happy. But I'm learning all these things about her this summer, and now, I just don't know."

"Like how that French dude is really your grandfather?"

"How do you know that?" I ask. It comes out as more of an accusation that I mean it to.

"Gray told me," he says.

"What else did Gray tell you?"

"Are you done telling me what you're scared of? Because it really doesn't sound like you have anything to be scared of at all. You actually sound like you're in great shape."

I take a big swig of iced tea and then I begin: "I'm afraid my kid will hate me. That I'll do the wrong thing. I'll try to do the right thing, but I won't succeed. I'm afraid I'll be a bad mom."

"Well, that's just silly," Hunter says. "You're going to be a great mom. I can tell."

"And exactly how can you tell?" I ask. This should be good.

"Because you're worried about it in the first place. When I interviewed Dr. Simon for this medical drama I'm working on—don't tell anyone about it, it's on the down low—he said that the doctors you have to worry about are the ones who never question what they do. That the worst doctors are the ones who think that everything they do is above reproach. That means they think they can't be touched."

"I know what above reproach means."

"Of course you do," Hunter says, giving me a tiny grin. "Well, anyway, Dr. Simon said that the best doctors are the ones who occasionally pause and wonder if they're doing the right thing. Which ultimately makes them stronger, not just as doctors, but as people. So, you're just like those good doctors. You're questioning everything, which means that you are totally ready to be a mom. And you're going to be really great at it."

"Thanks, Hunter," I say. "That really means a lot. Especially coming from you."

"I know."

Fifty-two

"I can't believe you're coming back."

"You don't want me back at the firm?" I ask Priya, feigning distress.

"Funny," she says. "You know I can't wait for you to come back; this place is so boring without you. I just didn't think you'd come back."

"It's time to get back to real life," I say, and as I say it, I wonder which one is actually my real life: the one I had before in the city, the one I ran away from, or my life out here?

"And you think you'll have a better life working at a New York City law firm?"

"Well," I answer, "I've got maternity leave coming up before you know it, so taking care of a baby will be a welcome break."

"Yes," Priya says. "I've heard that having a newborn is really relaxing."

We giggle and it dawns on me how many changes I've got coming up in my life. Before I came out here for the summer, I was completely stuck. No job. No relationship. No contact with my own mother. My life was stagnating and I didn't even realize it.

Now I'm living a completely different life. After years of barely speaking, my mother and I now actually talk, instead of just throwing veiled insults at each other. I think I'm beginning to understand her, and that she's beginning to understand me. And I really like having her in my life. I look forward to hearing her opinion on things, even though I know I'm not always going to agree with what she's got to say. This time with her has been precious. Now that I actually know who she is, I'll be able to tell my future child all about her.

What I want to say to my child is this: My mother loved me very much, and she loved you very much, before you were even born. She wasn't average, or even normal. She was extraordinary. And she thought I was, too. Even though she's not here anymore, she'll always be with us. A presence like Gray Goodman doesn't just go away.

My relationship with my grandmother has changed, but hopefully with time we can get back to where we were before. And now that Adan is part of her life, he's a part of my life, too. I didn't grow up with a grandfather, but maybe now we can make up for what I missed all these years.

I don't have Jaime anymore. But I have Nate. And Hunter, and even Skylar.

My life is moving in a completely different direction, and I'm not scared anymore. I couldn't be happier about what's to come. Maybe going back to the city will be a fresh start for me. Maybe it will be the start of lots of good things.

Priya and I hang up and I go upstairs to have lunch with my mom. She hasn't left her bed for the past couple of days. Nurses have been monitoring her every move, and she seems to be getting worse. She's supposed to be resting, but she has a steady stream of people coming to her room for meals and tea.

As I reach the door, Hunter and Skylar walk out of her room, holding empty mugs.

"Think she's ready for lunch?" I ask.

"I don't think so," Skylar says.

"We brought croissants from the Golden Pear," Hunter says. "Were we not supposed to do that?"

"It was so sweet of you to visit. It's great that you did that. Thank you," I say. "We can have lunch later."

I walk into the room and see my mom in her bed. She's hardly recognizable—Gray Goodman never relaxes. She's always working or thinking about working. It's strange to see her at rest like this. It's strange to see someone so headstrong have no choice in the matter.

"Hey," I say.

"You just missed Hunter and Skylar," she says. The look on her face shows me that it pains her to even speak. I make a mental note to ask the nurses later whether all of these visitors are making my mother feel better or worse.

"I saw them in the hallway," I say, and sit down on a chair next to her bed.

She props herself up on one elbow and asks me: "Do you think they're sleeping together yet?"

"Oh god," I say. "I really don't want to think about that."

"Maybe they're not," my mother says, nodding toward my belly. "Maybe your condition has scared them straight."

"That's not funny," I say, and my mother lies back down in her bed with a big smile on her face.

"Who's ready for lunch?" my grandmother says, opening the door. Her chef follows her in and begins unloading a huge tray of food onto the desk.

"Hunter and Skylar just stuffed me full of pastries," my mother says. "I'm not really hungry."

"Well," my grandmother says, "you have to eat. It's important to keep up your strength." She looks at the nurse for a show of support, but the nurse suddenly seems very interested in her fingernails. "Well, I don't want to hear any excuses from you, mademoiselle," my grandmother says, her attention now focused on me. "You're eating for two."

I get up from my chair and take a peek at what the chef has sent up. I grab a roll and take a nibble and then pour myself an iced tea.

"There is something that I want from you," my mother says to my grandmother.

"What's that, honey?" my grandmother asks, and folds herself into the chair next to my mother's bed. She takes my mother's hand, and I can see in her eyes that there isn't anything she wouldn't do for my mother. I know that my mother never really let my grandmother mother her very much. She never lets any of us really take care of her, even now, and I can see my grandmother's maternal instincts at play. "Whatever you want."

"It's my dying wish that you marry Adan."

"I beg your pardon?" my grandmother says.

"You know you love to throw a party," my mother says.

"I'm not exactly in the mood to throw a party," my grandmother says, nervously laughing. "And I don't like this talk of dying wishes. Don't speak like that."

"You have to make me legitimate," my mother says. She smiles and I can't help but chuckle. I turn to look at my grandmother and she's pursing her lips.

Fifty-three

My mother can't make it out to the pool today. She can barely get out of bed. So instead of following through with our plan to eat lunch outside, I've brought sandwiches on a large tray up to her room.

"Today we have fresh turkey breast with baked brie and honey mustard on croissants," I say, playing the role of chef. "The turkey breast is fresh off the bone and the honey mustard and croissants are both homemade."

My mother doesn't laugh, in fact she doesn't respond at all. She just lays still in her bed, looking out the window.

"Mom?"

"Oh, yes, Hannah," she says, turning her head toward me. It seems like the very act of turning her head is painful. "Hi."

Her skin is paler than it's been and her eyes are bloodshot. Her hands are so thin they look like paper—you can see her veins popping out. I avert my eyes and concentrate very hard on the pitcher of iced tea. I offer my mother a glass but she either doesn't hear me or ignores me, I'm not sure which, so I pour two glasses and set hers down on the tray next to her bed.

"It's a lovely day out today," I say. She doesn't respond, so I repeat it a bit louder. She still doesn't respond, so I ask her if I should open her window.

"Isn't that breeze great?" I ask.

"It's too cold," my mother says, and I pop up to close the window.

I sit back down and take a bite of my sandwich. I chew slowly, since there's nothing left to talk about. Nothing left to say.

I used to run away from talks with my mother, never wanted to hear anything she had to say, but now I would give anything to have a real conversation with her. Now I would love it if she could just muster up the energy to speak. If the marijuana didn't knock her out so much that all she can do is stare out a window all day.

Is this what will be left? When she's gone, will I be left treasuring the old times we had together? Will all the bad memories turn into joyful ones? Do we turn the old unhappy memories into blissful ones we can treasure for the rest of our lives? Or will I end up longing for one last argument with Gray?

I finish eating my sandwich and offer my mother some of hers. She declines with a slight flick of the wrist. Not knowing what else to do, I pack up the tray and leave.

"This is it, isn't it?" I ask my grandmother. "The end?" She's standing by the edge of the pool, looking out into the ocean.

"It would appear that way," she says, taking a sip of her cocktail. My grandmother never drinks during the day; it's one of her life rules. Today, however, she sits outside in broad daylight drinking vodka. My grandmother's not drinking to enjoy today. She's not drinking to be social. She's drinking to get drunk.

"Think a sip of that would hurt the baby?" I say.

"Don't even think about it," she says back without looking at me.

I'm about to explain that it was just a joke, but then she continues.

"You're going to see, the love you have for this baby will be unlike anything you've ever felt before."

"I've been in love before," I say. "I think I know what love is. I love you."

"Still?" she asks, looking at me. "After everything?"

"After everything."

"Well, that's good to hear. But you'll love your baby in a different way than you love me, or your mother, or Nate. It's something you've never experienced before. It will take your breath away."

"Is that how you feel about my mother?"

"Yes," she says. "And the way I feel about you."

"That's how I feel about you, too," I say.

"No, it's not," she says with a gentle smile. "But you can't see that yet. You will, though. You'll see."

"This must be so difficult for you," I say.

"It is," she says. "You'd think that someone who's experienced as much death as I have would know how to deal with it by now, but each time I lose a loved one, it hurts just as much as when I lost your grandfather. It never gets easier to lose someone you love. And now, your mother . . ."

She trails off for a second as her eyes tear up, dabbing at her eyes with the linen napkin that was wrapped around the highball glass.

"Your mother and you are the most important things in my world. Men be damned, all I ever really cared about was you two. And now, to be losing your mother. It's almost too much to bear. I know she hates me—"

"She doesn't hate you," I say.

"I've not made her last days any easier, and I'll never forgive myself for that."

"I forgive you," I say. "She forgives you."

My grandmother turns to me and opens her arms wide. I go to her and get inside the space her arms have created and let her hug me. I just stand there, breathing in her gentle scent while she squeezes me tight. She kisses my head and I put my arms around her.

"I don't know about that," she says, and I tell her that everything is okay.

"It's not okay," she says. "My baby is dying."

I hear her cry. Softly, barely making a sound, but I can feel her chest heaving. And then I start to cry, too. Only I don't do the soft gentle cry. I'm sobbing uncontrollably, and my grandmother breaks from our embrace to hand me the half-used linen napkin from around her drink.

"We'll get through this," she says. "Together. I just wish she wasn't in so much pain. It's hard to watch her suffer like this."

"Didn't you once tell me that this is the best possible way to die, as far as dying is concerned? You find out you're dying, but have time to get your affairs in order, say good-bye to the people you love?"

"I guess I did say that once," she says as she puts her hand to my face. "I'm glad I got to see her, and I would like to think that you'll treasure this time with her as well. Am I right?"

"Yes," I say.

"Well, then, I suppose that's something."

Fifty-four

My mother would have hated her funeral. A packed house—it is everything she ever said she didn't want. Seven major newspapers are here to cover the event, and so many people came that we need four guest books just to record everyone's names.

I suggested that perhaps a small graveside ceremony with only family might be more in line with what my mother might have wanted, but my grandmother wouldn't hear of it. She insisted that her daughter get the love and respect she deserved, and the pageantry that such an occasion merited. My grandmother feels it's important to mark off milestones—happy or sad—in a grand way. "If you haven't celebrated someone's life with a funeral, it's as if they never existed."

I wonder for a moment what she would want for her funeral, but then realize that if the Nazis couldn't get her, my grandmother won't be dying any time soon. And anyway, she's probably already planned the whole thing out with her party planner.

Jewish funerals take place quickly—it's imperative that you get the person into the ground as soon as possible after their death—so my mother's funeral is held just two days after she dies. And because we had no time to go out and buy clothes that weren't white, my grandmother has her personal shopper come over the day before the funeral. I can't believe life is actually going on the day after my mother has just died, so I don't come downstairs to see the personal shopper. Instead, I just let my grandmother pick something out for me. I know I'll never be able to wear the outfit ever again, so what does it matter what I wear?

The black shift dress she chooses for me is uncomfortable. When I first tried it on, it fit well enough; it is only after wearing it for more than ten minutes that I realize that the back seam is digging into my skin. But I don't really mind. Somehow it seems right to be physically uncomfortable for the occasion.

The funeral director informs us that, before the service begins, the immediate family will gather in a back room to have time alone with the body. Then, we'll step out into the funeral home to greet guests and accept condolences. But my grandmother already knows all of this.

After she has her time alone with my mother, it's my turn. I promise my grandmother that I'll follow her out, but I never leave the back room.

I sit down and just stare at the casket. Before she left, my grandmother put photographs of us into the casket. She said that she didn't know what happens after you die, but just in case you go to see a higher power, she wanted that higher power to know that Gray Goodman was loved.

I don't really know what to do with myself. I can't bring myself to peek inside the casket, as the funeral director suggested, and I don't have anything to put inside of it anyway. But I can't go outside either. I just can't face anyone. I can't even face my friends who have driven two and a half hours from the city to be here for me. Somehow it seems right to just sit here, with my dead mother, by myself.

The door opens, and I search my mind for something to tell the funeral director when he asks me why I'm still in here with my mother. Maybe I can tell him that I'm praying?

But it's not the funeral director. It's Hunter.

He opens the door and when I see his adorable face, it makes me well up with tears. I tell myself it's just the pregnancy hormones, that I'm really not this emotional, but I know that I'm lying to myself.

"I brought you a handkerchief," Hunter says. He extends his hand and I take the handkerchief. It's embroidered with his initials.

"This is your handkerchief," I say.

"But you'll need one today," he says. "You don't have to give it back to me."

I stand up from my chair and walk over to Hunter. Without saying a word, I hug him. I begin to cry, but I can't stop hugging him. Hunter doesn't try to pull away. We just stand there, two motherless kids, hugging, until the funeral director comes in and tells me it's time to take my mother.

"Do you need more time?" he asks me.

"No," I say, using Hunter's hankie to sop up the tears. "I think I'm ready now."

Hunter and I walk out of the room, holding hands, and Nate is waiting for us on the other side of the door. He grabs my free hand and asks if I want to walk out with him. Technically, I'm supposed to be walking out with just my family, but I'm so happy that Nate is there that I don't want him to leave.

"I think that Gray would have liked for both boys to walk with you," my grandmother says.

So that's how we walk into the funeral. Led by my grandmother and Adan, I walk to the front row with Hunter on one side, Nate on the other.

I try to scan the crowd as I walk down the aisle with Hunter and Nate, but it's hard. Priya is waiting for us when we get to the front row, and she hugs me before I sit down. The rabbi gives a beautiful sermon, and then it's time for people to speak.

First up is one of my mother's editors, and then her agent gives a tearful good-bye. A few friends speak, and then the ceremony is almost over.

Nate leans over and asks me if I want to say a few words, but I shake my head no.

"You don't have to," Hunter says, and grabs my hand.

"Thank you," I say, but then I find myself standing up, headed toward the altar anyway.

"My mother would have hated this," I say. The crowd erupts into a fit of laughter, which calms my nerves a bit, but I realize that I have no idea what I'm about to say.

"My mother and I didn't always get along. In fact, for most of my adult life, we barely spoke. She never really understood me, and I never really understood her, but spending all of this time out here together this summer, something happened. It's like we were both able to step outside of ourselves for a minute and really see the other person. For the first time in our lives.

"Now that I'm having a baby of my own, I understand what's really important. My mother once told me that she named me Hannah because Hannah means 'grace,' that I'm a part of her. Just as this baby will be a part of me. But the truth is, this baby will also be a part of her.

"I know that I'll miss my mother with all my heart for the rest of my life, but I can take solace in the fact that I'll always have a part of her inside of me, and so will my child. So, in that way, she will never be forgotten. She'll always be with us."

The rabbi shakes my hand once I'm done and I go back to my seat. Nate grabs my hand and I sob uncontrollably.

Fifty-five

Shiva is the weeklong period of mourning in Judaism. It begins immediately after the funeral. Traditionally, family members and close family friends gather at the home of a family member to mourn. It is customary for neighbors and close family friends to supply the food, as mourners are not supposed to eat their own food, especially on the first day of shiva. Mourners do not bathe or shower, nor do they wear leather shoes or jewelry. Any and all mirrors in the house are covered, and the mourners themselves are supposed to sit on hard stools or low boxes.

Shiva in the Hamptons is an altogether different animal.

My grandmother's house is completely filled with people, and I can barely get through the crowd without one person or another stopping me to tell me how sorry they are. The entire town of Southampton has turned out. Jaime does not show up.

I didn't really expect him to.

The house is crowded with all of the guests, but my grandmother told me that she didn't want to do it outside, since that would be more festive than the occasion merited. But still, it's not an entirely somber scene. But for the fact that it is my mother's shiva, it would be quite a nice party. A caterer's been called in, and my grandmother's party planner is flitting about. I wonder for a moment whether she's ever planned a soiree on such short notice. Is it possible that they started planning this a few weeks ago? I try not to think about that and instead stuff a puffed pastry in my mouth, courtesy of a passing waiter.

I look around the room and don't know quite what to do with myself. I feel completely empty inside. Like I'll never be able to feel anything ever again. How am I supposed to be with all of these people right after my mother has died? I don't want to make small talk. I don't want to talk about how amazingly talented she was. If I hear one more person tell me that her work will live on for the rest of time, I will shove a stuffed mushroom cap right into his or her face.

Skylar fights through the crowd and finds me. She gives me a cold glass of water and tells me that we should sneak out to meet the boys outside. That's exactly how she says it, "the boys," and I can't think of anything else I'd rather do. An escape. The perfect plan. I know that the new me doesn't run away from things anymore, but surely there's an exception for the day you bury your mother.

"That's a fantastic idea, Sky," I say, and she grabs my hand to lead me through the crowd. I notice that her fingernails are painted hot pink. I decide that I should paint my fingernails hot pink, too.

"Oh," she says, turning back to face me. She grabs both of my hands, looks me straight in the eye, and says: "I'm really sorry about your mom."

"Thanks, honey," I say. I know that it was hard for her to say these words, and that only makes them more meaningful.

She gives my hands a little squeeze and then turns again to navigate our way through the crowd. Through the myriad of faces,

I catch a glimpse of Adan, sitting on the couch. He's surrounded by people and deep in conversation, but I can tell that he feels terribly alone. I recognize this because I feel the same way.

"Mind if we make a quick detour?" I ask Skylar. She nods— a "whatever you want" sort of gesture—and we head toward the couch.

"Hannah," a familiar voice says, and I feel his hand on my arm.

"Tim," I say. I try to hide the surprise in my voice, but I'm shocked to see such a senior partner from my firm here.

"I was so sorry to hear about your mother," he says.

"Thank you," I say as Skylar comes to stand by my side. Did Hunter tell her that she was not allowed to leave me alone today? "This is my friend, Skylar."

"Nice to meet you," Tim says, and now it's his turn to hide the surprise in his face. I know he's wondering why I've made friends with a fourteen-year-old, but I try not to think about it.

I think of my mom as I instinctively look down at Tim's hands. Still prep-school-boy perfect.

"It was really nice of you to come today," I say.

"You know how I feel about you," Tim says. I don't want to tell him that, in fact, I do not actually know how he feels about me. Does it even matter? "I know it's been rocky with the firm, but I'm here as a friend."

"Thanks," I say. I don't really know what else to say. Shiva talk is nothing if not awkward.

"For now, you should just concentrate on you," Tim says. "If you need anything, though, I hope you know you can always call me."

"I appreciate that. And I'm really looking forward to seeing you in the fall."

"We're all really happy to have you back," Tim says, putting his hand on my arm.

"Thanks," I say, and really mean it. "Thank you so much."

Forty minutes later, we've met Tim's whole family, along with a number of Adan's friends from his tennis club. Skylar is probably about ready to kill me, but I give her major credit, because she keeps smiling the whole time. When we're done talking to Tim and his family, I tell her that I want to meet her parents to tell them how wonderful she is and she tells me that yes, her parents are here, but no, I may not meet them because it is Time. To. Meet. The. Boys.

So I let her lead me out toward the pool. It's late afternoon already, that magical time when it's not quite nighttime, but it's no longer day. The sun is in just the right place in the sky and the breeze from the water is cool and refreshing. I could live in this time of day.

Nate and Hunter are sprawled out on lounge chairs, and as we approach, Nate sits upright and pats the lounge chair, telling me where he wants me to sit down. They've got two pitchers in between them—water and iced tea—and an open bottle of white wine. I pick up a glass and pour myself some iced tea. In an instant, I realize that this isn't the iced tea that my grandmother's chef has been making us all summer. This is the tea from China that my mother drinks. They must have steeped it and then let it cool down since they knew I'd be drinking the iced tea. I look up from my first sip and everyone's staring at me, just waiting for my reaction.

"It's delicious," I say. "Thanks, guys."

"Skylar made it," Hunter proudly says.

"It was Nate's idea," Skylar says, smiling toward Nate.

"Thank you," I say, and look up at Nate. He kisses me lightly on the lips.

Nate puts his arms around me, and we look out at the ocean together. His arms around me are like a blanket—they make me feel safe and warm. We stay like this awhile, just sitting silently and staring out at the ocean, listening to the waves crash on the sand.

"So, this is where the real party is."

We all whip our heads around to find my grandmother standing behind us, right at the edge of our lounge chairs. Nate and Hunter both practically fall over themselves to offer her a seat, but she says that she prefers to stand.

"How are you holding up?" I ask her.

"That's what I was coming out here to ask you."

"Not great," I say. "I feel like my insides have been torn out. But I'm trying to breathe again, so I guess that's an improvement."

"Same here," my grandmother says. She picks up the bottle of white wine and pours herself an enormous glass before sitting down next to Hunter and Skylar. She takes a few sips—gulps really—and looks out at the ocean.

I'm suddenly overcome with the desire to jump right into the water. It's as if I feel dirty and it will make me clean. As if immersing myself will make everything better, let me start over again.

"I'm just going to walk out to the ocean for a sec," I say under my breath, and get up to walk out to the beach. I hear Nate jump up behind me and then some grumbling as everyone decides to follow suit.

But I can't stop walking. I walk through the sand, faster and faster, even though the tiny grains try to slow down my feet. Nate catches up to me and I let him grab my hand, but I keep walking. I walk until I reach the edge of the water, where the waves lick the sand. I wade in, until the water hits my knees, and I'm vaguely aware that Nate must be getting his pants soaked, but I keep going. I don't want to stop.

And then we're in up to our shoulders, Nate and I. We're both completely submerged, and I can breathe once more. I release my hand from Nate's and bring it up to my face, splashing the cool water all over my face and my hair. I glance over at Nate and he's just looking at me.

"You okay?" he asks tentatively. He doesn't look scared exactly, but he does look a bit confused.

"Yes," I say. "Yes." I dunk my head into the water, and when I resurface, I see Hunter and Skylar coming into the water, too. Hunter throws off his sports jacket before coming in, but they both come in completely clothed.

The dress I wore to my mother's funeral is soaked, completely ruined, I'm sure, but I don't care. It feels right.

"My pants are really heavy now," Hunter says to Nate. Nate laughs and tells Hunter that his are, too.

I look back to the edge of the water and see my grandmother slowly making her way into the waves. I swim toward her, and we meet just as she's knee deep.

"We should turn back and go into the house to dry off," I say, trying to lead her back onto the sand.

"I want to go in, too," she says quietly, so we walk right back into the water, fully clothed, holding hands.

"Come on in," Nate calls to us, "the water's fine!"

The truth is, the water's a bit chilly, but my grandmother and I laugh as we swim out to everyone else.

"This feels good," my grandmother says to me as we wade deeper and deeper into the ocean.

"I know," I say back. I lean my head back and the cold water feels good on my head.

"Are there sharks out here?" Skylar asks, and for some reason, it's the funniest thing I ever heard.

"One or two sharks have been spotted out here," Hunter says, in all seriousness. "But they normally don't come this close to shore, so we should be okay."

I see Nate go under the water and I know what's coming next: a blood-curdling scream let out by Skylar, whose ankle he's just grabbed.

"That is not funny!" she screams, splashing water at Nate as he comes up for air.

"It was a little funny," Nate says, and looks to Hunter.

"It wasn't funny at all," Hunter says, swimming over to Skylar and putting his arms around her. As she hugs him and puts her back toward Nate, Hunter gives Nate the "thumbs-up" signal and smiles widely.

"I think we've all had enough," I say, and just like that, we all head back to the shore.

My grandmother has us all take off our wet clothes in the mud room and then provides a change of clothing for each and every one. And then, with our wet heads and makeup dripping, we go back to see our fellow mourners.

At around nine o'clock, the guests start leaving. Hunter and Skylar say their good-byes (although Skylar gives Nate the cold shoulder), and I tell Nate that I'd like to spend some time alone with my grandmother, so maybe he should head home for the night.

"I'm not leaving you," Nate says with a laugh, as if I've just suggested the silliest thing he's ever heard. "I'll go upstairs to bed.

You hang out with your grandmother as long as you like, but I'll be up there waiting when you're ready."

I don't really want Nate to go home, not really. I'm glad that he'll be upstairs waiting for me when I'm ready, but I wonder how he knows that. He kisses me on the forehead and then hops up the stairs before I have a moment to respond to him.

I walk into the kitchen and find my grandmother sitting at the counter, watching a kettle boil up some hot water for tea. I sit down next to her and don't say a word.

She puts her arm around me and says: "It's just you and me now, kiddo."

I used to love it when it was just my grandmother and me. In fact, I longed for times when I could have her all to myself. I understand why everyone falls in love with her, why men fall at their feet for the chance to be near her. Because that's how I feel, too. That's how I've felt about her my whole life. As I sit next to her at the kitchen counter, I realize that even with everything's that happened, her secrets completely exposed, the way I feel about her hasn't changed. I see her differently now, but I still love her. And I don't feel angry anymore.

Still, it's strange when she tells me that it's just the two of us. Somehow, that doesn't feel completely right anymore. I never felt it before, but now I feel my mother's absence, a weight hanging between us.

The teakettle screams and my grandmother insists on being the one to get up and take it off the stove. She sets out two teacups and pours.

"So, what is there left to do?" she asks me. "I need to be busy."

She said something similar to me when I first came out to visit her for the summer. Something about a project, and then the next

thing I knew, I was locked into Georges Mandel for five hours, trying on swimsuits and dresses. I'm really not up for being my grandmother's project again, so I need to think quickly on my feet.

"Well," I say, "you could act out your daughter's dying wish."

And there are those pursed lips again.

Fifty-six

Priya wasn't exactly mad at me for skipping out on the first day of shiva, but she wasn't exactly happy about it either. It's just that you're not allowed to really yell at a friend right after her mother's died. So she comes to the second day of shiva with a huge box of Tate's cookies. A delicacy she knows I cannot refuse. And it works—as long as she's holding the box of cookies, I'm seated right next to her, nibbling away.

Priya's out here with her parents for the weekend. Her mother has parked us at one of the couches in a central location in the living room, since she says that the immediate family must be accessible so that everyone can offer their condolences. Priya's mother has a strong sense of family honor, and I don't have the heart to argue otherwise. She stands near us, and refuses to sit down, so that she may direct guests toward me, the mourning daughter.

"I didn't know that a shiva call was a 'plus one' kind of event," I say to Priya in between bites, as we sit side by side on the couch. The crowd is considerably thinner than it was yesterday, so we're able to see through all the people to the dining room, where Detective Moretti is helping himself to the buffet.

"Didn't you bring Nate?" Priya teases back.

"Oh, that's different. I can't get rid of him," I explain. "He refuses to leave."

"I knew I liked him from the moment I met him."

I'm about to say "me too," but that isn't entirely true, and Priya knows it, so I don't say anything at all.

"You know," Priya says, looking around, "this is the nicest shiva I've ever been to."

"Yeah," I say. "I think my mom would have really liked it."

"Really? I think she would have thought it was a disgusting display of wealth and excess, and completely inappropriate to the occasion."

"True," I say, nodding my head in agreement. "But I hear the salmon's really good."

"It is," Priya says. "If Vince and I get married, will your grandmother plan our wedding for us?"

"You and Detective Moretti are getting married?"

"I said *if*. *Shhhh*," Priya stage whispers, just as Detective Moretti—I'm supposed to call him Vince now, but I just can't stop calling him Detective Moretti—walks toward us. He brings back a huge plate of food and I'm glad that someone is taking advantage of the enormous spread that my grandmother's party planner has laid out for today's guests. There are no cold cut platters or heroes in the Hamptons, just filet mignon, antipasto, and an entire poached salmon with the head still attached.

"Priya told me that you liked artichokes," Detective Moretti tells me as he sits down next to me and then thrusts the heaping plate into my lap. It's filled with a sampling of everything from the buffet, along with a ton of artichokes.

"I'm not really hungry," I tell him, "but thank you."

He ignores me and puts a linen napkin into my lap and then

holds out a fork and a knife for me. We regard each other for a moment. There's no way I'm giving up my chocolate chip cookies. Then he says, "I can't help it. I'm Italian. I just want to feed you until you feel better."

He eventually wins, and I take the fork and knife and pick at the artichokes.

"So, I hear you're going back to your law firm," Detective Moretti says. "Good for you."

"Thank you," I say. "But believe it or not, I'm thinking about taking a position with the State Attorney General."

"You are?" Priya asks, practically dropping the bag of cookies as she turns to face me.

"Counselor Sugarman is rubbing off on you," Detective Moretti says with a smile.

"I'm thinking about it very seriously," I say, turning toward Priya. "I was chatting with Tim yesterday and he's going to set up an informational meeting with them for me in a few weeks."

"I can't believe you're going to abandon me at the firm," she says.

"I'm sorry," I say.

"Well, it will certainly be better hours, I hope," Priya says.

"I think so," I say. "It won't be the money I'd be getting at the firm, but it will be a good income, and hopefully more free time to spend with the baby."

"And your new grandfather," Priya says, nudging me in the arm so that I can see Adan approaching. He comes over to the couch, and Detective Moretti insists on giving up his seat so Adan can sit down with us.

"How are you holding up?" he asks.

"Okay, I guess," I say. "How about you?"

"This is incredibly difficult," he says, "but I'm trying to focus on the good—that I got to spend so much time with your mother this summer. Not the fact that I've lost her."

"Easier said than done," I say. I've tried out the very same rationalization often over the past few days, with mixed results. It's easy to tell your head that you're happy for the little time you had with Gray—getting your heart to believe it is the real challenge.

"True," Adan says. "But now I have you in my life. And whoever's in your belly. So, it's the beginning of lots of wonderful things for our family."

Our family.

"Yes," I say. "It is."

Fifty-seven

"There's a short exam and then a sonogram today," the nurse tells me. She leads the way back to the exam room, and as I walk back with my grandmother, I realize how much has changed since my first appointment with the doctor. For my first appointment, I was with my grandmother and I was the only pregnant woman at the office without a partner. Today, I'm with my grandmother, again, but I don't feel quite so alone anymore. The doctor is pleased with my progress in the exam, so we head down the hall for the sonogram. The technician squirts some gel onto my belly and begins.

"Do you want to know what you're having?" the technician asks me, interrupting my train of thought.

"Yes," I say, without giving it a second thought. I look to my grandmother and she is nodding her head yes along with me.

"I'm just going to ask you to move a little to your side," she says. "I want to get a really good picture here."

"This family is big on good pictures," my grandmother says, taking my hand and smiling.

The technician looks confused for a minute and then catches on.

"Goodman," she says, looking at my chart and then at me. "You're Gray Goodman's daughter, aren't you?"

For the first time in my life, I don't hesitate. I just say yes. I am Gray Goodman's daughter. And it feels good to say it out loud.

"I was really sorry to hear about your mom," she says. "But I'm hoping I've got some news here that will make you really happy. You're having a girl."

My eyes well up with tears and I can't control it.

"A girl," my grandmother repeats. She leans down and kisses me on the cheek.

"What did you think you were having, Hannah?" the technician asks.

"I didn't know," I say. "But I'm so happy that it's a girl. I have the perfect name for her. Grace."

"Well, here's a little picture of her," she says as she hands me a printout of the sonogram. It's hard to see her, but when I squint I can just make out a tiny head and a tiny body.

"A baby girl," my grandmother says. "That's just perfect, isn't it?"

I want to tell my grandmother that I don't deal in perfect anymore. But I understand that this is a moment my grandmother and I will remember for a very long while. This is a time when we can burst out of ourselves, get away from the pain we've been feeling for so long after the death of my mother. So instead I say, "Yes. It really is."

Fifty-eight

It's only been a few days since shiva officially ended, and my grandmother and I really don't know what to do with ourselves. She decides to host a cocktail hour on Friday night to get everyone together before we all scatter for the weekend. I think she just can't bear to have an empty house.

All of the people I've come to know and love over the course of this summer turn up: Hunter and Sklyar, Adan, and of course, Nate. Always Nate.

All the usual suspects.

"I would like to show you all," my grandmother says, "for the first time, my great-grandchild."

She holds up the sonogram picture with a flourish, and everyone gathers around.

"Do you know what you're having?" Skylar asks.

"A baby, silly," Hunter says, and grabs her side.

"I know that," she says, wiggling out from his grip. "But a girl or a boy?"

"Yes," I say, looking directly at Nate. I wonder if I was supposed to have asked his opinion on the matter, but he's smiling from ear to ear, so it seems as if we're on the same page. "It's a girl."

My eyes well up with tears and I can't control it. Nate swoops over and kisses me right on the mouth. When he pulls away, I can see that he's tearing up, too.

"We're having a girl," he says, which only makes my tears flow even faster.

"It's a girl!" my grandmother repeats. She grabs for Adan's hand and he hugs her tightly.

"Pay up," Skylar says to Hunter.

"Oh, man," Hunter says. "I had good money on the fact that you were having a boy," Hunter says to me, taking out his wallet. "Are we sure it's a girl?"

My grandmother walks over and hands Hunter the picture.

"I'm not sure what Gray would think of the composition of this picture," Hunter says, and we all laugh. "I mean, what's the story you were trying to tell?"

"Actually, I think the composition is good," Skylar continues, "but why'd you decide to go with black-and-white, not color?"

"Color costs you more," I say with a smile as Hunter hands the picture back to me.

I look at the little picture of my growing baby and then look around the room. Everyone's smiling, happy. And I have to admit that in spite of myself, I'm happy, too. With all these people, do I have a choice? They force happiness on you, whether you want it or not.

Is this what family's all about? I never really gave it much thought, being an only child. Having a mother who was an only child. There weren't a ton of people around me as I grew up, no siblings to play with every day, no cousins to see at holidays. It feels strange to have this many people around me for an important moment in my life. But I've always had my grandmother. The one true constant in my life. And now, it seems, I've got a few more constants.

A month has passed and things are starting to go back to normal. Not normal, really, but it's just that after about a month, people stop asking how you're feeling and expect you to live your regular life again. It's one of the things that struck me most about Adam's death, and it's something that I've been discussing a lot with my new therapist.

Nate managed to find me a therapist who splits her time between Manhattan and Southampton, so I can continue seeing her once summer is over and we've moved back into the city. Where we'll be moving in together.

I'm nervous and excited and about a million other emotions about taking this huge step with Nate, especially since he lives on the Upper West Side and I abhor the Upper West Side, but Hunter says that everyone on the Upper West has a baby, so I'll fit right in. And he's especially happy that Nate and I will be living just a hop across the park from him and Skylar, both of whom live on the Upper East Side, so we'll get to see them all the time.

But for now, we're all still here. In the Hamptons. Summer has a few weeks left in it still.

"It's a wonder he isn't worried about marrying my grandmother," I tell Nate. We're out at my grandmother's pool, and from our chaise longues, we can see my grandmother and Adan on the porch with my grandmother's wedding planner. "It's like she didn't do him in the first time, so now he's back for more."

"You're such a romantic," Nate says, leaning back in his chair with his eyes closed. He has the tiniest smile playing on his lips.

"That's what you secretly love about me," I say, and his smile broadens.

My grandmother's planning the wedding for next summer. Yes, she's taking an entire year to plan, as if she were twenty years old and a blushing bride. She intends on inviting over six hundred people and wearing an enormous white ball gown. One of her famous simple garden parties just won't do for an event like this. No word yet on whether or not she'll expect a bridal shower and bachelorette party, but I hope so because I never did find that strip club out in the Hamptons.

Out of the corner of my eye, I see Nate's family arrive at the house for lunch. I didn't realize it was even close to noon yet, but I've learned that in the Hamptons, when you're lazing around the pool all morning, time tends to fly.

Even though it's Saturday, and Saturday lunch is sacred to the Sugarmans, Nate's mother was delighted to accept my grandmother's invitation. Nate's sister is in attendance, as is his brother, wife and kids in tow.

As we walk over to the patio to greet the Sugarmans, I hear my grandmother tell Nate's mom that she's so thrilled that they are all there, that the Mattress King's estate is simply meant to host lots of people.

After lots of hugging and kissing, we all sit down just in time for Hunter, Skylar, and Hunter's dad to show up, so everyone gets back up and the hugging and kissing starts all over again.

The chef doesn't get lunch under way until well after one o'clock, and I'm starving. Luckily, my grandmother's chef never disappoints, and today is no exception. A three-course meal is prepared—with a summer salad and gazpacho to start, followed by steaks fresh off the barbecue, along with corn, barbecued in their husks. Dessert is usual Hamptons fare: fresh fruit accompanied by homemade sorbet. Today's flavor is mango.

Somewhere between the gazpacho and the steaks, my grandmother tells Nate that he should go ahead and marry me so that she can give us the Mattress King's estate as a wedding gift. Nate wonders aloud whether or not said gift would come with the staff of five, and I tell Nate under my breath that we're not getting married.

I mean for only Nate to hear it, but Hunter hears it, too.

"So, you two are just going to live in sin?" he asks, and then takes a huge bite of corn.

"Yes," I say. "We're going to live in sin. But don't you live in sin."

"Why can't we live in sin?" Skylar asks.

"Nate and I are much, much older than you," I say. And then, just for emphasis, I say again: "Much."

"She's thirty-four," Hunter whispers to Skylar, and she tells him that she knows.

"So, you're not going to marry me?" Nate asks, mouth full of corn. I look for that tiny smile on his lips, but it's not there. There's a slight wrinkle to his brow, and I realize he is serious.

"Why," I say with a laugh, "are you asking?"

"Not yet, but soon."

"I can't marry you," I say. "You know that. Marrying me would be the kiss of death. In fact, you should get as far away from me as you can. Hasn't anyone told you about our family curse?"

"There is no family curse," my grandmother interjects, half to Adan, the other half to Nate's parents. "I don't know where she gets these crazy ideas."

"You can't get rid of me that easily," Nate says, and his face breaks into a huge grin. He leans over and kisses me gently on the lips. I try not to think about the fact that our entire families are around us, watching us, but I still do. I pull away after a second and take a sip of my iced tea.

All this talk about marriage makes me think about walking down the aisle, about the last aisle I walked down, at my mother's funeral.

Nate's mother breaks my train of thought.

"That's okay," Nate's mom says. "There's no pressure to get married. Whenever you're ready, we can just have a little garden party to celebrate your union. Nothing big. Just a few friends from the neighborhood."

"You can put together a wedding in a few weeks?" my grandmother asks. This question is clearly a test. I know what she's thinking: that she and her team of experts can put together a wedding in one.

"We're not getting married," I say. "There's no wedding to plan."

"Yet," Nate says. He doesn't even bother to say it under his breath.

"When a mother is motivated," Nate's mom says, "she can do anything she sets her mind to. But for the record, I've put together bigger parties in less time."

I look over at my grandmother and she is beaming from ear to ear. And just like that, Nate's mom and my grandmother are best friends.

"I love a good garden party," my grandmother says.

"Who doesn't?" Nate's mother responds, and they both dissolve into a fit of laughter.

I'm not sure if they're laughing at me, or laughing because they're so happy to have the families get along so well, since it's clear we're all going to be a part of one another's lives for a very long time. It doesn't really matter, though. I'm just glad they're getting along.

I used to think that my grandmother and I were cursed. I

don't believe that anymore. Now I try to take life day by day, to enjoy every moment. I've learned to savor an afternoon spent poolside with my grandmother where we discuss nothing more than the color of our toenails, just as I enjoy an ordinary Monday night when Nate and I stay home and do nothing but balance our checkbook. Because, as it turns out, life is made up of these little random moments, and appreciating them is the recipe for a happy life.

Acknowledgments

Words are not enough to thank my agent and friend, Mollie Glick. It has been so wonderful to be on this journey with you. Thank you for your amazing insights, endless support, and thoughtful guidance. You always have time for me and I am so grateful. And Katie Hamblin, it's been so fabulous to have you on my side. Your constant help and attention were just what I needed. Big thanks go out to the entire Foundry family, especially Kirsten Neuhaus and Stéphanie Abou.

To my editor, Brenda Copeland, I am so happy that *Recipe* found a home with you. Your insightful edits made this book what it is—every suggestion of yours made this book better and stronger. I knew that the power of Brendas was a very powerful thing, indeed! To Laura Chasen, I'm so thankful you are on my team. It's been wonderful working with you, and also getting to know you.

I'm so incredibly lucky to be at St. Martin's. I can't offer enough thanks to the whole team—this has been such an outstanding experience, and I'm so fortunate that *Recipe* is just the beginning of our journey together. Endless thanks go to Adrian C. James, Matthew Shear, Sally Richardson, Eileen Rothschild, and Laura Flavin.

Special thanks go to my parents, Bernard and Sherry Janowitz, and the rest of my loving family—Janowitzes and Luxenbergs alike. I couldn't do it without you.

Lynda Curnyn and Tracy Marx, you read through countless first drafts of this book and your smart observations helped to set me on the right track. You are wonderful friends and even better writers!

Shawn Morris, Jennifer Moss, Danielle Schmelkin—my first readers and my dear friends. Your constant love and encouragement help me to keep writing. You are exactly what every writer needs.

My wonderful writer friends who have been a constant source of support, encouragement, and advice: JP Habib, Kristin Harmel, Debbie Honorof, Ellen Meister, Lynn Messina, Saralee Rosenberg, Allison Winn Scotch, Melissa Senate, Alex Sokoloff, Alix Strauss, and Anne Trubek. And especially Karin Gillespie, Melissa Clark, Maggie Marr, and everyone at the Girlfriends Book Club.

And to my readers. Well, I just couldn't do this without you. Thank you!

Finally, the biggest thank-you goes out to my husband, Douglas Luxenberg. As Ben says, you are my honey. You are also my everything.

And to my children, Ben and Davey, you have taught me so much about what it is to be a mother, what it is to love, but even more about how to live a happy life.

1. Vivienne gives Hannah a lot of advice throughout the novel: about men, about beauty routines, about how to be happy. At the beginning of chapter eleven, Vivienne tells Hannah that "It's all about figuring out what someone wants and giving it to them." Do you agree?

2. Vivienne tells Hannah that for a marriage to work, the man must love the woman more. Why do you think Hannah was so upset by this advice?

3. Do you think Hannah and Nate should get married? Will they?

4. Vivienne offers to let Hannah stay with her and support her financially. If a close relative gave you such an offer, would you consider it?

5. Vivienne is a widow six times over. Hannah jokes that she is cursed, but part of her believes it's true. Do you?

6. Hannah finds out that Vivienne has been hiding an enormous secret for years. Did this change how you view Vivienne?

7. Gray tells Hannah that she gave her the name "Hannah" because it means Grace, and in many ways Gray views Hannah as an extension of her. But Hannah tells us, "I'd much rather resemble my grandmother." Do you think Hannah is more similar to Gray or Vivienne?

8. What is your recipe for a happy life?

For more reading group suggestions, visit
www.readinggroupgold.com.

St. Martin's
Griffin